Nathan Sheppard

Shut Up in Paris

Nathan Sheppard

Shut Up in Paris

ISBN/EAN: 9783337428686

Printed in Europe, USA, Canada, Australia, Japan

Cover: Foto ©Andreas Hilbeck / pixelio.de

More available books at **www.hansebooks.com**

BY

NATHAN SHEPPARD.

*SECOND COPYRIGHT EDITION,
ENLARGED.*

LEIPZIG

BERNHARD TAUCHNITZ

1874.

Dedicated

TO

MY CIRCLE OF FRIENDS.

"O thou resort of all the earth!
Checkered with all complexions of mankind;
And spotted with all crimes, in whom I see,
Much that I love, and more that I admire,
And all that I abhor, thou freckled fair,
That pleasest and yet shock'st me, I can laugh
And I can weep; can hope, and can despond,
Feel wrath and pity when I think of thee!
Ten righteous would have saved a city once,
And thou hast many righteous; well for thee
That salt preserves."

CONTENTS.

Page

SHUT UP IN PARIS.

The following journal was kept by me, while shut up in Paris, during the investment by the German armies.

Circumstances prevented the publication of this fragment of my notes before the civil war broke out, but I think they will be found useful to those who would either read or write about the causes of that crisis.

Many incidents of the hour noted down in the following pages acquire a sinister significance when read by the light of subsequent events.

THE FALL OF THE EMPIRE.

5th September, 1870. — I think it was Madame de Stael who said, "The French are quick to discern on which side power lies, and swift to range themselves upon that side; they love success before all other things."

On the morning of the 3rd the "discerning" people were at their wits' end, and their "ranging" disposition was utterly confounded. Public opinion was literally suspended.

The newspapers without news continued to assert that something tremendous was going to happen for the benefit of France. Meanwhile the boulevards and cafés were crowded; and the stream of passers-by was arrested by groups of people who stood still to talk and to gesticulate eagerly; while the loungers eddied round them for a little time, and then continued their own languid course.

There was no more singing or shouting, the strains of the 'Marseillaise' had died away. Even the gamins had ceased to whistle it. A feeling of restless suspense pervaded all ranks. The official news was in the stereotyped tenor: "Bazaine and MacMahon have made their junction; to-morrow we shall have glorious news."

In the evening came the news, that the army under MacMahon had surrendered, and that the Emperor was a prisoner. At first it was whispered as a secret from the War Office, and then it became public and well authenticated intelligence. The first thought of Paris was, "the war is over." For France, for their country, the Parisians had no thought; they had only two ideas, which found vent in the cries,—

"DÉCHÉANCE!"
"VIVE LA RÉPUBLIQUE!"

One felt an intense desire to have one's capacity for hearing, seeing, and comprehending increased a hundredfold; to be enabled to be everywhere at once; and to miss not one phase of the situation. I would have had wings to my feet, and eyes all round my head, that nothing might escape my knowledge. I kept my eye to the kaleidoscope with frantic eagerness.

The two cries were raised simultaneously about three o'clock this afternoon, Saturday, the 3rd of September. At first the cries of *"Déchéance!"* and *"La République!"* were hesitating and inconstant, nor did they become much more resolute or persistent before Sunday morning. I remarked early on that day that the prevailing feeling was a sense of uncertainty and timidity. The furtive glances and shy demeanour of the people were observable even as they dashed and spread themselves, and here and there raised their voices to a roar. A large proportion of the crowd were mere boys, who seemed to have no motive but frolic. The fall of the Empire was to them only a "cry," "an object in life."

They were dancing and shouting; two of them tumbled accidentally into each other's arms, and whirled off with charming ease and some grace; bystanders laughed. Pretty young women, with babies in their arms, and ugly old ones, with fists on their arms, alike took part in the comical-tragical spectacle. Some of the crowd went in a body to pay their respects to Jules Simon; others went to General Trochu, and sent in a deputation, asking him to take the sceptre, and to rule alone. The General calmly and gravely replied: "Gentlemen, you find me unprepared. I am ignorant of events. I cannot reply to you. I am a man of obedience and duty. I am charged with the defence of Paris, and defend it I will at the risk of my life."

The sergents de ville made a charge on the mob, some shots were fired, and there was a general vanishing away; such as only a Paris mob can execute. During the whole of the night there was commotion; but as yet little method in the madness.

At midnight a crowd assembled outside, while the Corps Législatif were sitting. It was a midnight never to be forgotten. None dared to cry *Vive l'Empereur!* and few ventured to cry *Vive la République!* A few mounted Cuirassiers were to be seen here and there, people not knowing which side they would take. The gendarmes and sentinels were silent and impassive. Inside the building the gal-

leries were crammed. No tickets were needed. All
the members were present, and the Ministers were
in their places. There was Palikao, with his granite
face and firmly closed mouth, clean shaven, neat
compact moustache, small imperial, grey hair carefully brushed, eye cold—freezingly cold—seeming
to say: "Now give me a regiment of chassepots—
just one—and we'll see who is master." I recall the
fate of the prisoners in the cave and shudder. He
would do just so by the Red Government looming
on the black horizon of France.

The President rises. The silence is intense. You
can hear your own breathing. President Schneider
has a handsome face, and white hair of aristocratic
silkiness. He looks out sadly over the Assembly,
and says: "Adversity has brought us together at this
unusual hour. [It was now past one o'clock, A.M.]
I have been in all haste to call you together to deliberate upon the crisis of the hour." After saying
this, the President takes his seat—sinks heavily into
his chair. Then all eyes turn to the crowded minis-
terial bench. Silence ensues as the old Count rises.
He is not an orator—except in the sense that all
great soldiers are orators, just as all great orators
are possessed with the martial *esprit*. He announces
the disaster at Sedan, and says: "In the presence of
such intelligence it is impossible for the ministry to
enter upon a discussion until to-morrow. It is but
a few minutes since I was called out of my bed to
attend this sitting."

Cries of "*Oui! oui!*" The President asks the
voice of the Chamber upon the adjournment. Gam-

betta makes some exclamation. The President repeats the question whether postponement would not be the wisest course. Cries of approval, when up bobs the bushy head and out rolls the rough voice of Jules Favre, who makes a proposition with three articles— the dethronement of the Emperor, the nomination of a Government commission and the continuation of General Trochu as Governor of Paris. The signatures are those of the extreme Left only. The proposition is received with surprising indifference. Favre makes no speech. A member of the Right says they cannot pronounce the deposition of the Emperor.

The Assembly adjourns at 1.30 A.M. to noon of the same day.

At five o'clock we find, upon making a reconnoissance of the city, that all is quiet in boulevard and street.

The sergents de ville pace their beats in quartettes, eyeing us angrily and talking in suppressed tones. They know, and we know, that this is the stillness which precedes the storm.

Snatching an hour or two of slumber on the back of a nightmare, *à la* Mazeppa, I rose early and was up and dressed, and armed (with my passport), hurrying hither and thither. Thousands and thousands came pouring into the vast and glorious Place de la Concorde, and I soon heard the cry of *Vive la République* repeated everywhere, without fear of the sergents de ville, who were nowhere to be seen. They belonged to the Empire, and had passed away with it. The Garde Nationale press their way

through the vast dense throng of turbulent rejoicing.
See! they are carrying their guns butt end up. That
means, we won't fire on the people. The people
cheer and dance and weep for joy. The two cries
of "*Déchéance!*" and "*Vive la République!*" are universal, and the excitement is frantic.

I suppose I must have been possessed, for as the
clock of the Tuileries strikes a quarter to eleven, I
find myself, to my astonishment, not to say terror,
with my arms folded, leaning against the lamp-post
nearest to the Pont de la Concorde, crying, "*Vive
l'Empereur!*" at the top of my voice. I think it was
the last time that cry was heard in the streets of
Paris. I was brought to my senses by the threatening looks and gesticulations of those around me,
and I left my position as soon as an opening in the
crowd gave me the chance.

All the statues appeared suddenly to be stuck
over with little red flags. A little urchin, who had
climbed up to place one on the gate of the Tuileries,
finds himself suspended by his trousers on the tall
iron spikes.

Young fellows with the old cockade are buying
tricolour badges and red bows.

The little Italian girl from whom I bought a
white rose yesterday, offers me to-day a crimson
ribbon for my button-hole. She knows I am an
American, and infers that I am in favour of Parisian
Republicanism.

The Garde Mobile are scattered here and there,
armed with muskets, without order or commander.
The blouses are carrying muskets, yelling "*Vive la*

République!" They look like bandits. A distant group starts the 'Marseillaise.' It is caught up by all the immense concourse.

There are no words that can express the effect of the tones of the 'Marseillaise' at a moment like this; it drives men wild, and turns even an indifferent spectator into a revolutionist for the moment. There are tones in it that seem to be wrung from the heart of a whole people.

The day is bright. The sun is kindly. The blue sky smiles. Turn round once at the Egyptian obelisk, and you shall see the Arc de Triomphe, which may cover the venerable head of King William one of these days; the Madeleine pillars, standing sentinel against the angry horrors of the hour; the palace of the Tuileries, with the flag of the Empire still floating from its top, and the Corps Législatif, where all the interest has now concentred, while beyond it the gilded dome of the tomb of the other exiled Napoleon glistens under the blaze of noon. The fountains are playing as usual. The flowers in the avenue are as yet undisturbed. It is touching to see the rough fellows step over them. The love of these people for flowers and animals is one of the redeeming peculiarities of their volcanic nature. One of the massive statues in the Place is called Strasbourg. The stately figure is crowned with the red cap and the red flag.

The Tuileries clock strikes twelve. The flag is not down yet. The Empress is still there. Crowds assemble—and so does the Corps Législatif at twenty minutes past one. The National Guard and some mounted sabres protect the bridge and the approaches.

Again the galleries are packed to overflowing. No ventilation, great smell of unclean democrats. The Diplomatic Corps are in full force. Wonderfully magnificent ladies, and the time-honoured revolutionary dames of dauntless front and enormous diameter. The Corps Législatif are debating. In a few minutes there is a fearful uproar outside— soldiers and people fraternise, and in the briefest time the edifice is inundated with soldiers and people, young and old, both men and women, as well as little boys and girls; they burst through the door opposite the President's desk, and fill the chamber, shouting "*Déchéance!*" and "*Vive la République!*"

Some are in the costume of the National Guard, some in that of the Guard Mobile. Many carry chassepots, and some short swords. The women carry only their native arms, bare and brawny, and uplifted. There is the usual proportion of these masculine dames, and of young women with their babes, and of family men, taking no part particularly, simply smoking and watching, and of boys laughing and shouting. It is an indescribable tableau; and after all attempts at description, one returns to the only adequate one—it is French!

President Schneider rises, looks down upon the tumult with a most disconsolate countenance, not unmixed with disdain, rings the bell nervously, and says, "All deliberation is impossible under these circumstances, I accordingly pronounce the sitting at an end."

The President puts on his hat at about 3·20 P.M., steps down, and disappears, followed by all the deputies present, except those of the Extreme Left, several of whom, and particularly Gambetta, in vain endeavour to control the new "government."

The owners of the blouses, petticoats, and shirt-sleeves continue to dance and howl, to brandish fists, babies, and chassepots, as it may happen; they cry "*Déchéance!*" "*Vive la République!*" Little dogs chase one another over the hall; for wherever there is a Frenchman there is generally his dog also.

Jules Favre tries to pacify them by saying, "Union is necessary; the Republic has not been declared, but it will be presently."

The noise grows more unearthly—dancing, howling, babies screaming, women and men gesticulating, dogs joining in the chorus of cries with all their might, till the "extreme Left" are driven to their wits' end. Some of the National Guard mount the President's rostrum; a villainously ill-looking fellow takes the chair and shakes the bell; the green sprigs in the muskets are waved; one man in a blue shirt mounts the tribune and makes a speech, but it is inaudible. Some men seize the pens and ram them into the inkstands, and pretend to write; but as they do not know how, they can only "make their mark," and spill the ink around. The ill-looking man rings the bell furiously; the members of the "extreme Left" continue their exertions on behalf of "law and order;" but at length they give·up in despair, and depart, leaving the mob in possession.

The "extreme Left" is succeeded by the extremer

Left! Somebody thinks of Rochefort, and cries "To St. Pelagie!" Nobody stirs however. But the next cry, "To the Hôtel de Ville--to proclaim the Republic!" carries all before it; and they move tumultuously and noisily to the Hôtel de Ville.

In one of the rooms of the Hôtel de Ville the members of the "extreme Left" assemble and declare the Republic, and themselves its rulers. Favre chooses the Portfolio of Foreign Affairs. Gambetta prefers that of the Interior. Trochu is continued Governor of Paris. The Legislative Body and Senate are pronounced dissolved. All political prisoners and exiles are pardoned.

A *pronunciamento* is voted:

"The people have anticipated the Chamber, which was hesitating. They have demanded the Republic. They have placed their Representatives, not in power, but in peril. The Republic conquered the invasion in 1792; it is therefore proclaimed. The Revolution is made in the name of public safety. Citizens, keep guard over the city which is confided to you. To-morrow you will be with the army, the avengers of your country."

But the citizens will not wait till to-morrow. They avenge their country then and there. They make a perfectly successful attack upon a portrait of the Emperor, painted by Vernet. They bayonet it. They trample it under their feet.

While the upper branch of the Government is deliberating in one portion of the noble building, the lower House is busy in their mutilation of another. They burst into a thousand infinitesimal fragments the door which is adorned with his Majesty's head. Benches are smashed; busts are knocked on the head and captured.

Rochefort appears; he is rapturously received, and immediately incorporated into the Government, on the ground, says Favre, that he will do us less harm in office than out.

Finally the National Guard induce the mob to leave the edifice, and the doors are closed and guarded.

Gambetta proclaims the list of the Provisional Ministers, and says they are to be only a "transitory power, designed to defend the nation against the foreigner."

The crowd, gathering numbers as they went, joined the crowd already assembled in the Place de la Concorde.

As the clock of the Palace struck half-past three, the flag of the Empire was taken down, and cries arose: "She is gone! She is gone! She will escape!" "*Déchéance!*" "*Vive la République!*" "Down with Badinguet?" "Down with Madame Badinguet!" "To the Palace!"

The gates were not locked, and the multitude poured through them. A few sentinels stood at the doors of the Palace; they looked irresolute. An officer came out and said something in a low voice; the sentinels vanished. Then there were shouts of "Open the doors!" "Let us in; the Palace belongs to the nation!" "They are getting away!" "They are robbing the Palace!" An officer appears in parley with the foremost of the crowd; but he retires.

The fence is scaled, the last gates are burst open, and, screeching, howling, and laughing, the crowd rush headlong in. One man tumbles over another man's dog; he jumps up, pats the dog, begs its owner's pardon, and then continues the chase.

The edifice seems to be occupied by the National Guards, who beg the people to spare the "National property." Everywhere these words were to be seen written in large white chalk letters. The National Guards did their duty admirably and successfully, and the people deserve the credit of listening to them. They roamed through the Palace; but there was no pillage, nor any damage worth mentioning. Indeed there was little or nothing to tempt the covetous. On a bed lay a toy sword, half-drawn; in another room a lot of empty jewel cases were strewn on the floor, and on a little table some bits of bread and a half-eaten egg.

No soldiers are left to the Empire; the few that remain in Paris are apathetic; they do not cry "*Vive la République!*" nor anything else. The National Guard and the Mobile Guard fraternise with the people.

This Sunday after the disaster of Sedan is a fête-day in Paris from the morning till the night.

ESCAPE OF THE EMPRESS.

ON Sunday, the 4th of September, the Empress had her last official interview with Count Palikao, who told her that he and his colleagues, and the whole Assembly, had been driven out by the mob, and that the Extreme Left and the mob had gone to the Hôtel de Ville, to proclaim a Republic, and themselves its Ministers, with General Trochu for President and Commander-in-Chief. The Count declared his willingness to see what could be done, if a reasonable number of troops could be found who might be depended upon to make a stand for her. The Empress replied promptly and firmly, that not one drop of blood should be shed for her or for her family. She resolved to depart at once, if it were still possible.

By this time it was about 3.30 in the afternoon, and the crowd which had gathered round the palace already filled the palace grounds. The old Tuileries resembled a gigantic ship in a heavy sea. The roar of the human billows echoed through the deserted halls and apartments. Voices could be heard on the main staircase, and the clatter of muskets on the stones below. The flag on the cupola had been hauled down; perhaps in the hope of diverting the attention of the mob, by suggesting that the Empress had already got away. But it had no such effect; the voices and tramp of footsteps came nearer and nearer—there was not a moment to lose. Accompanied by Madame le Breton, sister to General Bourbaki, Prince Metternich, M. Nigra, and a few members of her household, the Empress began her attempt to escape.

To reach the street through the courtyard, which was divided by an iron fence from the Place du Carrousel, was impossible, for the Place was full of people. They were obliged to return, and to hurry along the whole length of the gallery of the Louvre. The party by this time had dwindled down to the Empress, Madame le Breton, and the two foreign ministers; the others had dispersed to seek safety in their own way.

The Empress and her friends reached the door opening into the Place St. Germain Auxerrois, opposite the church of that name. Outside the gate there is a short passage with a tall iron railing on each side, leading to the street. But that street was full of people crying "*Déchéance!*" and "*Vive la République!*" The little party paused and hesitated, before they ventured to open the door; but there was nothing to be done, except to go forward.

The crowd could be heard behind them; to return, would have been to fall into their hands. The venture must be made. The gentlemen opened the door cautiously, looked out into the street, with dismay, and the two ladies stepped forwards. They were not studiously disguised; indeed, they were too thinly veiled, for one of the inevitable *gamins*, catching sight of the ladies, cried out, either in jest or mischief, "The Empress!"

Fortunately, no one heeded the cry, and still more fortunately, a close fiacre was drawn up by the kerbstone of the pavement. The Empress and Madame le Breton entered it, and giving a fictitious address to the driver, rode away in safety.

It was a most critical moment, and one shudders to think of what would have been the fate of these two women if they had fallen into the hands of that excited mob. The recollection of a narrow escape gives one a pang of terror sharper than any felt during the danger itself.

The perils of the Empress were not yet over; as they drove down the Boulevard Haussmann the Empress asked her friend if she had any money, as she herself had not her purse. Madame le Breton brought out hers, and found that it contained three francs only, and then the terror seized them, that they would not have enough to pay the driver. They decided to alight at once, to avoid all danger of a dispute, and they pursued their way on foot to the house of Dr. Thomas W. Evans, the celebrated American dentist.

They had to wait like all other visitors until he could see them. Some time elapsed before they were called, and then, being ushered into the presence of the doctor, Madame le Breton closed the door and turned the key, and, warning the doctor to make no exclamation that might be heard, she introduced the Empress, and told him they had

come to seek protection under his roof, until they
could leave Paris.

Dr. Evans was more astonished than might have
been expected, for, engrossed in his patients, he
was ignorant of the sudden and complete change of
affairs. At first, he could not believe that there were
any grounds of alarm for the personal safety of
her Majesty. He asked the ladies to remain, and
putting on his hat, he went into the streets for a
short time.

On his return, he was quite convinced that the
Empress had not left the palace a moment too
soon.

He behaved like a most loyal and gallant gentleman; counting the risk to himself as nothing.

He desired them to remain his guests until such
time as he could compass means to get them out
of Paris.

Fortunately, two ladies (strangers to his servants)
were expected to arrive in the course of a few days.
The Empress and Madame le Breton were to per-
sonate these ladies—arrived unexpectedly. Mrs.
Evans was in the country, and the Empress, as an
invalid, kept her room.

As soon as it was practicable, the doctor went
out in his carriage, ostensibly to pay professional
visits, as usual—in reality to prepare the way for
passing the barriers.

He drove to the Pont de Neuilly, where he was
stopped and questioned; he declared he was going
to see a patient, and ought neither to be stopped
nor questioned. He announced his name and pro-

fession. One of the guards recognised him, and said he ought to be allowed to pass without question or passport. The doctor begged them to look at him well, that they might recognise him, as he would probably have occasion to pass and re-pass the barrier frequently. He drove on, and returned after a while, without hindrance.

The Empress and Madame le Breton remained at the doctor's house. The doctor put his wife's wardrobe at their disposal, as they had escaped without any provision of necessaries.

When Dr. Evans considered that the barrier might be passed by him with tolerable safety, he informed his guests of his plan. The Empress was to be a highly nervous patient, whom he was taking to a *maison de santé;* Madame le Breton was the friend who had charge of her. On reaching the barrier the carriage was stopped, to account for the doctor's companions. He pointed to the Empress, and made a sign that she was a person of unsound mind who must not be excited or alarmed. The guards, who recognised Dr. Evans, courteously drew back, and made amicable signs of wishing him a safe journey.

This first danger passed, the carriage proceeded to St. Germains and Maunt. There the doctor drove to an hotel, and having told the proprietor that one of the ladies in the carriage was a patient whom he was taking to a *maison de santé*, requested him to find a room that could not be overlooked, and furnished with shutters to the window and locks to the door—a request which was very willingly obeyed

—and here the Empress and her companion gladly took refuge while the doctor and the friend who accompanied him went out to make arrangements for continuing the journey. He sent his own carriage and horses back to Paris.

After their departure he engaged another carriage and pair, with a careful driver, to be ready to start in an hour for a certain château, belonging, as the doctor said, to a relative of the afflicted lady.

While the fresh carriage was being prepared he returned to his charges and made them take some refreshment. The Empress was told of the destination of the carriage, and she was desired to show a great objection, and to become so angry and restive that the route would have to be changed for another, which the doctor would give at the proper time. After they had left the hotel and proceeded some distance on their road, the Empress began a lively quarrel with the doctor, and the altercation between the "insane lady" and her friends became so violent that the doctor desired the carriage to stop, and tried to persuade the lady to alight and walk a little, which she refused to do, and objected vehemently to going in the direction of the château, whither she seemed to know they were taking her. The driver remonstrated, and said his horses would take fright if such a clamour were continued, upon which the doctor, apparently driven to despair, ordered the horses' heads to be turned and driven to the town on the next stage, where the carriage was sent back.

The same precautions were used at the hotel as

before. Another carriage and driver were procured, and the party proceeded on their journey towards their real destination, which was Déauville, where Mrs. Evans was then staying for the benefit of the sea air.

At each stage a fresh driver and carriage were hired and the other sent back. The party had one cr two very "narrow escapes," but the Empress was more fortunate than Marie Antoinette and the royal family in their attempt to escape. She was never recognised, and at the end of two days, fatigued and harassed, and with dangers and difficulties still before them, but so far safe, the little party arrived at Déauville and drove to the apartments of Mrs. Evans. Here the ladies remained, and found such repose as they were capable of taking; while the doctor, accompanied by his friend, went to see what means existed to enable them to leave the port and cross the Channel.

There were two yachts at anchor in the harbour. They first went on board the larger of the two, but the owner was absent. They then went to the *Gazelle;* it belonged to Sir John Burgoyne, Bart. On telling him their story and begging him to give a passage to the Empress and her friend, he at first absolutely refused to be mixed up in the matter, having possibly some fear that it might somehow become a source of national complication; but the perilous situation of the fugitives was urged, and it was insisted that all risks should be run to perform an act of common humanity. Sir John at length consented, only stipulating that the Empress and her friends should not come on board until the last possible moment before the vessel was ready to sail, in order to avoid the danger of the yacht being detained if attention were attracted to her passengers.

It was a prudent arrangement, for vague suspicions were afloat in the town, and the *Gazelle* received visitors who were not "welcome guests;" but as no one was on board save the rightful owner and his crew, the baffled searchers went their way; the Empress and Madame le Breton, accompanied by Dr. Evans, got safely on board, and the *Gazelle* set sail.

The perils by land were over, but the perils by sea had yet to be encountered. A fearful tempest arose, the most terrible and destructive that had for a long time been known in the Channel.

It was in that same storm that the fine new ship the *Captain* went down with her commander and all her men: a catastrophe which moved the heart of England more than the loss of a battle. The commander who then perished was the son of the venerable Field Marshal Sir John Burgoyne.

The little *Gazelle* behaved gallantly, but the peril was fearful. The ladies were lashed in their berths and there remained during the whole passage. At midnight all hope of saving either the vessel or the crew was given up. But the storm that destroyed the *Captain* spared the *Gazelle*, a little craft not more than thirty-five feet in length.

Seldom have those in perils of "the great deep" had a more wonderful or unhoped for deliverance.

The *Gazelle* rode out the storm and reached the harbour of Ryde about 3 o'clock on Thursday afternoon, the 8th of September.

That afternoon the party went to Brighton, and there Dr. Evans learned that the Prince Imperial was at Hastings, and thither the Empress insisted on going that same evening. For many days the mother and the son had been ignorant of what had become of each other. Not one human heart in the whole world but must sympathise in that meeting of the mother and child, after events in which all their grandeur and pomp, and the very empire of France itself, had been broken to pieces and vanished away.

As soon as possible Dr. Evans endeavoured to find a suitable residence for the Empress and her son. Finally Camden House, at Chiselhurst, was agreed upon; the owner, on learning for whom it was desired, offered very generous terms, and at Camden House the Empress and the Prince Imperial found a haven of rest, and the hazardous task which Dr. Evans had undertaken was successfully completed.

———

RUBBING OFF THE LANDMARKS.

HAVING disposed of the Second Empire the Parisians proceeded to obliterate its footprints from "the sands of time." Shopkeepers were allowed only a few minutes in which to remove the imperial decorations from their windows, while the new rulers, the Mob, stood by, making grimaces and antics, and uttering every imaginable species of street cry, mingled with an occasional menace to accelerate the proceedings. The medals of the Exposition Universelle, with Napoleon III., Empereur, on one side, and MDCCCLXVII. on the other, with the familiar device of little winged boys carrying a tablet between them, underneath which was the Napoleon eagle, and over all the Emperor's head, were peculiarly exasperating to the "governing class." The words, devices, and recollections they suggested were like a red flag before the eyes of an infuriated bull. I saw, however, instances in which the destroying fist was arrested before the representation of a London medal bearing the effigy of Britannia and her Lion, and the inscription, "Londini, 1862," which showed a touching discrimination. The busts of the Emperor and Empress were thrown out of the windows of the houses in which they were found; and on one ladder I saw a well-dressed *bourgeois* effacing the street name of the Boulevard Haussmann, and substituting that of "Victor Hugo."

The great gilt "N," taken from the Academy, left a conspicuous mark behind. "The substance is so powerful that the shadow is ineffaceable," whispered an old officer near me.

It was sometimes difficult to know why certain places and things should be selected for demolition; for instance, one window had only the word "*modes*" inscribed over it, and that one word was effaced—because, as a genteel youth told me in reply to a mild inquiry, "the shop is suspected of having furnished flowers to the Empress:" so the forget-me-nots which were growing in the vase on which the obnoxious word was inscribed were thrown into the street. The crowd are like children in their love of being aimlessly busy.

6th September.—Victor Hugo arrived to-day, and received an ovation at the station. Among those who went to receive him was to be seen the humorous face of Laboulaye, who was driven out of his lecture-room last spring for having accepted office under the Emperor, and the handsome white head of Michelet, and the two clever sons of Hugo. The old man's fiery eye has not yet become dim, and he is evidently good for much hard service in verbal pyrotechnics.

"Paris," exclaims Victor Hugo, "must not be sullied by invasion. To invade Paris is to invade liberty. It is to invade civilisation. No such invasion shall triumph. Paris will be saved by the union of all souls, all hearts, all arms in her defence. The defeat of Paris means new hatred, new resentments, new barriers between people and people. Paris must be victorious in the name of fraternity, for only by making the fraternity of all possible can the liberty of all be gained."

The speaker points to the United States flag, and says: "That banner of stars speaks to-day to Paris and to France, proclaiming miracles of power, which are easy to a great people contending for a great Principle: the liberty of every race, and the fraternity of all."

"Fudge," sneers an American; "the United States Republic has about as much sympathy with this one, as a well ordered family circle has with a lunatic asylum."

Jules Favre publishes his circular to the diplomatic agents. "We will not cede one inch of our territory, or one stone of our fortresses. . . . After the forts the ramparts: after the ramparts the barricades. Paris can hold out three months and conquer. If she succumbs, France, rising at her call, will avenge her. She will continue the struggle, and the aggressor will perish."

Paris strikes the café table with her fist over this, and says, "Now the war will commence, and not a German will get back home alive." Belleville yells with "noble rage." Only here and there a Frenchman shrugs his shoulders and hints the misgivings he dare not speak.

7th September.—Vinoy arrived at 4 P.M. with thirteen trains of artillery, eleven trains of cavalry, and fourteen trains of infantry; in all about 20,000 men. His jaded columns of red legs and disordered mass of guns and waggons, looked like nothing so much as the floating in of a wreck upon the beach.

8th September.—Trochu proclaims that "the defence of Paris is assured," and Paris feels a dangerous sense of security. Does it never occur to her that the defence of the investing army may be equally "well assured" one of these days?

SYMBOLIC PATRIOTISM.

———

September 8th.—Jules Favre says, in his circular:
"When they piously lay crowns at the feet of the
statue of Strasbourg, they do not merely obey an
enthusiastic sentiment of admiration: they adopt
their heroic *mot d'ordre;* they swear to be worthy
of their brethren of Alsace, and to die as they have
done."

This flowery swearing has been going on ever
since the 4th. I have watched these pious devotees
with profound curiosity. There is something inex-
pressibly exhilarating in watching these crowds.
There may be a strong leaven of the histrionic
faculty in all this, for which the French are pre-
eminent; but it gives expression to a real instinct in
human nature. The chivalric and the poetical spirit
go together. Poets have been gallant fellows on the
field. The history of France is particularly full of
their renown. The dreamy eyed youth I saw go
up to kiss the pedestal of the statue of Strasbourg,
will fight heartily when the sentiment has to be
transformed into hard blows. The pretty little
maiden in her white cap, who sells bouquets, would,
I believe, desire nothing better than to fall beside

her lover in the front of battle. The old soldier who has hobbled on his wooden leg from the Invalides with his wreath of immortelles—he knows what bravery is and what battle means. The French easily become intoxicated with phrases; they are so addicted to the dramatic, that the sternest realities become to them only more or less a drama or a "situation." It is difficult to guard against unfair judgments; but the histrionic genius comes out sometimes in such intensely absurd and grotesque touches, that no mortal can help laughing. Even the French laugh at themselves. Their artists and their authors gather into their books and illustrations more absurdities than a foreigner can discern; and they have an exquisite expertness in delineating French character that none but they can attain. But there is a hard and cruel element in the French caricaturists. The fun is not genial, it is biting; and there is venom in their laughter. It is not all who bring their offerings to the foot of the Strasbourg statue of whom we can hope that they are carried away by enthusiasm, or who "swear" in any pious sense at all. The gigantic statue is now covered with yellow wreaths, small flags, and bouquets. Her head-dress looks like the many-coloured bandanna of a negress. Mottos, and indecipherable ditties cover the pedestal; and there is a picture of General Uhrich, framed in a wreath, in the front.

Hundreds of people assemble and stand staring before it. National Guards in large detachments stack their arms there and lean on them. I asked one of them what was their object in remaining.

He replied: "If the tide should turn against General Uhrich, the statue might be demolished, and it was best to be on their guard!"

"But is the tide likely to turn?" said I.

"It is certain to do so, if he fails."

"THE CRY IS STILL, THEY COME!"

September 9th.—"The Prussians are advancing on Paris in three *corps d'armée.*" This is the official announcement. How does Paris take the situation? The fête day over, the stupendous humiliation at Sedan has been succeeded by the apathetic bewilderment which preceded that event. The frolicsome Sunday has been followed by a week of nonchalance. The boulevards are packed all the long evenings, and you must keep a sharp lookout, or you will never get a seat among the cognac-sippers, there to watch and muse upon the two opposite sluggish tides of insensible people. Here and there you will see a group of from twenty to sixty gathered round a couple of men who are discussing the war, or one man who is reading aloud the news from an evening paper. The infrequency of such incidents gives effect to the mournful spectacle of universal apathy. All day long and all night long there are squads of men with muskets on their shoulders in the dress of workmen, and of men in regimentals without arms, lounging about the cafés, or sauntering leisurely through the streets. I can count citizens armed and unarmed, and soldiers partially armed, by the thousand, lounging about or sauntering along.

Victor Hugo sends a letter to the Germans, in which he informs them, that "Paris is a city," and that "in ruining her they sanctify her. The scattering of the stones will be the dispersion of ideas." They "will take the forts," then "the fortification," then "the barricade," and then "mined sewers will blow whole streets into the air." "We will draw from the scabbard an idea." "Do we say this to frighten you? No; you are Germans, you are not frightened!"

10th September.—Our wives have left us, and our children, too, have fled, and we are as forlorn as the patriarch under the juniper-tree. We only are left to tell the story of the city's doom. We wonder and wonder what that doom will be.

Yesterday I made another tour of the forts and of the camps of our defenders. This is in itself significant. How is it that four of us in an open voiture could survey the defences and defenders at our leisure, and return unmolested through the gates of the imperilled city? To make the case all the stronger, I can add that a party of Englishmen were, on the same day and the same route, arrested, not by a sentinel, but by a mob. The cabman became entangled in a network of vehicles, refused to proceed, and called for his pay. Remonstrance was met by the new and fashionable remark that Anglaise and Allemande are one and the same language. The "Government" is as omnipresent as it was before the 4th. It interfered, and the English gentlemen were glad to pay up and make off. I myself always take to my heels when I see the "Government" coming.

An endless line of vehicles of every description, size, and sort, and with every species of contents, came winding in to-day from the country. Paris has become a city of refuge. Women were dragging their small load of household goods in two-wheeled carts. The perspiration rolled down their brown faces—or, were some of the drops tears? Poor Jacques had more to carry than his little legs could well get on with. In the midst of the furniture sat an old woman, too old to walk, surrounded by grandchildren, too young to trust on the crowded thoroughfare. There were piles and piles of hay, of something in sacks, of wood, of everything. Sometimes our road was blocked for a half hour, baffling the strategy of our energetic Jehu. But finally we got into the Bois de Vincennes, in some parts of which we could take a breath of refreshing and uninterrupted quiet. But in other parts of it the fine trees were cut off half way up the trunk, and the tops were made into abattis. Houses that would obstruct the view of the approaching enemy, or shelter him when he came, were being demolished bit by bit with pick-axes and hatchets, as though time, that one element which Napoleon I. said was the all valuable thing in war, were perfectly at the disposal of General Trochu, who tells us in the midst of all this chaos that the defence of Paris "is assured."

Nobody stopped us, nobody spoke to us, nobody seemed to care whether we were King William's spies, or Uncle Sam's inquisitive children, or John Bull's "busybodies in other men's matters."

We saw "the well established enceinte, the well provisioned forts, and, above all, the breasts of 300,000 combatants, determined to hold out to the last."

Marshal Marmont, who commanded the defences of Paris in 1814, said: "Whatever may be the consequence of the most disastrous campaign, the scattered remnants will always amount to from 80,000 to 100,000 men, and supported by these the forts are unassailable."

If this could be said in 1814, how much more reason there is for saying it since the improvements of 1841?

"UNDER THE BOWS, WITHOUT A LIGHT."

IT is the same here as it was in Metz, when I was there in August, although then there had been only a little of the crash and wreck which has since overtaken France. I remember vividly the carnival of vanity at Metz, when the armies of King William were coming over the Rhine. Spurs jingled and glasses tinkled, at the little round tables under the shade of the trees at the *Hôtel de l'Europe*. The new saddles creaked and the new buttons glittered. It was difficult to get out of the way of the officer you met upon the street. He was so absorbed in the act of looking down upon his new suit of clothes, that he would run right against you if you were not agile. He, like his country, recalled that startle which one gets sometimes at sea in a dark night, or in a fog, when the shout comes up from the forward deck: "A ship under the bows, without a light!"

Such conceit, such vanity, as there was in Metz, in August, there is in Paris to-day. All seems like an allegory, with its fantastic scenes and solemn moral.

I believe the vanity of France will survive every calamity, and rise superior to every humiliation. Is there not something akin to the heroic in even this? But there is the silly giggle and complacent simper which drives you distracted. At any rate, a vanity so vital never was seen before on the face of the earth.

France, these Frenchmen tell me, is an idea, a sentiment, a civilisation. She is the world's teacher and guide. The world could not get on without her. She will now sweep these insolent Vandals from her soil, and come out of the fiery ordeal mightier than ever.

I am told here what I was told at Metz: "Oh! we shall clean them all out. These reverses are the best thing that could happen to us. They have roused us. We shall drive them out of the Vosges and over the Rhine to Berlin."

The person who talks thus to me, so soon as he ceases to speak, drops into his chair in the café, the very personification of a mollusc; he has not the least symptom of possessing a back-bone, moral or physical; he has no "grit," as the Americans phrase it. He is like a schoolboy, coming in from his frolic to declaim an "oration" on "speech-day"; with this serious difference, that in the schoolboy there may be the making of a "man," but that sonorous "patriot" will never be anything but what he is.

If Germany could have been conquered by the tactics which reduced the walls of Jericho, the entire army of the Empire would now be encamped in the suburbs of Berlin. The war has been carried into Gascony, however, and I must have seen, without knowing it, the officer whose "bed is stuffed with the whiskers of the men he had slain in battle!"

American gasconade is neutralized by its rollicking humour, but the vain boasting of France is the only serious habit of the people. They believe everything they say about themselves. The only pertinacity they show is in following the devices and desires of their own vanity; all the energy they have is exhausted in the pursuit of the Will o' the Wisp, created by their morbid self-conceit. Their future is a mirage of *gloire.* It would seem as if every beverage they drink were a decoction of strong delusions. *"Disillusionization"* is one of their enormous words, but it is an experience to which they never attain. They always complain, and with perfect propriety, of being "deceived." But they never see the deceiver; because they never look into themselves in search of him. In like manner they always complain of being betrayed; but they never recognise that they are their own worst traitors. In their own experience, infidelity and deceit are common; so they naturally suspect easily.

Leader and follower, politician and people, general and soldier, monarchist and republican, are all equally involved in this inextricable labyrinth of deception with respect to being "ready" for the war.

France is beaten, therefore "deceived," "betrayed." From the Emperor down they are all crying, "Is it I? Is it I?" And upon my word, I also cry in bewilderment, "Lord who is it?" Upon second thought, however, I have concluded to cry, "Who is it not?"

With the French, a battle and a duel are the same thing, differing only in degree, not in kind. The duel expresses both their motive and their method in fighting. "Wounded honour" calling for "satisfaction," and proceeding to obtain it according to all the rules and regulations of the "chivalric" code—two picked armies of equal size on an open plain, led by picked men of equal reputation, whichever falls is wrong, whichever survives is right — this will settle which was the most to blame in the Hohenzollern quarrel.

"If it is a challenge we accept it," says Jules Favre.　Such is bituminous France.

"My people," says King William, "My people will with me make all sacrifices to conquer peace again for the nations."

Such is anthracite Germany, slow to catch, but when ignited and united, inextinguishable and all consuming.

"Forty centuries are looking down on you from the tops of those pyramids," is blustering French.

"England expects every man to do his duty," is Anglo-Saxon common sense.

"INVESTED."

———

14*th September.*—The Mayor of Paris appoints a commission to revise the names of the streets of Paris.

La Rue du dix Décembre, to be called, Rue du quatre Septembre.

The Orleans princes were at the *Hôtel Bristol* one night, but were ordered off by the Government, and returned to London. Their swords are no more acceptable to the Republic than they were to the Empire.

Some members of the Legislature made an attempt to meet at a private residence. They were admonished by the Favre cabinet that no conversation among ex-deputies could be tolerated which related to politics. They could talk social ethics or domestic economy, but politics is a forbidden theme; whereupon the *Gazette de France* observes, "All governments are alike. The administrative atmosphere perverts the feelings and corrupts the most deeply rooted convictions."

The Red papers want to know why there is no "blouse" in the cabinet, and why the Government does not ornament its proclamations with the words,

"Liberty! Equality! Fraternity!" and why it has dared to make a prefect of police out of a Count.

Uneasy lies the head that does not wear the crown—in France.

17th September.—The whole eastern horizon is full of Uhlans—hurtling clouds that portend the hurricane and tempest. Saw some in the distance on the road beyond Versailles, whereupon we retired rapidly into Paris with a feeling curiously like that of fleeing for shelter from a storm. The gates of the city closed after us.

Our last letters were received by this morning's post. The old moustache, with his awkward leather box, which he carries before him, said he believed he should take a short vacation.

19th September.—The last train went out on the Orleans road at 1 P.M. We hear that it was attacked by the Uhlans. The last telegram was received at 11 o'clock. They would not undertake to send one for me. Said the wires were cut. They shut up the office as if business were at an end.

This news of roads cut, wires cut, and Prussians closing in from every point of the compass, causes a noticeable flutter on the boulevards and in the cafés. Paris betrays nettled vanity and alarm, which her bluster cannot conceal.

Félix Pyat opens a subscription in his *Combat,* for a *fusil d'honneur* to be given to the man who shall take off King William; and meanwhile Jules

Favre goes to King William to confer on the question of an armistice.

The *Institute* protests against the destruction of the museums and monuments by bombardment. Everybody seems to anticipate bombardment.

Rochefort is made president of a barricade commission, which is going to make "a second *enceinte inexpugnable*, on the interior of Paris."

Former landmarks are to be restored. M. Gaultier-Boissière is instructed by the Government to put "Liberty, Equality, and Fraternity" on the public edifices.

Victor Hugo consoles us with the information that "Paris has an angry civilization fermenting within her. The red furnace of the Republic blazes in her crater, and it is full, this powerful Paris, of all the explosions of the human soul. Tranquil and terrible, she awaits the invasion. A volcano needs no assistance."

4*

AN OLD HUGUENOT.

LAST night I made another reconnoissance of the pleasure-world of Paris, in order to see how it was taking the situation; and I found it was taking the situation joyously. The "gardens of delight" were crammed with the lovers of pleasure—dancing, sipping, smoking, chatting, sauntering. But there was the usual absence of drunkenness and boister-ousness. In this respect Paris contrasts favourably with London, and this race to ours. In all their carousals, they are remarkable for ebriety and quiet.

"No, Monsieur—no; not one of the Cossacks will get back alive;" and the young man who said this, immediately upon saying it was summoned back into the whirlpool of waltzers by the music of the band.

As I wandered about among the throng, I was surprised to stumble upon an old Huguenot, or rather, the venerable and eccentric man who is called a Huguenot because he is proud of his descent from ancestors who suffered for their faith under Louis XIV., when the Edict of Nantes was revoked, which drove away the best and most earnest of Frenchmen, whose loss is felt in the national character to this day. France would have been a different country had the stern Huguenot element been retained.

The old Huguenot whom I met in my ramble that night is what I imagine to have been the old Puritan type. He has a mouth to be remembered —it is the mouth of a "good hater;" it has a biting expression both in repose and in action; the upper and the lower lip are kept scrupulously shaven, though the operation has been somewhat unskilfully performed, as they are generally cut in one spot or another; the teeth are sharp, projecting, and angular; chin and cheeks are covered with scraggy, coarse iron-grey hair. The eyes are, however, singularly soft and gentle, and little children and poor people believe in the eyes, and do not pay any heed to the hard mouth. There is the same contradiction in the man's character; he revels in the denunciations of the Old Testament against sin and wickedness; he quotes, with passionate earnestness, the awful threatenings of the Prophets; be believes that the Day of Vengeance is at hand, and that judgment is gone out against Paris, and that the blood of the Huguenot persecutions is about to be avenged; but he is generous, charitable, and gentle in practice, thoroughly religious, and full of earnest convictions. He talks out his own ideas with a rugged bigotry that is impressive, and which is a complete contrast to the sonorous phrases and glittering generalities in which most Frenchmen indulge. His dress is in keeping with himself; it does not follow the fashions. The hat resembles a chimney-pot; in some places it is bare and napless and brown, but it is scrupulously brushed; his coat is old-fashioned, and he wears a large white neck-cloth with ruffles at the bosom of his shirt; and he wears sharp-toed shoes. His figure is tall and gaunt. But the kindly look of the eyes, and the grim expression of the mouth, combine to give the impression of the whole character of the man.

Such was the manner of man who startled me with his unexpected presence in the gardens last evening. His first words were: "All this does not look much like preparing for its doom, does it?"

"Then you believe there is a doom impending!" said I.

"Certain! certain! The Lord has a mighty and strong arm, which, as a tempest, shall cast down to the earth, the land, with the Crown of Pride. I have lived fifty years in expectation of this day. I have gone about this joyous city, weighed down with a sense of all this appalling shame and corruption. See how they are dancing on the brink of a precipice: nothing will awaken them but the fierce wrath of the Almighty, devouring them with fire and sword. 'The destruction of transgressors and of sinners shall be together; they shall both burn together; and none shall quench them.' But we are observed: we must part: we will meet again. Mark, as you go out, that young thing in the pink dress. She is the victim of Paris. Poor thing! poor thing!"

I looked back as I turned away, and saw the old Huguenot with tears in his eyes for the people over whom he had just been breathing forth such terrible threatening and woe.

FIGHTING AND NEGOTIATING.

20th September.—First battle of the siege yesterday. It is difficult to get at the distinctions which the newspapers intend when they call one conflict an "*Affaire*," another a "*Bataille*," another a "*Reconnaissance*," another a "*Combat*," another a "*Sortie.*" And then one is still more philologically bothered when all these words are used in the course of a description of the same contest of arms.

The *affaire* of Chatillon-Clamart seems to have been an attempt to occupy some heights in that vicinity, with the design of making them as useful as they are now annoying.

An officer, who took part in it, says: "If all the army had fought as well as the Breton Mobiles, the Artillery, and almost all the Line, we would have had a beautiful success."

The fugitives here alluded to never ceased their retreat until they fetched up on the Boulevard Saint-Michael, where they entertained great crowds with stories of their rout and panic on the heights of Chatillon and at the forests of Clamart. They declared that the "Breton Mobiles, the Artillery, and almost all the Line," shared in their stampede, but had rested under Fort Vanvres. Several were arrested as deserters, and were carried off amid the boisterous reprobation of the *gamins* and of an old Red hag, who brandished her long bony fingers in their faces, while she called them cowards and scoundrels. Their excuse was that they "have no leaders." Nor had they on this occasion. "Perhaps you left your leaders at the front," the Red hag suggested.

Supposing this *affaire* to have been designed to try what the forces are made of, we may make up our minds that the situation is disheartening, that we are now completely invested by an alert, resolute, and powerful foe, and completely dependent upon an army which cannot be depended upon for anything except for its facility in getting back behind the walls of the city in the smallest possible space of time.

We seem to be at once fighting and negotiating. Paris is effervescent, Belleville mad. "Manifestation" at the Hôtel de Ville, led by National Guards and recruited by deputations from the clubs, to protest against "Peace," "Surrender," "Armistice," against everything but "War *à outrance.*"

Jules Ferry promises "to consider." Crowd dissolves to wreak its wrath in spy-hunting.

I met a squad of *moblots* with an alleged "*espion.*" Boys and women follow, shouting and dancing. A cabbie slashes at the prisoner with his long whip. A huckster-woman loaded with baskets stops on the kerb, shakes her enormous fist at the captive, and declares she would like nothing better

than the opportunity of biting his head off. One
of the Guard aims his chassepot at the back of the
same head, prancing and dancing, grinning, and
grimacing.

The venerable Marshal Vaillant was strolling
about the fortifications. He was seized by a gang
of Mobiles (who were also strolling about the fortifications), and hauled, dragged, and jerked along
to the nearest Mairie, where he showed a permit
signed by Trochu. This was an aggravation, because a disappointment. The old Marshal was
hauled, dragged, and jerked to the Governor's head-
quarters, and there he was recognised. One of the
Provisional Government endeavoured to assuage the
patriotic rancour of his fellow citizens, who, after
hanging about for a long while, reluctantly dispersed
in pursuit of other game.

The female *espionomaniacs* are more savage if
possible than the male of their species. They
uniformly demand summary execution. Their features recall the days of the Reign of Terror, when
women were always foremost in the bloody fray.

One of the victims was hounded with the cry,
"He speaks German! He speaks German!" He
finally succeeded in getting his back up against a
shop window, and exclaimed, "Yes, I do speak
German, and Italian, and Spanish, and that isn't
all. I speak better French than any man in this
mob. I am a born and bred Parisian, and that is
more than can be said of any of you. Mon Dieu!
Things are coming to a fine degree of liberty,
equality, and fraternity if a Frenchman cannot walk

the streets of his native city without being run down
by a lot of ruffians from the provinces."

The boldness of this speech cowed the mob.

"And now," exclaimed the man at bay, "if a
passage is not made for me at once through this
crowd I'll make one."

The gentleman doubled both fists, made a dive
and a plunge. The villains fled precipitately, illustrating the proverbial fact that no mob is at once
so devilish and so craven as that of Paris.

21st September.—General Trochu denounces the
soldiers who "compromised the combat of Chatillon,"
and "turns over to the military tribunals those who
were found in a state of inebriety, talking scandal-
ously, and dishonouring the uniform they wear."

The police swoop up a lot of *demoiselles* on the
boulevards. The impertinence and aggressive disposition of this class now is in striking contrast
with their retiring behaviour heretofore. This is
one of the signs of our times—night times.

I observed on the doors of the *cremeries* to-day,
"Closed for the want of milk." I expect this will
be found on the cradles too one of these days—a
sad feature of the siege to come so early in it.

Several thousands of boys march along the
boulevards carrying a flag and singing the 'Marseillaise.' They call themselves "The pupils of the
Republic," and have evidently got a Republican
lesson or two by heart already.

22nd September.—The Garde Nationale "mani-
fest" at the Hôtel de Ville against the armistice.

Jules Favre responds, "We are a government of national defence and not of capitulation." The manifesters disperse, crying "Death to the Prussians!"

A reconnoissance to "feel the Prussians," near Creteuil. The Prussians feel strong, and the French feel like retiring, whereupon they retire.

A deserter fires on his captain, who in turn fires, and kills the deserter.

THE RELIGIOUS DIFFICULTY.

23rd September.—I find the following on the walls to-day:—

"Monsieur le Curé,—In consequence of the notice of the Mayor of Paris, which orders that the device, Liberty, Equality, Fraternity, shall be replaced on the public edifices, I ask *(j'invite)* the curés to give M. Gaultier-Boissière, who has charge of this work, all the facilities necessary for carrying out his mission in so far as it concerns the churches.

"✝ G., Archbishop of Paris."

As I looked upon the defilement going on at Notre Dame, I was suddenly awakened from my reverie by a hand on my shoulder and a voice—

"Oh! well, you know, the Kingdom of Heaven is as a net cast into the sea. It must yield with the tide lest the tide break it, and in trying to catch all it catch none."

This was said by the handsome curé with whom I have had some talk, amid the roar of the battle and in the lonely streets of old Paris. He is one of those rare souls, who, with brilliant intellect and the highest attainments, devote themselves to the drudgery of their profession. He is learned in literature, in science, and in the human heart. He is nobly born, and has consecrated a fortune to the service of the poor. He loves his calling with an enthusiasm which is never expressed in words, and which is none the less conspicuous and all the more fascinating on that account.

"And that is your explanation of that fellow's work, is it?" (I said, pointing to what was going on under "the royal towers.") "It isn't an epitaph, is it?"

"No, my good friend, it is no epitaph, I can assure you. That man's chisel, you see, does not go in far. His mutilation is shallow. He touches no artery. A few veins bleed, that is all. The wound will soon heal. If such as he could reach the heart of the Church, she would long ago have bled to death. See how careful he is, and with what a malicious delight he prosecutes his work! It is not pleasant to see, but as there is no depth to the chisel's mark, there is no depth in its wound. The wound heals, and the mark will pass away."

"Of course the consent of the Church is not given with goodwill, is it?"

"Certainly not."

"She yields rather than do worse?"

"Precisely so, my good friend; the net yields rather than break. Our divine Lord is explicit upon this point, you know; when the alternative comes of bending or breaking, we are to bend. When pursued we are to flee; when we can become pursuers we are to do so. That wall yields to the chisel, which it cannot resist, as our wills yield to the tide, which we cannot withstand. The Church is founded upon a rock which does not yield, but she herself is necessarily of a more pliable substance. The foundation standeth sure, but the superstructure is shattered. The rock is secure, and so is the house on it, for that matter, but it cannot escape damage from rain and wind."

"Especially in the midst of this Red Sea,—eh?"

"True enough" (laughing); "but when the Red Sea has spent itself the house and the rock will both be safe and tranquil and beautiful—a shelter and a repose. The waters will part some day, and we shall go over dry-shod."

"I suppose you apply your idea of the net to the events which seem to be impending in Rome, do you not?"

"Oh yes—well, yes—that is, I suppose those who set much store by the temporal power do. For my part I have no concern over its loss. I believe, if it ever was necessary (and I admit that it was), it is necessary no longer. It has been means to an end, and the end is gained."

"What is that?"

"Universality of dominion. The temporal power has secured a kingdom and dominion to the Church throughout the earth. That achieved, she may safely, and I think profitably, lay down the temporal sword, and devote both hands to the spiritual sceptre. At any rate, when brought before governors and kings,

whom she cannot withstand, she must yield in
obedience to a holy command."

The evening came. The man descended from
his half-finished work. As I parted with the curé,
I overheard a workman say, "The good father hates
that operation as much as we hate the good father.
Heaven speed the day when there shall be no more
priests or churches!"

We all took a parting look, as we went our different ways, at the sad old cathedral standing there
in the twilight, with its half-written inscription at
the top of the ladder,

"LIBERTÉ, ÉGAL——"

Jules Favre publishes his interview with Bismarck.
I am satisfied that but for the insane populace, or
the monarch in the red crown who rules in this
city, the terms of Bismarck would have been accepted, revictualment abandoned, and the Assembly
called together.

The official journal, after saying that the armistice negotiations have failed, says, "There must be
no more tumultuous manifestations at the statue of
Strasbourg."

To-day we had an "*affaire*" at Villejuif, which
was occupied by the French under the fire of the
forts.

A soldier at Villejuif will not retreat with the
rest. Has a hand-to-hand struggle with a spiked
helmet. Bullet through the lungs. Falls. Bullet
from a window designed for the Frenchman mortally
wounds the Prussian. The two are borne away on

the same *brancard*, and are laid off for a moment near together. They wake from their swoon. They recognise each other, shake hands, smile, and die.

24th September.—Price of bread fixed at 45 centimes the kilogram. The Government of Jules Favre begins the publication of the private correspondence of the Government of Napoleon III.

Newsboys prohibited from crying anything more than the titles of their journals.

Reconnoissance at Nogent, Petit-Brie, and thereabouts.

Municipal elections, fixed for 28th inst., adjourned. Ditto those for National Assembly.

National Guard to have 1 franc 50 centimes a day.

Government requisitions the horses, and promises to deal out horse-meat at a reasonable and uniform price.

General Trochu arraigns the National Guard for behaviour unbecoming the gravity of the situation, and enjoins fewer political and poetical "manifestations," and more military discipline.

There is hardly a semblance of military etiquette among the Guard. A private soldier will rush up to his colonel or general without so much as touching his hat, and make a request concerning some grievance in the most familiar manner.

26th September.—Twenty-one soldiers of the line attempt to desert to the enemy from the artillery of Mont Valérien. Caught. Walked through the streets

with these words on a piece of paper on their caps:
"A miserable coward, who deserted before the enemy,
and deserves to be spit in the face by all good
citizens."

And the good citizens paid the debt with ala-
crity and vigour.

The Arc de Triomphe and Louvre, and most of
the monuments, are protected from the anticipated
shells by boards and earthworks.

City gates to be closed at 7 P.M. and opened at
7 A.M.

LEDRU ROLLIN COME AGAIN.

27th September.—The Communists clamour for the municipal elections, and Ledru Rollin makes his first appearance for twenty years in his *rôle* of agitator. He advocates the "Commune" as the panacea for all the ills that France is heir to.

He calls upon the Garde Nationale to sign a demand for elections to be held on the 2nd and 3rd of October. He declares himself in favour of the elections, government or no government, and advocates the appointment of a committee in each arrondissement, who shall proceed to hold them, under *la surveillance du peuple.* He says:—

"A member of Government has come to me and said, 'I also wish for the Commune, and the Government will yield if the *chefs de bataillon* energetically demand the elections.' 140 *chefs de bataillon* having gone to the Hôtel de Ville, with the protest, which had received 180 signatures, the answer of the Government is—an adjournment *sine die.* Citizens! your reply to this decree must be the assertion of your right. If you believe that the Commune will give you more strength to sweep away the insolent enemy that threatens you, insist—act—vote! We will be worthy of our fathers. We will do our duty by imitating that great people, and that great Commune, which, in 1792, saved France, and created the Republic!"

The advent of Ledru Rollin recalls the Red-letter days of 1848. Time has not yet diminished his strength; his natural force seems to remain un-abated; his sixty-second birthday has not brought him increase of wisdom, but it has found him as strong for mischief as ever; and there is no doubt of his being a most successful witch for conjuring the deadly elements of the political cauldron. He is aging, certainly; but he is still fine-looking, and impresses one as forcibly as of yore with his rotund and commanding presence, his sonorous voice and masculine delivery. He speaks with as much energy as ever, but perhaps with a trifle less of impudent audacity than in 1851. Jules Favre, who was formerly his secretary and coadjutor, is now at the head of the Ministry, and will hardly rejoice at his return.

Ledru Rollin has been twenty years a refugee in England, whither he fled from before the face of Louis Napoleon, who for a time rode on the whirl-wind and directed the storm which Ledru Rollin had raised; but now Louis Napoleon is at Wilhelms-höhe, and Ledru Rollin has come back to resume his place at the "cauldron."

The newspaper called *La Patrie en Danger*, contains to-day a thoroughly '95 editorial article, to which the name of Félix Pyat is attached. He charges everybody, except himself, with "betraying the Republic."

The Bourbons are not the only people who "have learned nothing and forgotten nothing" during all these years.

"We must have no mercy," says Pyat, "but cover the traitors with their own blood. Down with Mirabeau! *Vive Marat!*"

28th September.—M. Courbet, in a public *réunion*, advocates the transformation of the Vendôme column into its original cannon. He says it is a monument of imperialism and conquest, and expresses a sentiment wounding to republican sensibilities. He announced that a statue of the First Napoleon had been taken down at Courbevoie, by order of the mayor. He is in favour of removing every trace of Napoleonism from the city.

SOWING AND REAPING.

A LOOKER-ON at a siege obtains an insight into the condition of the people which he could never have gained in the normal state of society. The vivacity and quickwittedness of the French, their genius for acting and public speaking, is well known; but few are aware of the ignorance that prevails in France.

It is said that not more than one in twenty-four of the Parisians can read and write, and that not more than ten of the educated men of this city can speak or understand the English language. Indeed, it is quite) the fashion among the *literati* here to parade their ignorance of the English language and of English literature.

You can hardly be surprised at this absence of common-sense, while its source is unfrequented. Vanity must be in its full maturity, if it has not reached its dotage, when it glories in insularity, and makes an affectation of ignorance.

The French are very vain of the fact that their language is "the Court language of the world," and are just now exceedingly nettled, because Bismarck and von Moltke have the impertinence to communicate with Paris in their own tongue.

I find that reading (as that word is understood in Great Britain and the United States) is little practised here. There is no intelligent mass of any class; there is no well-read or well-informed class in France.

The lowest class cannot read, the highest class will not read, and the intermediate class do not want to read. All classes prefer a boozy lounge, or a silly chat, or a lascivious dawdle, to reading or reflection.

The erudition of the French is as exceptional as it is respectable. So in generalship, and ruler-ship, and statesmanship, so in literature and learn-ing, one man rises to an abnormal superiority, and the rest are left in a proportional depth of darkness.

The aristocracy of France are as ignorant of books as her democracy are of sobriety. Both classes are equally destitute of common sense.

M. Pelletan's disgust for what his ill-read coun-trymen and women do read is becomingly intense: "A detestable novel has reached its fourteenth edition in less than a year, and do you know through what inspiration of genius? Through a night-scene beheld through a key-hole." If his wife had read this novel in his (Pelletan's) absence, "he would demand on his return the re-establishment of divorce."

He is quite right. Nothing in the way of litera-ture could be more nauseous and enervating than the common reading of Paris. It suggests another point of resemblance between the present situation here, and that which we find when we read of the decline and fall of ancient nations—monarchical and republican.

One is constantly reminded here of what one thought and saw among the ruins of Pompeii. Material splendour and vicious indulgence flourish side by side. But the latter, which the Second Empire compelled to observe a certain amount of reticence and retirement, is now stalking abroad and literally fattening upon the "liberty, equality, and fraternity" of the new Republican regime.

In 1848, about a month before the Revolution, De Tocqueville said in the Assembly: "Public morality is in a state of degradation which will shortly, perhaps almost immediately, hurry us into new revolutions." The prophecy was fulfilled. To make it now is to see it fulfilled again before our eyes.

The most grossly obscene *brochures* are cried upon the boulevards by young women and little children. Some of these are so abhorrent, that one feels, upon glancing at them, that no calamity could be too great for a city which has neither written law nor lynch law equal to the task of removing so odious an abomination.

In the shop-windows of the most unfrequented streets in the most licentious cities of Italy or Spain, you will see nothing more villainously filthy than the caricature I saw an hour ago, dealt out to merry purchasers on the boulevard by an equally merry young woman of about 18 years of age, with a pretty and unblushing face.

Books make their appearance in the shop-windows, which heretofore were concealed under the shop-counters; and engravings which formerly were only shown to the initiated on the sly, are now within reach of the lads and lasses who accompany their mamma or the servant. A shopkeeper said to me, "Let me show you how rapidly we are progressing." And pulling out a pile of *cartes de visite*, he continued: "Look on the back of it. That is the name of the most fastidious photographer in the city. Before the war he would have prosecuted the man who should have charged him with publishing such a picture, and even upon *cartes* of the ordinary departures from decorum he would not have put his name. Then as to selling, any shop that should have been caught selling such a picture as this would have been closed, and its proprietor punished."

On the tents of the soldiers I have seen words and sketches of the very last degree of flagrant indecency. The songs of the camp cannot be repeated in the presence of a lady. An officer said, on my comparing notes with him as to this: "Yes —and the conversation of my comrades is no better. It is so obscene and profane that I, without making any pretension to religion, am shocked and repelled. With you I know it was different; I was in your country during the war. Your camp-songs are sung in the drawing-rooms—ours are too abominable to be tolerated in respectable society." I have had abundant confirmation of this officer's testimony.

My French friends, when we talk over these things, shrug their shoulders, and say: "We make

no pretence, like you Anglo-Saxons; you are hypo-
crites, and are in reality as bad as we are."

There is just one step lower than a bad practice,
and that is a bad theory. Alas for a people who
say unto evil, "Be thou my good!" When a nation
takes that step, it has reached the lowest depth.

It is a curious trait in the character of the French
that, while they will acquiesce in whatever blame
you may lay on society, they themselves will accept
none of the responsibility. They make scapegoats
of their rulers, the men whom they themselves elect
and gladly follow; but they, the individuals, have
no sense of shame or self-reproach. "France," say
they, "is white with innocence; her rulers and
leaders are black with guilt!" But what constitutes
"France," or in what it consists, nobody can tell.

To hear a Frenchman discourse upon his favourite
"scapegoat" (each man has one which he believes
to be the source of all evil) is like listening to a
discussion as to "Who struck Billy Patterson?" or
"Who killed Cock Robin?"

At the present time the scapegoat, not only for
the war, for the insatiable thirst for dominion and
military glory, but the one who has also bewitched
her out of all moral sense and common sense, and
made her—the pure "France, who is white with innocence!"—the involuntary source of all these nasty
caricatures and vicious habits, is Napoleon III.; on
him and on his head they lay all their sins as well
as all their misfortunes.

"The French," say they, "do not read, because

they have been discouraged from reading." Who brought down the brain and soul and understanding of France to its present condition of moral and intellectual putrescence? Who is the sorcerer that has exorcised this nation of its pluck, its manliness, its veracity, its virtue, its chastity, its self-respect, its self-reliance, its love of home, its respect for woman, its faith in religion (heathen and Christian), and its fear of God? It is Napoleon III.! No other Bonaparte, no Louis or Charles, no "child of the people," and no people, had a hand (or sword) in it. It all began and ended with Napoleon III. He did it all, and he did it in eighteen years. He had power over the past, the present, and the future— and infinite power too. He must have exerted it before he was born, and he exerts it now that he is a captive!

What hope can there be for a people who "rend" each one his neighbour's "garment" instead of his own, and who imagine that to lay the blame and shame of "the unclean thing" upon one another is equivalent to doing each his own share in putting it away?

Republicanism cannot survive where there is not a certain degree of public intelligence, a certain amount of virtue, and a certain measure of self-reliance. The masses here have none of these. They have no confidence in one another, and have less to fear from a ruler of their own choice than from themselves in the experiment of ruling themselves. The worst ruler France can have is—"France." In the United States, and in Great Britain, every man stands upon his own two solid legs. Here every man leans against every other man, and all have an ineradicable desire to lean against some one man.

"TOIL AND TROUBLE."

1*st October.*—We have now made up our minds that our bodies are shut up in Paris. This consciousness of being cut off from the outside world must be like the first sensation of being shut up in a cell in solitary confinement; it is very chafing, and makes one feel very impatient: there is a sense of suffocation.

The Prussians have sent in the body of General Guilhem with great solemnity. The bier was covered with flowers and evergreens.

Go where you will, when you will, and you see troops drilling. There is no reason why we should not have a well-drilled army in another month. Then we have a rare opportunity for military rehearsals, since we can fight a little, and run a little, and do a little of everything known to the science of war. Wimbledon is nowhere in comparison for sham-fights and counterfeit campaigns.

Rochefort's Barricade Commission have done their work well, thanks undoubtedly to Dorian, who is the best organizer in the Government. He is a man with great executive faculty and good capacity for achievement. There is a prodigious amount of work in him. He is also as modest as he is efficient. He never speaks, always works. To him we are indebted for the enormous amount of skilful work done on the outer defences of the city.

A small number of Parisians look on these symmetrical mounds of earth with misgivings, when they think of what the Parisians are; and are hopeless of the barricades being any hindrance to an army which must have previously carried the forts and moats and walls, and iron spikes and abattis, of the outward defences. But by far the greater number of the inhabitants believe them, as well as the other defences, to be—impregnable!

6th October.—The day before yesterday we had our first "armed manifestation." The Belleville National Guards, with Flourens at their head, came to make a series of "demands" upon the Government; the first of which was, that every man should be armed with a "chassepot," and that there should be a *levée en masse*, with one or two other items, concluding with the proposal that the Commune should take upon itself the direction and distribution of food.

General Trochu came out and said, somewhat nervously, as he looked out upon that sea of upturned bayonets, that it was not desirable to make the *sorties* demanded without having a precise object in view, and without hope of a useful result, and without the necessary drilling in the use of artillery. This information was received with some murmurs and commotion, which quickly subsided as the burly head of Gambetta appeared. He was greeted with applause until he said his say, which was as brief and as unsatisfactory as the reply of General Trochu, for the remaining requests were also refused.

. There was a great surging and roaring of the thousands of armed men, and it was generally supposed that Flourens meant to board the Palace and take command. On the contrary, he threw up his command, and his regiment dispersed. There was a prodigious feeling of relief in the second story, doubtless, at this collapse of the manifestation.

Flourens' eyes are the wildest and maddest I ever saw out of a lunatic asylum.

He has withdrawn his resignation, "to preserve order and tranquillity!"

We have received another letter from Victor Hugo, who says:—

"O Paris! thou hast crowned the statue of Strasbourg with flowers; history will crown thee with stars!"

Louis Blanc writes a letter. He adheres to the visionary socialism of his youth, and although not to be classed with the sanguinary Reds, he is scarcely to be preferred as a leader to Victor Hugo or Ledru Rollin. To say the truth, these three gentlemen know nothing about the government of a republic. A will-o'-the-wisp would be as safe a guide. "The beginning of the words of their mouths is foolishness, and the end of their talk is mischievous madness."

LEADERS AND FOLLOWERS.

POOR M. Cremieux, at Tours, is getting an awful newspapering.

I had better turn my camera upon him before he is unseated, for he is a "child of the people," and when his parent dismisses him, there is no resurrection for him in this country.

He was Minister of Justice in the Provisional Government of 1848. He was in the prime of his fine abilities during the Revolution of 1830, and figured brilliantly in the law courts throughout the reign of the citizen King. He took his seat in the Chamber of Deputies in 1842 on the extreme Left, where he was resolute and effective in opposition to the Government. When King Louis fled Cremieux advocated the regency of the Duchess of Orleans, and was the author of the appeal of the Duchess to the people. Failing in this project, he took a powerful oar in the Revolution and Government of 1848, and was the originator of many of the most beneficent reforms and measures of that period. He played an important part in the Constituent Assembly. He was one of the arrested at the *coup d'état* of December, 1851, but was released in twenty days. Since that he has been a not very conspicuous, but very vigorous, opponent of the Second Empire. One of the revenges which the whirligig of time brings round is its tossing of M. Cremieux back into one of the seats at the council-table of the Republic. But he was born in 1796, and hence can hardly be expected to fill the post, which he should not have accepted. Like nearly all the able men who struggle and fret their hour on the stormy stage of French politics, his moral ideas are lamentably mixed, and he will pass behind the scenes presently with a very indefinite conception of the part he has been playing, or the object he had in playing it.

8th October. — A newspaper of this morning says: "France needs only one thing at this moment —a solitary military will, which nobody may impede or question, and which has no superiors, colleagues, or committees."

The press gives utterance to that yearning of the French for a supreme will, which alternates with their longing for the complete supremacy of the whole people.

Another "manifestation" to-day at the Hôtel de Ville. The fall of Toul and Strasbourg has disquieted the evil-minded, and disheartened everybody. The Reds were out in great numbers, and such a fermentation as we had!

The Government was on the ground betimes, however, and covered the immense square with troops it could, or supposed it could, trust. They soon up-ended their muskets and brandished the

butts, to signalise the innocence of their intentions
toward the people. It was the signal, too, for a
tremendous burst of "*Vives!*" and "*Vive la Commune!*" Several immense pieces of white paper, inscribed with the word "Commune," were hoisted
on the ends of canes and umbrellas. Trochu rode
along the line followed by his staff, and was greeted
by enthusiastic cries. It was evident that the majority
were with him for that moment, anyhow.

The booming of the guns of Fort Mont Valérien is distinctly heard. Could it have been timed
to impress the dramatic imagination of the Reds,
and turn against the enemy their sanguinary patriotism?

Jules Favre exclaims, "That sound proclaims to
us the post of duty!" He deprecates such manifestations in such a crisis. There are cheers and
cries of *Vive la République! A bas la Commune!*

Favre retires, but the crowd of ten thousand
people in all uniforms, and of all ages, and both
sexes, and every description of odd character, sways
to and fro—a vast hum like millions of bees, and
an awful swell of tumult like the roaring of the sea
admonitory of a storm.

What a conglomeration of human eccentricity
and inflammability indeed did that great mob contain! I saw little boys not over ten screeching at
the tops of their voices, and old women shaking
their forefingers under one another's noses while
they discussed the merits of socialistic democracy,
or descanted on the good times coming when the

poor and the rich would have all things in common.

A brawny-faced workman carried a babe on his shoulder in the midst of the dense mass. The wee thing had a bright face, cunningly set off with a clean white cap, and there it was looking out placidly on the turbulence and uproar. Not a change came over its pretty countenance—no feature moved. It was an emblem of purity and repose standing conspicuously out in the foreground of that picture of unrest and discontent.

A Paris *émeute* is a panorama of such contrasts. You always see nurses drawing babes about, and genteel-looking families—father, mother, and children—sauntering through the conflagration.

A moblot carries a Prussian spiked helmet through the crowd on his bayonet. The rejoicing is intense. If the siege were raised, and the King's army driven away, these people could not dance with more delight, or shout with more ecstasy, than they do over this captured helmet. Well-dressed, good-looking men and women find in this trophy a source of the most demonstrative satisfaction.

The "clouds in the evening sky more darkly gathered." The rain came down. It rained for the first time for a month, and rained as you might expect it would upon such a spectacle—furiously. The father huddled his babe into his arms. The old women ceased to argue and fled. All fled. It rained hard; then the clouds dispersed, a blood-red sky covered the Prussian camp, the sun went down, and the moon shone silently on the deserted square, and the lonely sentinel paced back and forth before the statue of King Henry. Troubled Paris slept.

Minister Gambetta went up in a balloon yesterday to join Minister Cremieux at Tours, where we have a branch government. So our Minister of the Interior becomes Minister of the Exterior. He has a morbid horror of travelling by balloon. He shilly-shallied for three days, putting Nadar in a tempest of impatience; and when the moment for departure came, the eloquent Minister became as white as buttermilk, and his knees smote together as he took his seat in the basket that had been enlarged and otherwise revised to suit him. However, up he went, and a pigeon returned to-day to tell of his safe arrival beyond the Prussian lines.

An intoxicated franc-tireur kills one moblot and wounds another in a restaurant. A member of the National Guard, being suspected for a spy, kills one of his comrades, and comes very near being torn to pieces by the mob before he can be locked up. These incidents are indicative of a change for the worse coming over our situation. And I can see other symptoms here and there of increasing demoralization. One is, that the English language is about as unpopular as the German.

10th October.—The Red papers call Favre "another Palikao," Gambetta "Ollivier II.," and denounce Trochu, Kératry, and Thiers for designing Orleanists. They call the Government organs the "journals of the reaction," and accuse them of secretly conspiring for the overthrow of the Republic.

The administration papers return the compliment by charging the Socialist wing with breeding the discontent which Bismarck predicted.

One of the Red journals is edited by Blanqui, who is called "Blanqui the Younger." So I suppose he is not the original of that name which is familiar to readers of French history. Was it the father of this man to whom Lamartine alluded when he said, "I conspire with Blanqui as the conductor conspires with the lightning?"

The present Blanqui is grey enough and mischievous enough to be the old forked shaft himself. He calls the President "Trochu *le Pieux*," and the Préfect "Kératry *le Chouan*."

There is a general demand for a sortie.

The *Electeur Libre* says: "Strasbourg and Toul have fallen, and we learn of the incapacity of the members of the Government at Tours. And in the presence of this grave news what does the Government do? It orders the statue of Strasbourg to be cast in bronze! Is this the way to avenge Strasbourg?"

The same paper says, "The capitulation of Toul and Strasbourg has been received with a courageous *sang-froid*."

Paris reads the announcement on the walls without a change of countenance or an interchange of observation. Paris is as torpid as a frog in midwinter. But Victor Hugo says: "To her all transformations are possible," so we live in constant expectation of one of these "transformations."

Eighteen new daily papers have been started

since the 4th of September, five of which have
stopped.

Several persons have been arrested for using
violent language against the Government.

Our Government announces 160,000 men marching to our rescue from the Provinces, but nobody
believes a word of it. We believe we are played
out.

The fifty days' heroism of Strasbourg must be
imitated, and the failure of it "avenged." We are
to hold out one hundred days, and then descend
into the last ditch, which is to close over us, leaving
the city to its fate, and the Prussians to the city.
The truth is, according to the heroic rhetoric of
our press, that "Strasbourg fallen is greater than
Strasbourg victorious." Catch our French public
mind if you can! They will swear when Paris
caves in, and Metz follows the example of Strasbourg, and the whole country lies at the feet of
the conqueror, that France has been betrayed and
will be avenged, and is just going to rise and snort
and soar.

There has been a praiseworthy attempt on the
part of the military authorities to restore order and
decorum to our demoralized population by keeping
the soldiers out of the streets. The order is bearing good fruit in increasing sobriety.

The cafés are all closed at 10 P.M., and the
stray moblots are picked up by a squad of muskets.
So that, while we have still to deplore the multiplicity of these loungers in regimentals, there is a
decided improvement in the aspect of the boulevards.

A MYSTERY OF PARIS.

WALKING out with my friend, the Barrister, he suddenly said: "Now for a leaf from the book of human life. Do you see that woman and child? We shall meet them. Take a good look at that child, and I'll tell you her story when she has passed." We meet. We stop.

I looked earnestly into the bright face, and sighed in advance at a venture. They passed. "Now, I'll tell you," said the Barrister. "The mother was a member of one of the highest families in France. She lived at Orleans. The father, too, was of noble lineage. She fled to Paris—an every-day thing in this country—to hide herself and her impending shame. The child was born at the house of the woman who leads her by the hand. The mother died an hour after the child was born. Poor thing! She was very gentle and beautiful and ami-able. I knew her in the provinces. I had some business with the family. Her remorse was poignant from the first. It increased as the shame approached, and when the shame came human nature was not equal to both tortures. Mind and body gave way together. Even the physician, who was an old Parisian practitioner, and thoroughly familiar with

kindred incidents, was deeply moved, and told me
he never was so touched in his life. Such an expression of pathetic sorrow came over the lovely
creature's face, he says, as will never leave his
memory. The silence of the room, the babe, the
motionless face with its awful cloud, the impossibility
of doing anything to mitigate or soothe—it was al-
together a spectacle of rare gloom and melancholy.
So the physician tells me, and I can well believe it
all, for I recall the graceful form darting *incog.* here
and there along the streets in old Paris, and the
startling shadow that I used to see come and go
on that charming countenance. And you will see
that shadow on the child's face, if you catch it at
rest. Just now, it was chased away by the burst of
sunshine at seeing me, but there, it is and there it
will ever be."

THE BLIND LEADING THE BLIND.

12th October.—The day before yesterday the supply of meat was rationed by Government, and we have all been desired to send in the number of the mouths to be fed in each family. Every one leaves his or her name with the butcher of the district, who gives us each a card certifying the right of the bearer to receive about a quarter of a pound of meat every three days upon presentation of the card. Government has fixed the price, which is two to three francs for each portion of beef, and from two francs to a franc and a half for a portion of horseflesh. Horseflesh is at present the most popular.

The "*boucherie*" is now one of the characteristic scenes of the siege. Over the door you read "*Boucherie de cheval*," or "*Boucherie Hippogriffe*." There is a man, sometimes a soldier with a musket, at the door, who asks for and inspects the card. A *queue* of persons wait their turn with basket and ticket in hand. They are mostly maidservants in the more genteel portions of the city, and the very common people in the very common portions. There is a prodigious prevalence of tidy white caps, interspersed with dilapidated old hats; here and there a black skull-cap fringed around the bottom with thin white hair. The old man totters up to his turn, takes his bit, and totters away. At his heels a lean small dog, who looks forward and upward for his share in the stipulated allowance. There is very little crowding or pushing. The *boucheries* are numerous, every district has its own, and so none are pressed by an unwieldy crowd. As the meat is tariffed by the Government, there is no dispute or wrangle over the purchase, so all goes on smoothly and quietly.

The beggars are a feature of the situation. They gradually multiply, and are one of the strongest of our reminders that the glory of Paris is departing. Those who recollect the rarity of mendicants heretofore can hardly believe their eyes when they see these filthy tableaux of deformity and disease.

As you walk along the boulevards now, you might almost imagine yourself in London.

Some of these mendicants are repulsive, but others tempt the hand of charity by their transparent candour and remarkable neatness.

The old blind woman who sits on a chair knitting at the entrance of the Palais Royal, looks for all the world like a piece of waxwork—she is so tidy, trim, and pleasing.

As to giving alms on the street, it is right for me, whatever it may be for other people. Thus I have the poor always with me.

13*th* October.—A trifling *affaire* at Bagneaux. "The object being attained, the retreat was ordered," and we returned.

As usual, we have to deplore the loss of one of those who are so clamoured for by our rank and file—"leaders." In every *"affaire,"* however trifling, we invariably leave the leaders we are so much in want of, and never have, dead in their tracks, or they follow their followers to the rear on a stretcher. In this brush the fallen leader is the Count de Dampierre. He led a battalion of Mobiles, who wavered. He appealed to their patriotism, and then to their sense of shame. At this moment Dampierre fell, mortally wounded, from his horse. His men shouted "Revenge! revenge!" turned upon their heels and fled. At first it was thought that the rascals made something of a stand, but it appears they were so electrified by the heroic example of their commander that they immediately retired to contemplate it at their leisure.

The Count is deeply lamented. He was a general favourite. He was about thirty, bright-eyed, high-spirited, handsome, and resolute. He had many amiable qualities which gave a charm to his character, which was not without those stronger traits which insure vigour and dash on the field of battle. His stable and stud were the admiration of the country. When the Mobiles of his department were organized for the defence of Paris, they chose him for commandant. He had received a military education, but had never been under fire until to-day, when he was ordered to capture the fortifications held by the Prussians near the hamlet of Bagneaux.

I have made up my mind after considerable listening and reflection, as to what this clamour for

"Leaders" means on the part of our garrison who do not follow the leaders they have.

It is, in some cases unconsciously, in most cases consciously, a confession of helplessness,—the helplessness of children. A towering and autocratic spirit is what these helpless people desire. They have a most natural longing for Somebody to rise up from among them and galvanize them. What they mean by a "Leader" is an irresistible Galvanic Battery.

The soldiers of the First Napoleon declared that when he rode along their lines something electrifying came out of him into them. This something electrifying or intoxicating is what our garrison is waiting for, and they have waited thus far in vain to see or feel it come out of Trochu.

This suggests another difference between this race and ours. In the late civil war in America there was indeed that cry for "leaders" which is simply the traditional exercise of the free speech of a free people, but in so far as it was founded upon reflection (which it seldom was), it meant: "Give us men who can organize and make the best possible use of the material we put into their hands." It is like the proprietor of a great manufactory, or rather the workmen themselves, desiring a foreman, or a ship-owner looking up a captain.

That proud feeling of self-respect which animates the Anglo-Saxon resents any other meaning than this in his use of the word "Leader." It is a demand, not of helplessness but of the most sensible self-reliance. We need a veritable human leader, not a two-legged battery of animal magnetism.

I have asked several of these leader-worshippers how they could have endured Washington and his years of failure, or the leaders in our late civil war who were anything but the "favorites of fortune" at first. Neither Grant nor Lee would have stood before this French test of leadership. Washington, so far from sending an intoxicating influence into his troops, was complained of for frigidity and reserve. Those plodding fellows had simply a dogged confidence in their plodding leader.

Lamartine said, "the revolutionary vertigo intoxicated him like wine." Washington never could have said that. Nor could Cromwell, nor Marlborough or the "Iron Duke." These men were not Galvanic Batteries, they were not dependent upon the intoxication of "vertigo," they were "leaders" in a sense which, while it does not detract in the slightest degree from their renown, does reflect gloriously upon the troops which obeyed and followed them. Their followers did not desire and did not expect anything to come out of their leaders but a reasonable order.

They fought with a self-reliant courage which could retreat without despair, as well as advance without losing its head. They did not fight with that blind craze which upon the first reverse degenerates into a headlong panic.

As with the word "leader" so with the word "courage." The very difference in pronunciation of the word in the two languages indicates the dif-

ference there is in its meaning. The French mean
by the word *courage* an unreasoning "vertigo," we
a deliberate doggedness. So they mean by a leader
one who can impart this delirium, we one who can
handle this doggedness.

This difference in race explains the difference
in history. The French leaders have always been
Personal Rulers, often tyrannical Rulers (especially
those who overturned tyranny). The Anglo-Saxon
leaders have always been to some extent and are
now entirely (perhaps too much) ruled by their followers, who will "stand no nonsense" from their
public servants however valuable or illustrious. The
one race resents despotism as an insult to its self-
respect, the other race has an ineradicable hanker-
ing after a despot from sheer lack of manly self-
reliance. The extremer the democrat here, the
more pronounced his despotic disposition. Extremes
meet—Personal Monarchy and Impersonal Republicanism.

Then to make a bad matter worse as far as
Republicanism in France is concerned, the French
are as inflated with self-conceit, as they are deficient
in self-reliance. They are at once self-conscious
and self-distrustful, spasmodically brave, habitually
cowardly, vain-glorious and sneaking, forever prancing up to an obstacle and (if the battery be absent)
forever galloping away from it. The consequence
is that they have none of the advantages and all of
the disadvantages of Republican Individualism.

To say the truth the simplest conditions necessary for a Republic are wanting here—individual

self-reliance, content with hum-drum peace, industry, public virtue, stability of character, common sense, common honesty, and common religion.

On the other hand there is every condition here necessary to a Monarchy and a Personal one in that —helpless feeling of public dependence, vanity in being ruled; passion for *gloire* and militaryism, and the pomp of royalty; chronic discontent; partyism, suspicion, treachery; instability of purpose; infidelity toward everybody in heaven above and in the earth beneath; theoretical as well as practical licentiousness; absolute absence of common sense, and common honesty and common religion both in theory and in practice.

The French and the children need a father for a ruler and a ruler for a father. Or if these people attempt Republicanism they will need a "Personal Monarch" to administer it.

1 5*th October.*—The topic of the day is the *"plan Trochu,"* and the letter which the General has written to the Mayor of Paris.

It has discouraged us all, for it is full of himself and the history of his forebodings when the war began; though he says truly enough "that in the noisy manner of entering upon the campaign, as well as in the means brought into requisition, he perceived the elements of a great disaster;" and he made his will on the strength of it. His only hope in a return of good fortune lies "in the great work of resistance summed up in the siege of Paris." He declares he will not accede to the pressure of public impatience; he will pursue his own plan and keep his own council; and he only begs from the Parisians one thing—their faith and confidence!

He might as well have asked them for the moon while he was about it; for faith, confidence, and stability are not the virtues of a mob—least of all of a Parisian mob.

16th October.—Garibaldi has arrived in the provinces at the head of a very motley following.

THE AMAZONS.

THE walls of Paris, with their wonderful placards, would furnish at once a history and a picture of the siege, if they could be photographed.

Just now everybody is standing still before an enormous green placard headed

"AMAZONS DE LA SEINE."

The placard sets forth that battalions of women should be formed, without distinction of rank, in companies of 150, to the number of 1200. They are "principally destined to defend the ramparts and barricades, jointly with the Garde Nationale Sédentaire, and to render to the combatants in whose ranks they would be distributed by companies all such domestic and fraternal services as are compatible with moral order and military discipline. They will also charge themselves with rendering on the ramparts the first necessary cares to the wounded, who will thus be spared having to wait for several hours. They will be armed with light guns, carrying upwards of 200 yards, and the Government will be petitioned to accord them the same daily indemnity of a franc and a half which is given to the National Guard. The costume of

the Amazons of the Seine will consist of a pair of
black trousers, with an orange-colour stripe, a blouse
of woollen stuff, with a cap, and a black képi with
an orange band, together with a cartridge-box fasten-
ing to a shoulder-belt."

Expenses are to be met by a general sacrifice
on the part of rich ladies of their bracelets, neck-
laces, and other jewels, which they are exhorted to
give, rather than keep them to be plundered by the
Prussians.

The women declare that, "more than men, they
are gifted with the divine fire of grand resolutions
which save, and the active devotion which sustains
and consoles."

The placard is signed "*Le Chef Provisoire du
premier bataillon,* FELIX BELLY."

He has already received 15,000 applications
and innumerable letters. A notice over the door of
his bureau states that each applicant must be accompanied by a relative or guardian, and any one giving false credentials of respectability will be prosecuted by law!

M. Belly might have achieved wonders, but before he could organise his movement he was "suppressed" by Government, and the plan was laughed
down.

The other day, however, there was a woman's
manifestation. The column marched with such a
heavy tramp to the Hôtel de Ville, and carried such
a mass of muscle and sinew, that I was afraid
Rochefort would faint when he came out to address
them. Their request then was that they should be

allowed to take care of the wounded while the "other sex" went one and all out on a sortie, and that there should be "an equitable distribution of subsistences." There was nothing more unreasonable or sanguinary in the manifestation than this. Poor Rochefort listened, and bowed, and promised, and was glad to get off without being carried off by the women.

Everybody knows who knows the *maisons*, the wine-shops, and the markets of Paris, that the common run of women here are superior to the common run of men in all that pertains to strongmindedness and stronghandedness. In nine cases out of ten the *homme* and the *femme* are unequally yoked together, and the woman is the better man of the two. She has more energy, more pluck, more pertinacity, more sense, more brains, accomplishes more, and often weighs more and eats more although, as M. Belly says, she drinks and smokes less, and therefore mopes less. Nobody can compare the two sexes as they sit together in the cafés or kneel together in the churches without coming to this conclusion.

The women are more religious and have more sense of virtue than the men. Men in Paris reach a depth of degradation to which women do not, and I believe cannot, follow them.

22nd October.—A sortie on a large scale (for us) yesterday in the direction of Rueil and Jonchere, under General Ducrot, with about 10,000 men and about twenty-five cannon. The fight begins at 1 P.M., and continues till about 4.30, when an "order is given for the troops to re-enter into their respective cantonments." The "results," which are not given, are said to be "very satisfactory."

But nobody cares for official bulletins: it is doubtful if anybody cares for anything. The public mind is getting callous. Paris is not at all thin-skinned now towards the "results" of *"sorties"* and *"affaires."*

"ON WITH THE DANCE!"

23rd October.—Sunday without amusements has become insupportable to the Parisians; so to-day they had a "Popular concert of classical music; given for the benefit of the wounded." Hundreds were unable to get in, and about 5000 francs were taken. The excellent music was extremely saddening at its merriest notes, and went to the very soul of some, I am sure, of the large audience. It brought the woes of their country vividly home to them. I saw several nice-looking persons drop their eyes and dash away the tears. The poor old soul adjoining me, dressed with such charming, old-fashioned quaintness, was breathing hard all the time, as if the orchestra were tearing her sensibilities to pieces, and the lips of the young woman in deep black, a little farther along on our seat, were working constantly as if she too were in torture, and I presume she was. I suppose it is very foolish for the afflicted or the sad-hearted to go to an entertainment like this, since the "soothing" influence of music, so much talked about, is mercilessly dispensed.

But such persons are morbidly drawn to what is certain to lacerate them. The concert was of more benefit to "wounded" bodies than wounded spirits.

25th October.—The *Temps* says: "Paris has not lost her *esprit* or her gaiety, and calls for *spectacles* and concerts." I think this demand for the medicine is a symptom of the disease.

The *bal masqué* dies for want of breath; the gaiety of the Maison Dorée betrays the artificial exertion it requires to keep it up.

But it is sorrowful to see that the only persistency shown by the Parisians is in their efforts to follow their old diversions, and to keep alive their animal pleasures in the matter of wine and women. In these latter days, drinking has become strangely and ominously prevalent.

The Théâtre Français was crammed to-day; and hundreds were unable to get in. The programme comprised the first two acts of Molière's 'Misanthrope' and the 'Cuirassiers of Reichshoffen.' The French know how to act. They act all over, and each player acts with all his heart. They are born artists on the stage.

M. Ernest Legouré, member of the Academy, gave a 'Conference' on the 'Moral Alimentation of Paris.'

To hear one of these *conférences* is to have heard them all.

They are theatrical entertainments from beginning to end, to which the orator and the audience equally contribute. One of M. Legouré's passages was:

"Paris uncrowns herself with her own hands of the forests that surround her, as a widow cuts off her hair in token of her grief."

The audience were moved.

The speaker caused some amusement by making fun of the "sacred word" *citoyen;* and also of the sacred pastime of changing the names of the streets and public buildings.

M. Henri de Rochefort, who was sitting on the platform, felt himself insulted by this, and he arose and strode with dignity out of the little back door that was the entrance to the platform. There was a universal titter at this incident, one angular looking youth tried hard to get up some applause; but the laughter prevailed.

Blanqui, in the leading article of his paper, "*La Patrie en Danger,*" is indignant at the continuance of theatrical entertainments; he is ashamed of the multitude who continue to flock to them, and declares them highly unbecoming in so grave a crisis.

This is all quite true and quite right. The witches who brew the "Double, double, toil and trouble," and who "round about the cauldron go," are no doubt fastidious about their ingredients.

Mégy, who was in prison for the assassination of the sergent de ville, and who was liberated and made standard-bearer of the 91st Battalion, has just had a fight with his commandant, and is under arrest for it.

The countenances of many of the National Guards are anything but encouraging to look at.

There are thousands of men in the ranks of these citizen soldiers whose appearance bodes ill for the future. It would be almost as safe to liberate and to arm the convicts of the prisons, as to place muskets and ball cartridges in the hands of these fellows. Every owner of property in the city must shudder to see these troops at drill or on the march. It is hazardous to go so low for soldiers; honesty and integrity are quite as essential in a soldier as in a citizen.

˅ Our second postal balloon went up to-day containing 100 kilogrammes of letters. Each letter must not be more than four grammes in weight.

We watch the ascent of our aerial post with lively curiosity not unmixed with anxiety, for it carries messages which, however brief, will be comfortable to some beyond "the circle of fire."

When I said to a cynical acquaintance of mine: "Well, we shall get no more letters," he replied, "Thank heaven! I've been praying for this day these ten years."

The Mayor of Paris decrees that the Boulevard Prince⁻Eugène shall be called Boulevard Voltaire, and that the statue therein of the prince (Eugène de Beauharnais) shall be displaced by one of Voltaire.

My friend the barrister, although a stiff Roman Catholic, confesses to a great admiration for Voltaire on account of his services to liberty.

The statue of the Empress Josephine has been removed from the avenue that bore her name.

Government announces a despatch by pigeon-post, bringing the news of "*la belle résistance* of Chateaudun." One feels a real affection for these little birds as one watches them coming in. There is something very pathetic in their wearied appearance and languid flight. The people are very kind to them, and some weep as they watch the faithful things alight on a roof to rest, and perhaps to take their latitude.

THE RED HAND ON THE SKY.

LAST evening, Joseph, our indefatigable forager, burst pale and breathless into the dining-room, where we were resting after one of the bankers' starvation dinners of delicious chciken, to inform us that an awful fire had broken out, and the blaze was covering the entire city. We seized our hats, bounded down the steps, and out into the street through the court, overturning the concierge's children in our headlong haste for the Place de l'Opéra, where we joined a big crowd to see the northern and eastern and western sky perfectly suffused with the deep rich red of—an Aurora Borealis! It was entirely different from any phenomenon of the sort I ever saw, and it was in some respects the most extraordinary one I ever saw. I have seen more variegated and more beautiful ones, but I never saw one so awfully red. It rose up out of half the horizon, hesitated, rose, recoiled, expanded, contracted, faded, deepened, broke into lakes of Red intenser than any I ever saw on canvas, or on the clouds at sunset. It shimmered out over almost the whole heavens. The darkness imbued it with a heavy tinge of gloom. It assumed the form of darting fingers. Upon my word—a Red Hand!

"*Mon Dieu*, it is Bismarck's bloody hand!" muttered the young Mobile to his companion. "Or Fate's?" replied the companion, and laughed. But I saw the restless twitch of superstition in his nerves. A Celt is superstitious while he laughs at superstition.

An officer standing by my side in the crowd said, "Oh, as for that, you know our common people are all superstitious." "And they are very uncommon people who are not superstitious," said the Doctor. "I know, if I had more of it, I would have more peace of mind. Better that than nothing. It is inseparable from religion. Without it there can be no religion."

I said to the old woman at the kiosque, You are not superstitious? "Not at all, Monsieur." If you were, what would all that mean? "Blood, Monsieur, blood! The Blessed Mother is vexed with poor France, perhaps." And the old newswoman told the story of her superstition in the act of denying it. A genteelly-dressed man, with a thoughtful face, gazed up long and abstractedly, and then said, "That is the blood which is to be shed in Paris. So I knew well enough that the newswoman and the officer and the man with the thoughtful face went home with the belief that they had seen the bloody hand of Bismarck in the Red Hand on the sky.

26th October.—The papers announce the death, from wounds received in the last battle, of Bérenger, formerly French consul at Stettin; Leroux, artist;

Guvillier, *statuaire;* and Vibert, author, all of whom fought in the rank-and-file.

A contractor of my acquaintance, who wished to supply the Government, asked a wealthy captain of the National Guard if he (the contractor) could depend upon the men buying their own muskets. The reply was, "Why, do you really think that the National Guard would fight for their country and buy their own muskets? That would be patriotism. There is no such thing in France now. The National Guard will not buy. You'll lose every sou of your investment if it depends upon any considerable number of even the rich buying their guns."

A venerable-looking fiery old Frenchman opened in my hearing a furious tirade of denunciation upon a lot of soldiers. Pointing to them he exclaimed, to those of us who stood by: "They are cowards and scoundrels. They won't do anything. There is no blood and no pluck left in France—no mettle, no heroism, no physical vitality. We are gone!— we are gone! Poor France! she is gone! When the war is over I shall go to Switzerland, become naturalized, and deny to my last breath that I am a Frenchman."

This declaration is quite the fashion now. You hear it frequently, and from the best class of Frenchmen; and, what is still more noticeable, those who have most to say about the desertion, and deception, and treason, and betrayal, and all that, to which "poor France" is subjected, are the first to declare that as soon as von Moltke opens the gates they are going to flee their native land, and leave it to its fate. Call you this backing your country? Is this the French "patriotism" of which we have heard so much? The worship of success, the only sentiment to which the French are faithful, kills patriotism, chivalry, and every civic virtue. A nation guilty of such idolatry must of necessity fall down and perish.

There are many Frenchmen here who wear the uniform of the National Guard and carry an American passport. I was pleased to hear the United States' Minister tell some of them that their place was on the other side of the Atlantic, though I must say I shall be thankful if they do not act upon the hint. May the "civilization shut up in Paris" stay where it is!

29th October.—It is asserted in *Le Combat* of yesterday that Bazaine is secretly negotiating with King William for the surrender of Metz. This has caused "a profound sensation."

General Bellamere reports the capture of Bourget with much elation, and says, "This enlarges the circle of our occupation," etc.

30th October.—Bourget has been recaptured by the Prussians. The French commander was in bed and asleep; the soldiers were in the wine-cellars, and mostly drunk. Those who were drunk were killed or captured; those who were sober ran away.

This disgrace makes a great sensation. The Government try to smooth the matter over by asserting that Bourget "formed no part of the general plan of defence."

1st November.—There was an interesting spectacle in the cemeteries to-day. It is All Saints' Day, when it is the custom to visit the tombs of departed relatives; and to-day, in the midst of all our gloom, people came in crowds, each to freshen up the little mound which covered the precious dead, now "wholly at peace and quiet." The dead, discoloured wreaths are replaced by living ones. The French are as reverent about their dead as the Chinese—their graves are never left alone or forgotten. One would say that the living strive to give their dead ones some share in the pleasant light of the sun, and to keep their hold of them even in the land of shadows.

ANOTHER ERUPTION.

WE have had another eruption of the volcano upon which we are living! It was brought on by three specific events—

The affair of Bourget;

The fall of Metz;

The negotiations of M. Thiers.

We have had one Republic taken captive, another Republic set up in its place, and the first Republic reinstated—all in the space of twelve hours. By ten o'clock Bismarck's "populace" were ominously astir, and Bismarck's prophecy seemed about to be fulfilled. People, and people, and people hurrying to the Hôtel de Ville—our seat of government—Robespierre's, and King Louis's, and King Mob's seat of government. King Mob's seat of government last night: ten thousand, fifteen thousand, twenty thousand, packing all the vast open space before the palace, and all the streets emptying into it. Women with big feet and ankles of prodigious circumference; maidservants, in their clean white caps; boys, as frolicsome as only boys can be, playing hide-and-seek among the forest of legs, followed by small dogs in full bark; old men, who totter as they hasten; frantic blouses, pipe going furiously, some with the moblot stripe down the legs; Mobiles and Nationals, in half uniform and full uniform, full-armed and half-armed — in they pour, and here they gather, and shout, and squeeze, and sway.

The Seine runs silently and swiftly by; the church-bells toll slowly and solemnly; Notre Dame stands near, on an island in the river. More history. What history upon history piled all round here! The spirits of Robespierre, and Danton, and King Louis (with King Mob's red crown on), gather about the equestrian statue of King Henry. That fearful hum again—that long, low, awful murmur of the human sea.

Detachments of the National Guard crowd through the dense mass with the butt-end of their muskets up. A pacific sign. They will not fire on the mob. "Better," says the spirit of King Louis. "Better not," replies the spirit of Lafayette, and the spirit of Robespierre concurs. Mirabeau would like to address them from the balcony, and Napoleon lead them against Blücher's successor at Versailles. But may not the butts mean surrender? The waiter from the café suggests that it may, the middle-aged woman with the thin nose fears it does, and exclaims *"Mon Dieu!* it shall never be. The women will never consent to it." "Never!" cries the lame man in the straw hat. "I will join thee, *citoyenne,* cripple as I am, and never yield till the Prussians are driven from France."

Large pieces of white paper are raised aloft, on which we read: "No armistice! Resistance to death!

Vive la Commune!" Wild cheers and frantic swinging of hats and caps. The ocean heaves, and swells, and roars. The clouds hang low. An un-intermittent drizzle. Sloppy streets. Dismal enough, look which way you will, up or down, to palace or cathedral.

A tall wellbred-looking gentleman, in officer's undress uniform, ventures to deplore such factious behaviour, and looks down haughtily on the ruffians who hustle up around him with menacing faces and fingers. But he folds his arms and continues to look formidable to his tormentors, who gradually skulk before his cool disdainful eye.

This combination of the sneak and the bully is only to be found in all its perfection in a Paris mob. Somebody of consequence, to all appearance, is recognised by the villains, one of whom wriggles up close to him, shakes five filthy nails in his face, and screams, "*Vous êtes un lâche! Vous êtes un lâche!*"

A French revolution thaws out some of the oddest and strangest-looking human beings that ever were seen on the face of the earth.

Delegations wedge their way through to the iron gates, carrying banners inscribed, "*Levée en Masse!—Pas l'Armistice!—Vive la République!*" The largest of these banners is snatched from its two poles by a gust of wind. "A good omen!" growls the tall officer. The woman with the thin nose grabs at her boy, exclaiming, "Look! I tell thee, child, the winds are against the Republic!" A shrill voice cries, "*Vive la République Rouge!*"

The clock over the entrance chimes the quarter-hour. The pleasant melody is sadly out of keeping with the angry and vindictive shouts. We are over-heard talking English, and a moblot takes his pipe from his mouth to remark, "We don't want to hear any language spoken that we cannot understand." "Then you'll not hear your own," growls the hand-some officer. But nobody minds what the officer says. We keep close to him. We hear it whispered, "An Imperialist! How he'd like to shoot us down with his master's muskets!" The answer was, "But it is our turn now. Look—they are forcing the gates."

So they are. The gates come open. The crowd pours in. Flourens, at the head of several hundred armed tirailleurs, leads the attack. There is a parley with the sentinels, who give way. Shots are fired, by whom, at whom, no one knows. They fire the mine. Ten thousand people run hither and thither, crying, "To arms!—to arms! They are attacking the Government. They are firing on the people." Now a spectacle of panic, stampede, and lunacy, such as only Paris can furnish. The ten thousand lunatics run down the Rue Rivoli, into the Boule-vard Sebastopol. Some spin round on their axis— just spin round, that's all. Others make frantic gestures. National Guards plunge into their shops, and rush out again with their muskets. The shops close magically. Paris shopkeepers excel in shop-closing. They can keep ahead of the rapidest mob. "Clap, clap, clap," all along the street. It is like a drill. Fastidiously-dressed Nationals are rolled over

in the thin slop. I sit suddenly on the kerb, with
an enormous woman in my lap. I slip out from
under, and leave my burthen in my place. I take
shelter in a restaurant. The handsome officer stands
still. The freshet goes round him like a brook round
an oak. I can see him wish that Napoleon were
ten years younger, and at the head of 50,000 men.
Such antics and frantics, such grotesque contortions
of rage, such gesticulating and perspiring, and
shaking of fingers and brandishing of fists and hats,
and such laughing and jesting, too! If a terrified
woman exposed her ankle in her flight, the lunatical
patriots would pause and stare. No male Parisian
would miss such a sight on his death-bed. You
would see a man suddenly stop running, take out a
pipe, light it, and become perfectly composed and
unconcerned.

We gather at the door of the palace again, and
rush in. The Government are in session in one of
the rooms, but break up in disorder. Flourens, with
his great wild eyes wilder than ever, mounts the
table and proclaims the Red *régime*. He calls out
a dozen names for the offices of state, Dorian for
president. He declines; not—such is the astound-
ing demoralization of everybody and everything—
because he holds an important office under the old (?)
Government, but because he does not feel competent
to form a new one. He is afraid he is not the man
to form a ministry, and he is sure it is not modesty
that induces him to decline. Trochu mounts a stool
in the passage, and exclaims: "Citizens, hear the
words of a soldier. Your city was in danger; I

have secured its defence. The enemy could have entered in forty-eight hours, now I can defy him." Cries of *"A bas Trochu!"*—*"No armistice!"*—*"Vive Flourens!"* The general is asked why he did not march on the enemy. He replies, because it would be butchery to do so. Jules Simon and Mayor Arago try in vain to soothe the lunatics. A scuffle occurs on the great stairway, so often trodden by the feet of revolutionists.

An officer gets slapped in the face. He draws his sword. It is snatched from him. Another shot outside, followed by the cry, "To the Seine—to the Seine!" It was proposed by the Trochu party to drown the man who had fired a revolver. He was rescued by some of the National Guard. There is an attempt to shut the gates; it succeeds but partially. They are forced back again. The iron banister of the stairway bends under the tremendous pressure. Furniture is smashed. A splendid plan of Paris, drawn up by Haussmann's engineers and Napoleon's Haussmann, is cut to pieces by the revengeful Reds. They break into the chamber where the twenty mayors are in session. The mayors flee. Din, racket, confusion, in all the rooms and in all the halls. Trochu is incarcerated in one of the rooms, with his coat mutilated and his decorations torn. Favre is also shut up. Rochefort is as pale as on the day of Victor Noir's funeral. Jules Ferry slips out, and rallies the National Guard for the rescue of the Government. The unwashed and uncombed crowd are addressed by Flourens, Pyat, and Blanqui. "The country is to be saved by the Commune. You workmen and artisans are to save it," and so forth.

While the mob inside is deliberating in this maniacal manner, the mob outside is deliberating in a manner no less maniacal. A shot is fired before the entrance, by a man who was grabbed and called a Prussian, because—as a wild woman exclaims, as she brandishes her fists in the man's face—he has light hair and light complexion. "Did you ever see such hair on a Frenchman?" vociferates the hag. "Never!" echoes the mob. But the supposed *espion* eludes his followers and escapes. While the clock over the door is chiming the quarter before five, slips of paper are thrown from the windows, announcing the proclamation of the Commune and the elections. Darkness adds to the entanglement and confusion. It is evident that the great body of the National Guards are on the side of the old (!) Government. There is an encounter with the white-bearded Blanqui. The old revolutionist is hustled and knocked hither and thither in the fray, and at last falls senseless over against the bench. The Reds hold the field, or rather floor, and carry off their wounded leader. Favre looks out of the window of his prison-room upon the sea of troubles, that looks all the more sinister and ominous by reason of the gloomy drizzly night. At one time the Reds have possession of the Hôtel de Ville on the inside, and the Trochu troops on the outside. So we have a siege within a siege. This was very comical, and was hugely enjoyed by the volatile Parisians, who forgot their sorrows in the enjoyment of the comedy.

For about five hours the Reds had control and held the quarter-deck, as it were, while they kept their opponents in the hold below. So Flourens followed the example of Favre, and "picked up the authority he found lying on the ground." The Mayor made a speech inviting the people to support the cause of order, and to abide by the result of the elections, which would take place on the following day. Dorian was declared president *ad interim*, and the Favre government would resign. The twenty mayors also met, and proclaimed the elections for the following day.

This was a capitulation on the part of the Favre government, but it was no sooner over than—lo! presto! change!—they found themselves out of the hold and on the quarter-deck, in undisputed supremacy.

Ferry's Nationals got the upper hand, and Flourens fell back down the great stairway, and has since declared, in the language of the official reports of the sorties, "having attained our end we retired." The crowd dissolved, the morning dawned, the river ran on, the clock on the palace chimed the quarter-hours, and all was quiet once more.

How the *émeute* passed off without bloodshed is a mystery even to those who are used to the caprices of fortune in a Paris "manifestation."

Certainly we are not indebted to either the Trochu or the Flourens party for our escape. It is no credit to any of them that "the Revolution" continues to be "bloodless." If it continues so to the end it will be a "Divinity" indeed that "shapes" it.

Rochefort has resigned his seat at the council-board of the Republic, but retains his stand at the barricades.

Rochefort is not either cruel or ferocious. The ugliness of his face is relieved by its drollery, and the savage chatterings of his pen are redeemed by their grotesque incoherence.

5th November.—Jules Favre tells us that M. Thiers spoke with Bismarck on the question of the re-victualling of Paris.

My morning paper has a gleam of sense, for it says: "We are expiating the blunders of the late (and present?) Government;" and it says also:

"It is time for illusions to cease. Now is the time to look the reality in the face. We are vanquished. France is beaten and prostrate. Can she prescribe absolute conditions? Can she speak as the victorious party? It is impossible."

Then the lunacy returns, and it goes on to say:

"Thank Heaven, we can subsist for awhile on our antecedents; they are sufficiently illustrious!"

This is something like the boy at the base of the monument at Bunker's Hill, who, being asked by a stranger "what people lived upon in those parts," replied, "Pumpkin Pies and Past Recollections."

CRITICAL PIETY.

ONE of the sarcasms of what Victor Hugo calls "The civilization shut up in Paris," is aimed at King William for using the name of the Deity so frequently in his dispatches to the Queen. But why should this awaken the jealousy of Paris? She should be content, one would think, so long as his Majesty does not appropriate her deity, or deities, or plagiarize her devotional phraseology. She might well complain if he should so far forget what is due an honourable foe as to continually harp on "The treason of fortune," or "The conquest of famine"—or rather on the fidelity of the god Fortune and the victory vouchsafed by the god Plenty-to-eat. Does not Paris speak quite as frequently (if not so fervently) of her object of faith and worship, as Berlin does of hers? Will we ever hear an end of French crowing and boo-hooing at the shrine of French fatalism? Surely the frequency of reference which is practiced by the worshippers of the god Fortune will not be denied to the worshippers of the Lord God of Sabaoth.

Picking up the "Figaro" we read: "France is the Christ of nations, for two months nailed on the cross." . . . . . "Paris exists as God, and as God she will live forever."

It is well enough for devout persons of retiring piety to deprecate what they may consider the bad taste of the King's words; but when I know that the horrified individual is sneering and leering in his very soul at what the king means, I instinctively take the side of the old monarch. Even if his language is objectionable, his meaning is right, or the New Testament is a delusion and a snare, and the Old Testament is a falsehood from beginning to end.

MENTAL HORRORS.

———

THE mental "horrors of the siege" are the most distressing to experience or to witness. It is the intolerable tension of expectation and the baffling uncertainty that besets every hour and minute of the day which tries us. One really knows nothing of what is going on, and there is an all-pervading sense of something that is going to happen, and which may come at any moment. This gives a sense of unreality to one's whole life. The strain upon, and the exhaustion of, both moral and physical energy, that this state of uncertainty and expectation produces, is not to be put into words. This vague expectation becomes, after a while, unendurable. Something is coming—is on its road—is impending. We know not what it is, or what it may be; nor how it will come, nor when it will come. The solid earth seems turned into smoke, and to be going away from under our feet. Bodily health and moral sanity are alike difficult to preserve under this prolonged state of things. Our grief for those who go out to battle and do not return has the horrible element of suspense. The certainty of death would be a blessed relief.

There is just enough of hope to keep the imagination keenly alive to the tortures of apprehension. One longs for a word, and dreads to hear it. The mind is haunted with melancholy suspicions. The silence becomes terrifying. Many have not heard from their friends since the siege. I hear one cry, "Oh, for a single word to tell me of my beautiful babes!" Another says, "I would give all I possess to hear from my poor mother, but it is so long since I heard anything that I dread what might come!"

In some cases the silence of months is broken by the worst of tidings.

The first news one young man has of his mother is that she is dead.

A lady, who had used every means to obtain information of her daughter, who was on her wedding-tour when Paris was invested, at last succeeded in hearing that her daughter was lying at the point of death, with the words always on her lips, "Tell mother to come." The next tidings are that all is over; the mother could not come.

Another learns from an incidental remark in a friend's letter that she has lost her only sister.

Such is the inner life of the siege.

A CHAT AT THE HUNGRY CLUB.

A SMALL company of us having floated together several times at the same restaurant in search of something to eat, call ourselves "The Hungry Club," and had some interesting chats there and elsewhere, over our *viande de cheval* or *ragout de chien.* It is curious to experience how friendly and communicative we become by being shut in with one another from the great world. I will recall some portions of a recent chat of "The Hungry Club."

The Barrister said he knew Sheridan Knowles well. His sister asked Knowles to write something in her album, and he wrote the following, which afterwards appeared in the Hunchback:

> "Love's not a flower that grows on the dull earth,
> Springs by the calendar, must take its turn
> To stem , to leaf, to bud , to flower.
> Love owns a richer soil and boasts a richer earth.
> You look for it and see it not.　You look again
> And lo! the beautiful flower is up and consummate in its growth."

Some one in the company said Knowles sold the copyright of "Virginius" for £100 to Macready, the actor, who made £20,000 by it.

The amount reminded the Barrister of Mrs. Jameson, whom he also knew, and spoke of with lively enthusiasm. A friend of hers made £20,000 by her "Diary of an Ennuyé."

"And what did she make?"

"Nothing! The story is very brief and very sad. She separated from her husband on the day of their marriage, you will recollect, and went immediately to Italy where she wrote the 'Diary of an Ennuyé.' On her return to England the manuscript was shown to a friend, who, finding the author unconscious of its merits, persuaded her to let him keep it, and gave her a guitar in return for it. So he sold his guitar for £20,000!"

In the course of the conversation, an American (there being no Frenchman present) picked up a copy of "My Novel," and read aloud this passage:

"*Mr. Caxton*—'The Frenchman has plenty of valour, that there is no denying; but as for fortitude he has not enough to cover the point of a pin. He is ready to rush out of the world if he is bit by a flea.'"

"*Capt. Roland*—'There was a case in the papers the other day, Austin, of a Frenchman who actually did destroy himself because he was so teased by the little creatures you speak of. He left a paper on his table saying, life was not worth having at the price of such torments.'"

"*Mr. Caxton*—'Sir, their whole political history since the great meeting of the *Tiers État*, has been the history of men who would rather go to the devil than be bit by a flea. It is a record of human impatience that seeks to force time and expects to grow forests from the spawn of a mushroom. . . . . . When they are nearest to democracy they are next door to a despot, and all they have really done is to destroy whatever constitutes the foundation of every tolerable government.'"

The Barrister, who has a tender side for the French, resented this sneer at their fortitude, declaring the common people of this city deserve the highest praise for the exercise of that very virtue. He then gave an eloquent and pathetic description of their privations, and of the patience with which these privations are endured.

"Torpor, torpor! mere torpor," exclaimed the English Colonel.

"No, it is not torpor," rejoined the Barrister, and returned to his defence of our besieged population as zealously as though he were addressing a jury. He could indeed point effectively to the general quiet of the city, and to the fact that we live in a state of chronic disappointment, inasmuch as the eruption we hourly expect is continually postponed.

One of the company said he was led instinctively to "renew his acquaintance with those literary Siamese twins—Erckman—Chatrian," and, taking a paper copy from his pocket—

"By the way (interrupted a voice) that double name—Is it genuine, or a *nom de plume?* I confess I'm confused on the subject. I used to think there were two authors, but I'll be hanged if they are."

"Then you'll be hanged," said an American, "as sure as Tweed deserves to be, because my father once met both of these French authors at a party in Marseilles."

"Oh, for my part, I have no doubt of these books being written by two persons," said our friend, who had now turned to the passage he wanted, and read what Yegof, the madman, said in 1814:

"We will restore Alsace and Lorraine to Germany, Brittany and Normandy to the men of the North, with Flanders and the South to Spain. We will make France into a little kingdom around Paris—a very little kingdom—with a descendant of the ancient race at your head. And you will no longer agitate yourselves—you will be very tranquil. Ha-ha-ha!"

"Some method in that madness—aye, Colonel?"

"Oh, yes, the Teutons have a rod in pickle for them, you know. But how noisy it has been to-day! An extra amount of cannonading, as it seems to me."

"Another sortie, think you?"

"No, I would have been informed of it."

"WHAT DO WE HERE?"

6th November.—Attended the concert at the *Cirque National.* There were, I should think, about 3000 people; many were not able to get in, and many of those who made good their entrance were unable to hear or to see. There was a preliminary discourse, delivered by the Protestant minister, Alphonse Coquerel. He has a good voice, a pleasing manner, and a prepossessing presence. The subject was "Mendelssohn and the Reformation." Here is one of the introductory paragraphs:—

"While they enclose us with a girdle of artillery, and with great trouble bring their enormous Krupp cannon from afar and put them in place against us, what do we here? We play their music. (Laughter.) You come to hear and applaud the grand works of Beethoven, of Weber, and of Mendelssohn—Germans all three. Is this, on our part, an infidelity to our country, a complicity somewhat with those who have so cruelly invaded her? Not in the least. These illustrious dead are not our enemies. The domain of the ideal into which they introduce us has no frontier. Their great works are a part of the universal patrimony of humanity."....

Coquerel is a good speaker; his discourse was

well delivered, and it contained a vein of poetic feeling, but there was nothing in the oration commensurate with the occasion. The orator paid a high compliment to Edgar Quinet, and called his work on the Revolution "the most admirable and useful work of our age," and he promised that, "when we are quiet and at peace," he would give a discourse upon it. Then he went into a critical and rhetorical disquisition on Mendelssohn, and on the peculiarity of his qualifications, of which he said the greatest was "that he was a fervent and modest Christian." One object of the discourse, perhaps, was to make its hearers understand that if they wanted to have gold prize-medals, and decorations of the Legion of Honour, they were bound to do something really good to deserve them; and that, unless good service has really procured them, the decorations and rewards are a mockery and a caricature, instead of an honour, which is all true; but the very phrases in which he spoke were so turned and decorated, that the meaning did not strike home to the heart sharp and stern, as it ought to have done.

The object of the concert and of the oration was to raise a fund on behalf of the wounded. After the music was over, the orator appealed to the audience, and said that if they had entered into the spirit of the music they had just heard, they would be moved by generous emotions to a patriotic impulse, from which the wounded would profit.

"If our ambulance beds are empty," said he, "we are no longer men, we are no longer Frenchmen, we are no longer anything———" The remainder of the sentence was drowned in applause; but there was a despairing intonation in the speaker's voice, as though he did not hope much from his hearers.

In a great national crisis oratory is a great power; but the orator must have a great faith and a passionate hope, for which, if needs be, he is ready to perish, so that he may rouse and fire men by the message he delivers. But in this siege-time of 1870 "the oracles are dumb," and there is no prophet left amongst us.

"NO THOROUGHFARE."

7th November.—It is plain, from the tone or semi-tone of the more reasonable newspapers, and especially from the unawed public opinion privately expressed, that the failure of the negotiations is a pungent disappointment. There was a widespread wish that M. Thiers would find a way for France out of her present predicament. Rational Paris longs for peace.

The thoughtful people, among whom, I have no doubt, all our leaders, civil and military, are to be classed, put the situation about thus:—

We are done for. There is now no prospect, scarcely a possibility, of succour from the provincial armies. They are so watched, hunted, and disintegrated by the enemy that it is not possible for them to consolidate sufficiently for a march on Paris. The most that can be expected of them is guerilla warfare, and in that there is little help for Paris. As for the army of Paris, it is quite incapable of coping with the Germans. Their insubordination makes even a reconnoissance perilous. We might as well expect the "foam on the waters" to break through the German lines and to raise the siege.

We can indeed hold out while there remain

9*

horses and bread to eat, and they may last for t
months yet; but this, without some good fighting
show for ourselves meanwhile, will do little towar
raising the foreign estimation of France.

The most propitious moment for obtaining
truce, and after that a peace, has passed away.

Oh! for an opportunity to escape!

This, I think, is the secret aspiration of all w
have not gone quite mad with Red fanaticism,
who dare to realize our situation, and among the
M. Thiers and Jules Favre, and many others of c
leaders, must be reckoned; but they fear the R
Indians of Belleville, and the favourable moment 1
coming to terms with the Germans has passed by

I ventured to hint at the possibility of capitu
tion to a National Guard shopkeeper, and he repli
"But as you value your life, be careful how you u
that word. You might as well drop a match in
powder magazine."

Just so; the war party *à l'outrance* rule the ci
and the rulers of the city show an energy whi
might go far to deliver the city if it were put
practice in the right place, *i.e.*, in front of t
soldiers before the enemy; but when it comes
fighting, they not only run away themselves, t
carry with them even those who are disposed
stand. They will not capitulate, nor allow the Gover
ment to do so. While the sober-minded deplore t
failure of negotiations, the men of Belleville a
jubilant in their *salles* and clubs over their o'
victory, and—Bismarck's! One of them, M. Veuill
writes in the *Univers:*—

"Let the black flag which now floats on the walls of Paris be henceforth the flag of France to the day of resurrection. Let this flag be the symbol before God of our repentance, and before the human race of our resolution not to survive our country!"

Rhetoric and epithets intoxicate the brain like strong drink, and render men incapable of right reason.

13th November.—The National Guards are being mobilised, that is, weeded, for fighting men to go to the front. Great commotion in the Guard in consequence. It is sickening to hear their remarks.

This mobilisation is due to the popular demand, which can no longer be disobeyed. The feeling of other sections of the army towards the National Guard is bitter and demonstrative.

To hesitate longer would be perilous, for it seems that the first duty of our leaders is obedience to their followers.

All men between twenty-five and thirty-five, who have never served, or who are unmarried and widowers without children, are called into service.

Far better would it be for France if all who have refused to serve could be draughted out of the ranks! If one half of the garrison could be got rid of, or sent as prisoners to von Moltke, there would be some chance of the remainder making a decent fight; as it is demoralization and cowardly fear of the enemy work apace, the whole lump is being rapidly leavened.

A German, English, or American army, half the
size of this army shut up in Paris, could not be
kept inside these walls if they wished to get out.
But the French soldiers are terrified at the sight of
a body of spiked helmets, and as they do not often
see this sight, they are the more frightened when
they do. The Germans have a way of being invisible, which affects the nerves of the troops, and
which is certainly remarkable.

Butchers now give only forty grammes of beef
or mutton to each person every three days.

The theatres are opening one by one. The
Ambigu tries to give some reflexion in its piece
of the great drama of which France is now the
theatre.

Crowds go to witness, *"Les Paysans de Lorraine,"*
but without any enthusiasm.

STREET LIFE.

THE Boulevards have long since lost their old order and decorum; they are now filled with street performances of all kinds and descriptions. Music upon every instrument that can make it; fortune-tellers, conjurors, gymnasts, dancing dogs, mountebanks—every conceivable device, trick, or sleight-of-hand for entrapping money.

The new policemen are among the delighted lookers-on at these entertainments. Two lads perform gymnastics on a carpet, a weazened old witch shows you cheap battles through a small hole in a pasteboard house; a brisk young fellow in the National Guard stripe performs innumerable tricks after a sufficiency of sous have been pitched into his ring. Two little boys and a little girl attract quite a crowd; one of the boys plays a harp, the other a violin, and the little girl sings. They make a pretty and pathetic tableau; the music is wonderfully sweet, and there is a refinement about the whole performance. There is something in it which touches a young and pretty "unfortunate;" after listening a few moments she turns in tears. A little farther on is a chiropodist, who has beguiled an old man into allowing him to try the magic efficacy of his "wonderful invention." A molasses-candy man finds plenty of customers for farthing portions of his sweets, as he shouts and screams their virtues.

Paris has become very like Naples in the character of the entertainments of its streets, and above all in the crowds of greasy and sometimes not un-picturesque beggars.

Trochu confesses with some bitterness that the *émeute* of the 31st ultimo nipped the armistice and the hope of peace in the bud. His proclamation deprecates any further "manifestations."

ESPIONOMANIA.

BISMARCK'S wonderfully early news from Paris, during his interview with M. Thiers, shows that Prussian spies ply their trade with skill and success. There is no limit to their audacity, and the Parisians are driven wild with suspicion of every body; and this universal suspicion has a curious effect. The possibility of being taken for a spy makes you feel like one. You return furtive glances with glances as furtive. You colour in trying not to colour. You become ill-at-ease in the endeavour to seem unconscious. If you have a passport or a letter, with the signature of someone in power, that is exactly the document with which a spy would provide himself. Whatever you say seems to be exactly what a spy would say. In fact, the sense of self-consciousness makes you feel as if you were bewitched into behaving like a spy! and the idea of being arrested and arraigned before one of the rough-and-ready itinerant tribunals of Red justice, more summary and less discriminating than "Lynch law," rouses one's indignation as well as one's apprehension.

Added to all this, the suspicion of being suspected for a spy turns one into an involuntary spyhunter. I strongly suspect that the man who just now urged me to buy a cane is one of von Moltke's agents. He dropped a sentence, *sotto voce*, in excellent English, to draw me out probably! I feel sure that the man who was so inquisitive in his conversation at Duval's yesterday was a spy, and perhaps he thinks that he discovered a spy in me!

The papers comment upon the increase of drunkenness; one certainly sees more now than formerly, nevertheless I am bound to say that I have seen three times as many drunken men in the course of one evening's ramble in Liverpool, Glasgow, or Edinburgh than I have seen in the course of three days here since the war commenced. "Everybody drinking and nobody drunk," is still the singular fact. A great deal is said, too, about the drinking of absinthe, and one of the newspapers warns its readers against "*cette funeste liqueur.*" But in Paris people sit at a table and sip their beverage, while in London or New York they stand at the bar and take it down at one fell gulp; so that, though the liquor may be equally poisonous in both places, there is a great difference in the quantity swallowed, and in the mode of drinking it.

I have walked the whole day long over Paris during the siege, comprising its worst portions, without seeing one man reeling through the streets.

In another such excursion I have seen three. I once saw five in a walk of five miles of crowded boulevard. And I have counted a half-dozen men in the cafés who, I thought, were boozy. But I must confess, after a large and studiously intentional observation, that the number of intoxicated people in this city is marvellously small.

The difference, indeed I may say the contrast, between the revellers in a Paris café, and a London 'public,' or a New York bar-room, is striking. To whatever lengths the Frenchman may go in his indulgences, he is at least quiet. Each circle keeps to itself. There is no such thing as an uproarious row, gradually rising from many centres, until the whole assembly becomes a mass of pugnacious brawlers. The French, on the whole, are quiet in their dissipations. It is only in politics that they are noisy. In their deliberative assemblies and in their public meetings they can play the drama of Pandemonium to perfection, but in the café or at the ball they seldom rise above a cheery chatter or a merry hum.

STIRRING THE EMBERS.

14*th November.*—A pigeon came in the day before yesterday, and soon after its arrival the walls were posted with its news:—

The army of the Loire is victorious!

Orleans retaken!

Von der Tann and the Prussian division driven back before the French troops!

Newspapers make the most of this success—so does the Government—so do the orators in the clubs. Everything is done to rouse the patriotism of Paris; but since the dismal affair of Bourget, we have been so inert that even this victory fails to rouse us. There is nothing approaching to enthusiasm, indeed there is something approaching to misgiving, if not despair, in the presence of the "first victory." Still the club orators gesticulate, stamp, harangue, and rave. But their pulmonary patriotism has quite lost its charm, and the audience, in full uniform, listens with apathy when they are told that the enemy must be pursued to his own country, where the flag of France shall be planted and made to grow! All falls flat.

I am surprised to find so much oratorical ability in these clubs. Most of the speakers have more or less of real power, while some of them speak with a vigour and wit, facility and felicity, which seem to be indigenous to this country, and inherent in its language. The French have the gift of speech enormously developed; they are in a chronic state of utterance; they are for ever saying something, whether they speak or not. Their shrug is a speech, and language is with them an end and not a means; they begin and end with "words, words, words."

At the representation of 'Esther' to-day, at the Théâtre Français, there was much feeling shown by the audience where the actress alluded to the calamities of France.

We have a report of the secretary-general of the committee of *la viande de cheval.* He says that horseflesh is one-sixth more nutritious than beef. The best parts of a horse bring two francs a pound.

Tried to see what we could do to-day in the way of a siege dinner, and here is our bill of fare:—

1. Soup from horse-meat.
2. Mince of cat.
3. Shoulder of dog with tomato sauce.
4. Jugged cat with mushrooms.
5. Roast donkey and potatoes.
6. Rat, peas, and celery.
7. Mice on toast.
8. Plum-pudding.

Expense: Twelve francs a mouth.

It would be difficult to take a restaurant meal

now in Paris, without being served with at least one of the above-named animals. The bland market-man tells you it is an otter, or a rare species of hare, or an extraordinarily small and odd kind of sheep; but still you go away with the suspicion that you have seen, and will presently eat, a cat in disguise. And, upon my word, they have a skill in this process of concealment which keeps one, I have no doubt, a constant victim of his imagination.

As to our appetites, they increase fearfully—everybody complains of his appetite. And we live in a state of misery, because we fear the day is at hand when we shall have less to eat than now, when we have barely enough.

EXODUS.

19th November.—About 200 English and Americans have left the city, with Count Bismarck's permission. General Trochu did not wish any of them to leave, as "the effect is so demoralizing to the army and the citizens."

Trochu is as much afraid of his troops as his troops are of the enemy.

The American minister Washburne spent two hours with him, arguing the cause of those who wished to leave. The fugitives left in nineteen carriages all in a string.

They did not receive even so much as a shout from the Red *gamins*, nor did they seem to excite curiosity in the sentinels.

The Government informs us that fresh beef has come to an end, and that henceforth we must be content with salt-beef and fresh horse alternately.

20th November, Sunday.—At a concert to-day, the young lady received, instead of a bouquet, a— piece of cheese. This seems practical, at all events; but for all that, Paris has no realization of her situation—none. Toward the crisis she is torpid; toward everything else she is jolly. On the ninth

Sunday of the siege, no stranger would mistrust that we are an invested population. Even the multiplicity of swell officers and the variety of strolling regimentals might be regarded as an indispensable feature of a frolicsome capital. It has been one of those superb days in which Paris excels, even in midwinter. The sun was just warm enough for comfort. The atmosphere was kindly. It thawed out the Parisians, and the Parisians, thawed out on an autumn day, are always a diverting spectacle. But on this autumn day, at this state of the siege, there was nothing dejected in the appearance of the crowd. On the contrary, nothing could be more indicative of satisfaction and contentment than the faces of the people under the genial November sun. They were each and every one the picture of self-congratulation. Their boots were polished and their bellies were full—thanks, so far, to the fortunes of war. The children were sportive from inability to comprehend the situation, and for the very same reason their parents sauntered along under the leafless trees without the least appearance of solicitude or apprehension. Do you see that group— always changing in persons, always the same in number—looking out through the opening made by the street opposite? They are watching, with all their native indolent intentness, the nothing that is going on at the outposts. The National Guard and the old gent in the big blue necktie, the two little girls chasing one another round the group, and the matronly lady who holds her puny lad by the hand, the maidservant in her white cap, the mobiles and the policemen—all look out over the tops of the houses upon the tops of the hills, with the hazy stare which seems to come from the haze that covers the hills.

At the Arc de Triomphe there is another crowd. An old man will give you a peep at the Prussians through his telescope for four sous.

An urchin telescope proprietor cries continually, "Here's a fine view of the Prussian batteries for ten centimes!" and a prodigious woman with a basketful of lorgnettes exclaims: "If you want to see old Bismarck, buy one of these; only twenty-five francs!" Chocolate and gingerbread are everywhere for sale.

The churches are open, and full of women and Bretons.

Two moblots were playing pitch-and-toss to-day on the steps of the Madeleine, an incident significant of our demoralization.

A woman's committee of the 18th arrondissement have "decreed" the "melting of the bells into cannon," an "immediate rationment," and "the abolition of the *ouvrières religieuses* and the *Maison de Prostitution.*"

Deleschuze, editor of the *Reveil*, invites the arrondissements to constitute a popular jury of forty members to search and try all officers who betray their country—not only Bazaine and his accomplices, but all traitors of all grades, civil and military.

Deleschuze is one of the educated Reds, who give respectability to the Communist party, and plausibility to their theories.

A RED CLUB IN SESSION.

21st November.—The clubs are the waste-pipes of the fermenting "civilization shut up in Paris."

Last night we had a *séance* at the Salle Favié, which was too characteristic to go unreported. There is where the Reddest of the Reds most do congregate. There you hear the most "advanced" sentiment of the "Universal Republicans," unembellished by the poisonous sophistry of Louis Blanc, and unobscured by the pyrotechnics of Victor Hugo.

The *salle* is filled to suffocation. The president smokes, the secretaries smoke, the orator takes his cigar from his mouth to address the assembly, and the assembly takes its hundreds of cigars and pipes from its mouths to hoot or applaud the orator. It is a sulphurous place for a stranger in more senses than one. It is a pandemonium, a zoological garden, a pantomime, a comedy, a backwoods' Fourth of July, and a Donnybrook Fair all combined.

The men are in the uniform of the National Guard, and all who are not are in the uniform of the Garde Mobile. We miss the blouses, but not those who used to wear them. There is the usual proportion of women in all their imposing proportions, speaking physically. That raw-boned, broad-faced, towering female form over in the corner I have seen many a time before in Red "manifestations." She is a fine specimen of the Amazon. I would like to see her under fire.

There is a fine old Red for you about half-way down the aisle—that cadaverous, sharp-nosed veteran with a pipe going furiously. How the old chap's eyes glitter! What a mixture of drollery and savagery in his face! There is Voltaire's monkey and tiger. Meet that man in Westmeath, and you would take him for a native.

There is a rising Red on the platform, who revels in the occasion. He is not without marks of gentleness and good-nature. He has, strangely and probably enough, stepped down from a higher social sphere to breathe this more congenial atmosphere. He leaves his gentle circle to join the *sans culotte*. But he, too, betrays the "tiger." Kindliness alternates with ferocity.

'The *séance* opens with an orchestra of oratory and a pantomime of shaking fingers. Everybody shakes his finger in everybody's else face. The president shakes his finger in the face of the audience, the audience shakes its multitudinous fingers in the face of the president. The president rings his bell, and rings it so furiously that it won't ring at all.

I catch enough that is said by the speakers to know that they propose to march *en masse* on the enemy, and make *a trouée*, on condition that the old *sergents de ville*, the *gardes-côtes*, the *aristocrates*, and the *seminaristes* shall follow, and if they are

allowed to go where they please and come wher
they please, and not be obliged to "go to the lef
when they wish to be at the right," and *vice vers(*
"simply because their officers desire it."

A speaker opens upon "the sluggards who carr
a red cross on their caps, and a white dish-clotl
for a flag." This is received with uproar. On(
cries, "This is an insult;" another "wants to knov
who shall take care of our wounded, then?" Th(
towering form in the corner screams, "The women
the women! ye *lâches!* Ye will neither let then
fight nor take care of the wounded."

The president takes the cigar from his mouth
lays it on the table, rises to his legs, shakes his bel
with one hand and his finger with the other; finall
he is heard to say that "Citizen Beaurepaire ha
discovered a new tactic against the Prussians, whicl
he will exhibit to-morrow to the citizens of Belle
ville. The proceeds of the conference will be givei
to the poor of Belleville."———The last words ar(
enough, for they are not Red enough.

The young Red on the platform shakes his fingei
the old Red shakes his finger, all the Reds shak(
their fingers, and all the Reds scream and stamp
The tobacco-smoke increases to a suffocating degree
and the whole question, whatever it was, seems in
volved in the same blue stifling haze. Everybod
coughs and blows their nose, and shake their fingers
and cry one thing and another thing and every
thing.

From the cries I learn at last the cause of th(
disturbance. "It is contrary to equality" (to devot(

money to this purpose). "Let us make powder and ball with it." "We don't want the bread of the aristocrats." "We'll starve before we eat their bread."

At this moment there is a cry from the back part of the hall—"A *mouchard!—a mouchard!*" and the whole audience jump up and shake their fingers at the *mouchard*, or at least where he is supposed to be. The president rings and shakes his finger, with his cigar burning like a chimney on fire.

"To the door with him!—out with him!" is the cry. The *mouchard* resists, and with success for a minute; but then trips, stumbles, and falls, and is borne out of the door instead of being murdered, as I expected he would be, and as the towering squaw in the corner demanded. "Kill him!—kill him!" she screams.

The storm abates. It is the relief of exhaustion. We settle back to business, and I take the opportunity to retire.

The *Club de Belleville* had one of their most maniacal meetings last evening. One of the orators said, "*Je ne crains pas la foudre, je haïs le Dieu, le misérable Dieu des prêtres, et je voudrais, comme les Titans, escalader le ciel pour aller le poignarder.*" A voice cried, "You can go up in one of Nadar's balloons," and there was a boisterous enjoyment of this wit; but here let us draw the curtain.

HISTORICAL PARALLELS.

THE departure of the new balloon "Archimedes,"
reminds one of the changes in the manner of "hold
ing out" in a siege since Syracuse held out agains
the army of Marcellus for two years, by means o
the wit of the wonderful genius after whom this bal
loon is named.

Now there was a siege in which human brains
rather than horse-flesh, may be said to have held
out, although (and here a parallel suggests itself) the
town was lost at last, because its inhabitants had
lost their heads.   While the venerable philosophe
was contriving and constructing new engines for
defence, his fellow-citizens showed their appreciation
of his ingenuity by giving the reins to their desires
in some *Jardin Mabile* or *Quartier Latin*.   It was
during this "sound of revelry by night," that Syra
cuse was, to use the favourite French phrase, "con
quered by famine," or fell a victim to that eminently
phraseological obstacle, the "treason of fortune."
We have no Archimedes, but we can furnish the
remainder of the analogy.

The spirit of the Parisians alternates between
effeminacy and ferocity.   Now they are prostrate
with despondency, and now they are towering with

savagery, reminding us of Voltaire's description of his countrymen—"A delightful melange of the tiger and the monkey." The "delightful" part of this remark I cannot concur in, nor can anybody else, I think, who has been hustled by a Parisian mob. The transition from monkey to tiger, and from tiger to monkey, is not without its element of the grotesque; and the monkey, when he does arrive, is undoubtedly droll; nevertheless you are always in danger of being devoured by the tiger while you are laughing at the monkey. In the course of a conversation on the war, your Parisian will, by turns, whine over the cruelty of his enemy, and swear to avenge it by—surpassing it!

They remind one of the ancient Athenians, also. They are always reminding you of some people or other who are dead and gone. There is nothing like being shut up in Paris for quickening one's memory for historical parallels.

The propensity for precedent is quite irresistible. A passage of Thucydides recurs to me perpetually, although I cannot recall its exact words. He tells us that neither the calamities of war nor the most dreadful plague ever recorded in history were able to compose the temper of the volatile Athenians. Inordinately elate with any success, they were deaf to the most reasonable overtures of peace from their enemy, and totally wanting in modesty or moderation. Correspondingly dejected with any defeat, they believed the enemy to be at their very doors, and threw the whole blame upon their commanders, who, when unsuccessful, were always treated as unpardonably criminal. As might have been expected, the demagogues who kept watch over the inconstant temper of the people adapted every circumstance to their own ambition. The result was, as every one familiar with the history knows, a perpetual war of factions, all vociferously patriotic, and all at the same time consumed with that peculiarly vindictive form of selfishness and self-seeking, which only great demagogues and great autocrats (often one and the same person) have ever been able to attain.

Was there ever a more striking or mortifying parallel? Did ever history repeat itself with more vividness or suggestiveness? Patriotism here has degenerated into partisanism. Devotion to party has (with some unconsciously, perhaps) taken the place of fidelity to country. As the party now in the ascendency were willing to sacrifice the country to get rid of the Empire, so they will now bite off their nose, which is their provinces, to spite their face—or rather their two faces, with one of which they make grimaces at their enemy, the victorious Germans, and with the other of which they make grimaces at their enemy, the overthrown Imperialists.

Montalembert, the greatest and the most patriotic of the anti-Bonapartists and Liberal Catholics, said: "If Louis Napoleon conquers the Rhine, I shall never open my mouth against him again." And this was said when the Empire was peace. The best thing that the patriotism of France has had to say for itself these hundred years is just what the Count de Montalembert said: Whip Germany, and a Bonaparte may reign, and ruin too (as we believe he will)! Grant us to see the German Empire humbled, and our opposition to the French Empire shall cease. "Ajax asks no more."

Another of the purest and foremost of the French Liberals, Prevost Paradol, writing in 1868, did not hesitate to say that he "regarded the war between France and Germany as inevitable. Prussia had started on a career which France must oppose."

Why? Because "the union of Germany, however effected, whether by the passive acquiescence of France, or after a victory over her, is tantamount to a surrender of the greatness of France! For what is France when she has at her gates a military power with a population of fifty-one millions?"

Such is the testimony of the highest conscience of modern France. The French have had no higher public conscience since Charlemagne lifted their forefathers by the main strength of Personal Government. And when he was taken from under, they all went back into the helplessness and ignorance in which he found them.

Robert Knox wrote both history and prophecy when he said, in 1850, "From Brennus to Napoleon I. the war-cry of the French has been, 'To the Alps! To the Rhine!' This game, which still engages their attention, has now been played for four thousand years."

This game still engages their attention, and will

be played just once more, although it has been played once too often.

The people who now cry, "Revenge for Sedan!" once cried, "Revenge for Sadowa!" What was Sadowa to them, or they to Sadowa?

No man knows all this better than M. Thiers, the most mischievous leader France has ever followed, except Napoleon I. He opposed, not the war with Germany—that he always advocated—but the time for making it. The time, not the war, was "ill-chosen." He has always been the champion of ill-chosen wars, as well as ill-chosen times for making them.

"THANKSGIVING DAY."

24th November.

,As good and loyal Americans we could not forget that this was the national Thanksgiving Day, nor neglect the customary observance of it. So we gathered round the traditional turkey for which we paid 55 francs, and which was not as tender as our recollections. There was also a ham which was strongly suspected of having made one of the constituent parts of a Newfoundland dog. There was an equally suggestive item of sausage, and an infinitesimal item of butter, and for dessert we had apples, pears, almonds, coffee and champagne.

There were twenty persons present. At one end of the table sat United States Minister Washburne and at the other Consul-General Read. On one side were Col. Hoffman, Secretary of the United States Legation, Mr. and Mrs. Wm. Bowles, Mrs. Kock, Mrs. F. Riggs, Mr. Todt, Mr. Washburne jr., Mr. May the artist and Mr. Beylard. On the other side sat Mr. Durand of Chicago, Mr. Hopkinson, Hon. L. Wingfield, Mr. Dreyer, Mr. Sheppard, Mr. Kock, Miss Chander, Mr. Hoffer and Mrs. Moulton.

The Minister responded to the toast, "The President of the United States and the Embassy in

Paris." He rejoiced in the occasion which brought us together, and recalled the old thanksgiving days at home, when turkeys were cheap, ladies were plenty and pumpkin pies abounded. The refreshment that he obtained from the social atmosphere of the occasion more than compensated for the deficiency in animal food necessitated by the siege. If our table was scant, our hearts were full to overflowing with love for our country; and it was especially agreeable to him, in the midst of such circumstances, on this sixty-eighth day of the siege, shut off from all communication with the outside world, to pay this genial and hearty tribute of affectionate loyalty to our native land.

In response to the toast: "Our Country," Consul-General Read made a speech full of patriotic allusions to the Fatherland, and pathetic allusions to the loved ones from whom we are separated by a wall of fire. He would always look back upon this occasion as under the circumstances the most memorable thanksgiving dinner that ever brought Americans together. The author of this Diary tried to say a word for the grand old faith of our forefathers in God, the Divine Providence. After toasts to "The Old Folks at Home"—"The American Artist"—and "The American Ambulance" the little company dispersed never to forget their thanksgiving dinner in Paris on the 68th day of the siege.

PIGEON POST.

———

24th November.—Two pigeons arrived to-day, bringing 1100 private depatches. We examined these microscopic letters with intense anxiety. This method of communication was suggested last October by J. J. Arnold, Esq., an English barrister, on behalf of his clerk, a young Frenchman, M. Chas. Mangin, who invented the material on which to print the despatches. It is quite flexible, and entirely waterproof, and so light that it can be affixed to the leg of the bird without annoying or overweighting it.

M. Mangin has even put the whole contents of a newspaper in a space which, as a Frenchman expresses it, "is not larger than the end of Voltaire's nose!" Another Frenchman (of Irish mixture) declared the letters "were so invisible that they could hardly be seen."

The potato-dealers at the Halle this evening were assailed by the mob, who seized their stores; the people were in such numbers that they only obtained about one potato to three persons.

25th November.—The queue at the Halle to-day must have been nearly a mile long; each person had a card marking his allowance.

Letter from wife in London through American Legation. She says she is "waiting on in dumb endurance," and "expects to see me come out a skeleton in a bundle of rags."

For my part I send off multitudes of the prescribed "four gramme" epistles in the balloons. It is like sending up prayers—some are answered, and some are not.

Perhaps I should not speak of smuggled letters, and I will not—only to say that if Count Bismarck will read, he will not burn the communications of the Americans and English. These "birds of the air will tell the matter" properly, as far as he is concerned. To say the truth the French behave so badly, that there is only one side to this contest.

ALIMENTARY.

——

26th November.—*Vive les Rats!* The Academy of Science, after sitting on our alimentative condition for some time, have pronounced—that rat is incomparably superior to horse, dog, or cat. Rats are indeed far from being bad to eat, and they are not indigestible; but cat is, to my taste, far superior. You may cook the rat in all sorts of ways; but rat *pâté* is a delicacy! These luxuries are not plentiful; there are only two places where they are sold, and only one shop where you can buy rat *pâtés*. Dogs and cats are difficult to meet with, except in the streets, when one wishes them hanging up in the butchers' shops!

The rationment announced to-day is—27th, codfish; 28th, salt-pork; 29th, codfish; 30th, beef and mutton; 1st, 2nd, and 3rd of December, beef.

We all seem to have returned to the days when we were little boys, and used to hang round the pastrycook's window! Now, however, it is the grocers' shops which are the attraction, and to look in at every grocer's window we pass, is one of the most exciting incidents in our daily walks. My friend and I have just secured the two last remain-

ing jars of Scotch marmalade in one shop—each
jar cost two francs and a half.

The greatest sufferers from the present state of
things are the poor little babies. In ordinary times
a baby is sent out to nurse in the country; "the
mother has no milk," or it may be that the baby
has no mother. Paris hates babies, and now, as
they cannot be sent into the country, and there are
hardly any milch-cows left, the poor little things die
like flies in cold weather. It may not be the worst
fate for them, but it is very sad to look on and see
them perish. Edmond About writes a very French
article on this topic, and calls the King of Prussia
"Herod."

30*th November*.—No gas in the streets—and the
petroleum lamps are a very dark substitute. The
Boulevards are in gloom; but the people who love
darkness rather than light are numerous and animated. The cafés, however, are brilliantly furnished
with lamps, and they never looked gayer, or were
more crowded.

A battle is impending, and we Anglo-Saxons are
unsuccessfully trying to feel neutral. I defy man,
woman, or child of our race to look on even at a
battle in the street between dogs, or cocks, or cats,
or a squabble among boys, without taking sides;
while as to a war between nations, which most
people can only read about, neutrality of sympathy
is quite impossible—we must express our feelings,
or die of their suppression! The contrast between
the French, and both Americans and English, is

remarkable in this respect. We are a fighting race by nature, and we never get anything worth having without fighting for it. The French are a military people, if you will, but they don't like a pounding match as we do, and cannot stand it, or stand up to it, as we can. With the French, "nothing succeeds like success;" with us, "pluck" stands before all things. Here, the unsuccessful are execrated; with us, we make men into heroes, if they only "die game." There is a significant difference between the two tests.

"FRANCE HAS HELPED NOBODY AND NOBODY WILL HELP FRANCE."

OUR newspapers have a new epigram: "France has helped everybody, nobody helps France." But it is a mal-quotation from a letter to the Emperor, (just made public) from the Queen of Holland, who, in pronging His Majesty into the present war, said: "France has helped nobody, and nobody will help France" in this war of aggrandizement and revenge. Certainly France has helped nobody without at the same time helping herself. Her proffers of alliance, whether made by President or Monarch, have generally been prompted by a duplicity which has sometimes ripened into audacity. Now the object is to fortify a throne, and now to pacify a people; now to acquire territory, and now to gratify the French passion for *gloire*. When the Emperor declared for peace in the Crimea, he knew that the war-spirit in France was on the wane, although he knew as well that the British troops were only just "in wind." And when he sheathed his sword at Villafranca, he knew that he had gained three great objects—the increase of French territory to please the French people, the unity of Italy to please the Italians, and a new lease of the Tuileries to please its tenant.

Not to speak of admonishing Prussia, which, however absurd it looks now, was at that time a rational end to have in view.

But look how the French Governments figure
in their alliances that have now become historic.
After entering with England into a convention for
the suppression of the slave-trade, France broke her
engagement in the most deliberate manner. The
French Minister of that day, M. de Villéle, said he
"would not conceal from the Duke of Wellington
the fact that the abolition of the slave-trade was
unpopular in France, not because any value was attached to the colonies, for he believed there was a
very general opinion in France that their colonies
were useless to them, but because the abolition had
been pressed upon the King by Great Britain!"

And the Minister informed the Duke that he
would deprive the English of all pretence for re-
sorting to the coast of Africa, by depriving them of
their colonies on that coast, and giving them in exchange some other colony—an exchange of a ma-
larious colony on the African coast, for the fertile
and healthful colony of Mauritius!

The truth is, that while France helps nobody
without helping herself, she expects everybody to
help her out of pure admiration for her. What she
gives to others for a consideration, she expects from
others as her due.

* II*

THE RED NOBLEMAN.

In my "meditative moods," I often "walk by
myself" through the narrow and picturesque streets
of old Paris. In the cafés and restaurants there I
meet with many strange and curious specimens, both
of people and of things, as in marine stores and
brokers' shops, one comes upon objects obviously
designed to adorn places of elegance and pleasure.
Torn from their original belongings, they have come
down in the world, and are jumbled in places where
their beauty of design and workmanship is neither
known nor recognised, unless some casual passer-by
can discern their value through all their dirt and
varnish, and the incongruous objects amongst which
they lie. One day I saw a quaint Louis Quatorze
mirror on the walls of a coal-shed, and a clock that
had once marked the hours for some fair dame of
the Regency in a cobbler's stall, reflecting dimly
the shapes of dilapidated boots and shoes, some of
which had also moved in good society.

The "human mortals" sometimes met in the
small out-of-the-way cafés are often, in their way,
as much removed out of their natural position in
the world, but their sordid surroundings cannot
obliterate

"The mark of that which once has been."

I had been wandering one morning, with "devious steps and slow," going I knew not whither, until, hungry and tired, I entered a small restaurant, which stood in my road. I asked for something to eat, and sat down at one of the tables. The place had a certain air of doing a thriving business in its own way. There were no tablecloths nor dinner-napkins; the spoons were of dull pewter, the glasses were thick and dim; the crockery clumsy, and the salt anything but white; but the table at which I sat was clean. My *plat* was composed of meat, which was possibly beef, but *légumes* and *pommes de terre* were the chief features; the bread was good, and the *vin ordinaire* might have been a great deal worse. It was not high-tide of business, for I was early; but several blouses were sitting in a distant part of the low room, which, even in the daytime, required a petroleum lamp.

At the table next to mine sat a young man whose appearance interested me. He might have been about thirty, was dressed in the uniform of a National Guard; but it was worn with a difference. His light hair hung in heavy masses, and would have been all the better for a comb—his beard for a razor, and soap-and-water would have acted beneficially upon his general appearance. But his skin was fine, and his features refined and distinguished. He kept on his hat, and seemed to affect slovenliness; yet, in all his movements, his manner of sitting on his chair, the shape of his hands and feet, and certain indefinable airs, all betrayed the secret, that he belonged to another grade of society, al-

though he chose to pass as an ordinary "Red," and
to associate with men of the Belleville type. His
face attracted me; it was pale, thin, and marked
with traces of fatigue and dissipation; but it was
touching in its expression of gentleness and refinement, and there was an eager restlessness in the
eyes which contradicted and disturbed the rest of
the countenance. The eyes were beautifully brown,
clear, and large; the mouth delicate and mobile;
and his voice and intonation were those of an
educated man accustomed to frequent cultivated
society.

I had seen him once before, and I knew him to
be a stiff Communist. I thought I would try if I
could get him into conversation, so I plunged into
the midst of things by saying,—

"Well, how does your party get on?"

"Oh, badly enough, citizen; we are no better
off under this Government than we were under the
Empire."

"But you have more opportunity to propagate
your views, have you not?"

"Yes, we have—that is true. And we mean to
make the most of that opportunity. We shall succeed; we will have what we want after the war."

"What is that?"

"The Commune."

"Well, what is the Commune? Pardon me; I
am a foreigner, and ignorant."

"A Commune is a body of men elected, for
example, by universal suffrage in Paris, who have
supreme control in Paris. They make and unmake

municipal laws, they control the National Guard, and, in short, perform all the duties and fill all the functions of a Government, and are responsible oniy to the people, who elect them at stated periods."

"Should their power extend beyond Paris?"

"That depends upon the people out of Paris. If they fall in with our system, every town will have its Commune, each having its stipulated and limited rights and prerogatives, the Paris Commune being supreme over all."

"That will leave the rural districts under the dominion of the cities?"

"Certainly, citizen. The centres of population, industry, commerce, and intelligence will rule the scattered masses of the ignorant, whose very isolation and disintegration renders them unfit for self-government, and much more unfit for the government of the great cities. Paris has had enough of being outvoted and oppressed by the provinces; it is high time she should assert her independence and natural rights."

"Suppose the provinces refuse to join in this scheme?"

"Let them. Paris will cut loose from them, leave them to their fate, and take her destiny into her own hands."

"Are there no other features peculiar to the Commune system of government?"

"Oh yes, citizen—several; but they are all to be considered."

"How about Socialism; is that an essential feature?"

"That depends upon what you mean by Socialism."

"Well, what do you mean by Socialism?"

"It means simply absolute equality before the
law—an equalization of property—so that no one
person shall get so excessively rich as to make any
other person excessively poor. Extreme poverty is
only the result of extreme wealth, and extreme
destitution of extreme luxury. I suppose you know
there is nothing new about this, citizen?"

"I presume you will refer me to some such
practice among the Romans—the Agrarian Law of
Spurius Cassius, perhaps?"

"Yes, citizen, quite right. We might go further
back than the Romans; but to stop with them. I
think Spurius Cassius was the author of what you
call the Agrarian law, was he not?"

"It is thought so; but his motives were none
of the best, you know. He was a demagogue; and
to curry favour with the people, and so elevate
himself, he———"

"Never mind his motives or his object, citizen;
he was preaching no new doctrine; and in recognising it as a dream of the people, he was but paying
tribute to their sense of justice, which is always
right, while the sense of justice in kings and nobles,
who have inherited their possessions from their bar-
barian ancestors, who began this devilry of royalty
and nobility, is always wrong. Cassius, doubtless,
who was a patrician, felt that the ideas of justice

which prevailed in his class were cruel and oppressive; hence his plea that the lands which had been conquered by the people should · be distributed among them, instead of being added to the already superabundant possessions of the rich."

"Well, now, suppose the property of this city were distributed in equal parts among its inhabitants, how long would it be before the old inequality would return?"

"Ah, citizen, that is an old question, but it is not a fair one. In the first place, so sweeping a measure nobody would approve; and in the second place, the measure that would be approved would not only be slow but sure, not only gradual but discriminating—or should be, at any rate. To begin with the doing away of one extreme would do away with the other. Luxurious wealth and squalid poverty would disappear together. Then it would be time enough to see what further could be done to equalize the product of labour."

"But would not the idle be put upon an equality with the industrious, and shiftlessness and thrift have the same reward?"

"No, citizen; not idleness and industry, but honesty and chicanery, would be put on an equality; or rather, honesty would be enabled to at least hold its own against chicanery. Depend upon it, citizen, it is artifice and not industry that now rules in trade. Trade is a game in which the sharper wins, and the simple are ruined. This is not equality or justice. It is a cruel injustice upon the honest and illiterate, and a reward· to the clever and designing. This,

Socialism would put an end to. No—no, citizen; we are not to be frightened by these spectres, which are raised by the timid and the selfish. It is not necessary to work out all the details of the Socialistic scheme before putting it in motion. Its first step would remove a great and wicked injustice,—the monopoly by a few of what they never earned by legitimate means, but obtained by fraud, or inherited from those who came into possession of it by rapacity or artifice. Why, look at it, citizen; the whole machinery of the state in Europe is worked with the sole object of preventing rich men's sons from becoming poor, and poor men's sons from getting rich. The laws hedge about the stupid child of noble parents, lest his stupidity should fail him in competition with the brighter child of the common people. The one is prevented from rising, the other from falling, to the place in which his natural calibre would place him. No, citizen; if all property were put up as a prize for the reward of industry and honest toil, my word for it, there would be a great changing of places in the world."

"But wouldn't that bring us back, in the future, to where we are now? Would not the new aristocrats be as objectionable as the old?"

"Ah, citizen, you do not understand. We would have no aristocrats. Socialism interposes to protect the weak against the strong, and the honest against the crafty, so that men should not get so far apart as to be divided into ruling class and servile class. There should be serving, but the servant of to-day should have every opportunity of becoming the master of to-morrow, and no law should hinder him, nor hinder the master's degradation, if he deserved it."

"I think I get at your idea, and am exceedingly obliged for your explanation; but before we part, pray tell me how it is that a man with such surroundings as these can show so much thoughtfulness and intelligence. You are an educated man, if I mistake not?"

"As you please, citizen. I will not deny that I have had more elegant surroundings, and that I have seen the inside of more books than one."

"You are not a nobleman?"

"I am."

"And a graduate of a university?"

"Yes."

"You excite me with a curiosity——"

"Which cannot be gratified."

"But you will tell me somewhat of your history; I am sure it must be one of great interest?"

"Oh no, not so interesting as all that. My case is not singular. There are not a few of such as I throughout Europe. You know Rochefort and Flourens: their career has not been dissimilar from mine. You will call us fools and fanatics, but we know what we are after. We can fight or think, carry on a revolution or edit a newspaper, as circumstances may require. We shall do our work and gain our point. We are the picket-guard of the new civilization. But I must leave you now, I have an appointment of great importance."

"Political, I suppose?"

"Political."

"Then you won't give me your name?"

"Yes; mine, but not my family's."

"Do you never hear from your relatives?"

"Never."

"Do you not care to hear of them? Is it necessary to immolate our natural affections, and natural ties, in order to serve the progress of society?"

"Yes, citizen; the cause is more to me than relatives. Our oath enjoins the sacrifice."

"Then you are under oath?"

"Yes."

"But the fictitious name?"

"No, citizen, not even that now; I have said too much. I can depend upon your never even recognising me, I suppose?"

"Certainly."

"Adieu."

"Adieu."

He bowed to me, and left the restaurant, now become unpleasantly full.

This interview confirms me in the opinion that these Communists have an "idea," as the French say, and mean to plot for its attainment. But it is impossible to imagine how a body of so much contrariety of social grade, and so little coherence, are to work together at the critical moment. If they had a leader who could weld them, and use them, they would become extremely formidable.

TALKING HORSE AND EATING HORSE.

NEVER fail to meet a man with a crotchet, if you have an opportunity—a Dr. Amboyne, for example —and if you would enjoy him, "put yourself in his place." The man with a crotchet I have just met is not a doctor; or, if he is, he is a horse doctor. In fact he is a horse-meatist—the horse-meatist, M. Decroix. His hobby-horse is a real horse—a living horse—but more particularly a dead horse. He is reputed a devout man, early at mass, in all the observances of the church blameless. But horse-meat is his strong point. His fame rests upon his having made the horse as serviceable after as he was before death. He introduced the eating of horse into the French army of Algeria; and he was the first to say, *viande de cheval* in France. He is absolutely enthusiastic over his invention or dis-covery, whatever it is. I heard him talk horse for an hour, and not a word did he say about fast horses, or handsome horses, about trotting horses or running horses. His topic was eating horses— that, only that, and that continually. Digestible horses, not tractable horses, is his being's end and aim. He tells me that he has eaten every disease the horse is heir to—every one! There's enthusiasm in science for you! His object was to try the effect of the horse's maladies upon the human system.

Well, what was the effect?

"No effect. They had no appreciable effect. They are harmless, Monsieur; perfectly harmless."

Could he count upon so fortunate a result in the case of every other person who should try the experiment?

"No, he could not; at least he would not say that. He would not advise any other person to make the experiment. But having demonstrated that even diseased horse was harmless, he had proved that sound horse was nutritious."

Had Monsieur subjected the flesh of a bullock or sheep to the same test?

No, he had not; but he "was quite sure that it would not endure the test."

Was there not something in the cooking?—for I had eaten a horse steak that I would have taken for beefsteak; but again I had eaten it when I could have believed it to have been taken from the rump of a rhinoceros.

"Yes, there was much in cooking—there was much in cooking any kind of meat. Horse-flesh did require a little more dexterity on the part of the cook—a little more watching, a little more time."

Was there not some difference in horses?

"The same difference as in other animals, the difference in age."

An old omnibus horse, for example; he would be rather stringy and tough, would he not? especially those stalwart stallions that draw the 'busses in Paris, eh?

"Perhaps so; but he begged to insist that a Parisian 'bus horse could be transformed into a delicacy by a trained French cook, and Monsieur would never suspect that the deceased had drawn an omnibus from the Palais Royal to Vaugirard for ten years."

Would he recommend the horse as a common article of food, along with the animals now in use?

"He certainly would. The introduction of horse-flesh would reduce the price of all flesh; and while it would never pay, perhaps, to rear horses on purpose for the shambles, they could be killed at an age when they would be more profitable to their owner on his table than in his stable. Then, as to the army, the killed or wounded horses that were now a dead loss might be made incalculably profitable. It was distressing to think how often soldiers suffer for animal food immediately after a battle, while an abundance of it is lying all around them."

This reminds me of the lines:

> " Was ever Tartar fierce or cruel
> Upon the strength of water-gruel?
> But who shall stand his rage and force
> If first he rides, then eats, his horse?"

Notwithstanding the spirited advocacy of M. Decroix, however, I will leave Paris with a prejudice against horse-meat almost as strong as the meat itself. I draw my conclusions from internal evidence. The night after my first dinner of horse, I believe I would gladly have died of any one of the three or four maladies with which I thought I was afflicted. It was as horrible a night as ever King Richard spent in the imagination of Shakspeare.

Of the donkey I can speak with more satisfaction—with entire satisfaction. No beef-steak could be more palatable or tender than the steaks of donkey I have eaten at the restaurant.

BREAKING THE CIRCLE OF FIRE.

3rd December.—On the 28th of November all was ready for the grand sortie. Paris was in great excitement, and my American friend and myself resolved to go out to see what we could, and to give what help we might to the wounded. It was lovely weather, like an Indian summer; our *voiture* arrived at five o'clock in the morning, yet the air was so clear that we could see far and near distinctly. The driver had got up both himself and his horse as though for a fête; the harness and the carriage could be seen to shine even in the dark.

Before we reached the ground across the Marne, we met a stream of wounded and retreating soldiers; and as we drew nearer to the scene of battle, the crowd of wounded brave men and cowardly skulkers increased greatly. No need to tell all the terrible and pitiful sights we saw. One young fellow, lying wounded in the hall of a house, beckoned to my flask. He smiled the thanks he could not speak. A little dog was curled up asleep on his breast, and did not stir. The French soldiers are wonderfully attached to their dogs. The Zouave and his dog go into battle together, and it is remarkable how few of the dogs get killed.

The French had made progress; the village of
Champigny was captured. Alas for the pretty homes
deserted and laid desolate!

History again; new battles on old battle-fields.
This little town (a very little town then) was taken
in battle by the Armagnacs, in the year 1418. This
plain old church is not so plain inside. It was built
in the thirteenth century, and in the interior pleases
the eye; and just now, amidst this din of war, re-
freshes the mind with thoughts and hopes and dreams
of peace, if not in this world in another, where
none shall hurt or destroy in all His Holy Mountain.
I have seen no battle yet that had not its restful
church.

I do not wonder at the military spirit. It is
certainly one of the deepest of our instincts. There
is a tremendous fascination in the thunder of artillery; a battle charms, enthuses, crazes, and there
is an unspeakable enjoyment in the craze. Cannon-
balls went whizzing by, and a great shell rushed
hissing and sweeping over our heads, but we did
not care, nor think that we might be hit. The sound
of the mitrailleuse is like nothing so much as the
ripping-up of thousands of planks. Musketry—cannon—what a din there was, and yet it was terribly
fascinating! The soul rises with the awful majesty
of the strife.

There were no officers, or very few, in the stream
of fugitives, but there were a great number picked
up among the wounded.

An officer, rode slowly up to our place of observation. "What news?"

"Bad at the right, better at the left. Ducrot is

doing well, as you see. We are making headway. We have advanced a quarter of a mile, but on the right we have been driven back. Our troops fought well at first, but afterwards broke, and we retired in some disorder on Créteil. Have you seen anything of Trochu?"

"No."

"He was at Champigny just now; ah! here he comes."

Sure enough, at a brisk trot, the staff of the Commander-in-Chief came up. Trochu looked calm enough, and we could not but feel a deep sympathy with him.

The sun at last went down, and the cannonade gradually died away. There is no silence like that after a battle. The cold soon became intense. The indefatigable corps under the Geneva flag searched woods and houses for the wounded. It is extremely sad to find the miserable beings, silent and suffering, and watching for the lantern. There are few groans heard on the field of battle. The wounded seldom groan. Sometimes from the slightly wounded may be heard sounds indicative of pain; the worst wounded are the least complaining. In truth there is little noise on the battlefield besides that of the battle itself. Now and then a shout from commander or men, but mostly all goes on silently. The marching and countermarching, the advance and retreat, the picking-up of the wounded, even the rout, has a muffled sound. The voices sound suppressed. Awful stillness and awful storms of sound and fury go together in a time of battle. A battle is like nothing else in the world, either for noise, or the silence that succeeds to it.

There was a cessation of hostilities on Thursday, but on Friday, the 2nd of December, the terrible roar and thunder again reverberated through the city, and throughout all its once beautiful but now desolated and deserted environs. The day was fine, the scene was grand. The landscape comprised, as on Wednesday, a vast extent of hill and valley and river. The Marne makes a horseshoe behind the French positions. These were Champigny and Brie, which the Germans attacked at day-break. The French were furnished with artillery and redoubts, besides having the thundering assistance of three forts. The day passed on; suddenly there was a panic among the French troops, but the day was not lost. Thousands and thousands of the troops turned and tumbled back in appalling disorder to the very banks of the river, and artillery came tumbling after. A river is said to be a great disadvantage to an army; in this instance it brought the fugitives to a stand, and to their senses. A general, who was near when the panic began, rode up to the affrighted mass with such resolution of language and seriousness of front, that his presence was at once a reproach and an inspiration. He said little but did much, and what he said was said calmly. He cried—"Follow me, men, where duty as well as danger calls. Let us save France, whatever becomes of us." To everybody's surprise the men rallied, and followed, and, for a while, fought bravely, but it was only for a while. The French were driven from all their positions of the morning, and from more than all the ground they had gained the day before; and at night it was a pitiful sight to see the whole French army, 100,000 strong, recross the Marne under cover of the guns of the forts. The next day the Parisians are consoled by the "orders of the day," and official announcements, which soften the bad tidings as best they may; but it certainly taxes their powers of diction, and the fact remains that the "Circle of Fire" is formed by soldiers, and only soldiers can break through it.

The Ambulance Corps have their hands full; they are in very diverse garments, from magnificent regimentals to the most grave and quaker-like costume, but they have all one heart to animate the many hands. On the battle-field they are indifferent to danger, and they range over the field of battle from the extreme front, where they have no business to be, to the extreme rear, where there is no business to do. As to the nurses, there is no doubt of their hard-working fidelity and instinctive skill, but I would prefer seeing some aged and ascetic maiden aunt of a friend engaged in this philanthropy, than any one nearer or dearer to me. Whether this prejudice comes of my jealousy or of the wounded Zouaves' demonstrative affection, I cannot tell, but there it is.

There is something painfully humorous in the scientific enthusiasm of the surgeons. One of them who conducted me (only once) through his hospital, had some of his favourite "compound fractures" suspended by a rope and tackle which he would pull in order as he said to "illustrate his point," while his subject was going mad with torment and I with consternation.

"By just giving that string a twitch like that I (bring forth a yell) procure the elongation of the (yells and) sinews so as to enable me to (get another yell and) adjust the ligaments and in short afford nature every opportunity for (yelling and) healing."

By this time I begged the skilful surgeon to excuse me as I had an urgent engagement.

The wounded die off rapidly, in spite of care and skill. In every church, at all hours of the day, you see the burial-service going on over many coffins, and you meet the hideous-looking black hearse coming many times a day out of the court of the Grand Hotel, where death and suffering now reign supreme. What a change since this time last year! The deaths from amputation alone in the Grand Hotel are said to exceed twenty per cent., and not more than one in ten who are taken there return alive. The burials, numerous enough by day, are still more numerous at night.

Among the dead in the late sortie were found several "Brothers of the Christian Doctrine." These *brancardiers* exhibit the greatest coolness and deliberation in lifting and carrying off the wounded under fire, which requires more courage than going into the battle to fight, for they have none of the delirium which sustains the soldiers. Many soldiers and officers have told me that after the first round they knew no more, and that coming out of a battle was like recovering from a brain-fever, or the effects of a blow on the head.

A DREARY SUNDAY.

———

5th December. — This is Sunday evening. I am sitting shivering by a little grate-fire in the fourth storey, with the fumes of a cup of tea drifting into my face. The thermometer is at zero. The moon-shine makes the night seem colder, and the crisis drearier. The forts are silent—everything is silent. The city rests from strife. We have had a cold, bright, dreary Sunday.

There were many sad faces and dark dresses in the Madeleine to-day. The organ was in sympathy with them. It touched the deepest feelings. It groaned and moaned. It sighed with an awful sense of bereavement, and sang with a divine ex-pression of relief. There were some soldiers present, mostly Bretons. You can pick out a Breton. He is always rooted where he prays. He looks neither to the right nor left. The Bretons have many jests made on them by their Parisian compatriots, for being so religious, and for wearing a little cross in their kepis. Trochu is a Breton, and goes to mass; so the Red papers call him Saint Trochu, and sneer at his piety. Paris has a great contempt for reli-gious people and religious things.

The leading article in *Le Combat* of to-day, signed Félix Pyat, has the following paragraphs:—

"A battalion of the National Guard has made use of the liberty of Béranger under the Republic, and has attended mass before going to the battle. It is even said that they received the sacrament, not of wine, but of punch, which has not diminished their ardour. A drop of brandy by no means spoils the blessed water, and makes a good grog, which has happily succeeded in the case of this battalion."

*　　*　　*　　*　　*

"The proclamations of our chiefs are unfortunately more deist than republican. They are really professions of faith rather than '*ordres du jour.*' They sin both by admission and omission; they avow themselves without opinion, but not without religion. I should prefer opinion. They preach God, and are silent upon the Republic. I should prefer the Republic. They have more faith in Gospel than in social agreement. Gospel may make a man a good Christian, but certainly not a good soldier. Jesus is only a God, not a hero.

"Fight for France; die for her faith, her life, her laws, and her holy dogmas, which Danton and St. Just, Hoche and Marceau, have professed even in dying. Fight for that universal religion that has had its apostles and its martyrs, its professors and its heroes—this Trinity in the future, of which France is the word: Liberty, Equality, Fraternity!"

To be shut up in Paris, or, I suppose, any city besieged and invested, produces the dreariest feeling of home-sickness that it is possible to conceive. The loneliness of a large house, echoing to the footfall of a solitary owner, is more depressing than to be shut up in a cell, for it is more suggestive of home, and friends, and family. To be one of a vast mass without an intimate friend is to realize Byron's solitude in a crowd. You feel so "cut off from the congregation" that you long even to be once more under the surveillance of "Mrs. Grundy," who certainly has the credit of feeling an interest in her neighbours' business! It is very lonely and dismal to know that nobody cares in the least what becomes of you.

DEMOCRATIC SOLDIERS.

7th December.—General Thomas, commander of the National Guard, publishes the *"Tirailleurs de Belleville,"* who "have in a cowardly manner taken to flight in the presence of the enemy." Their brigade commander reports that "such is the hatred between them and the 147th Company, that they have established in the trenches a kind of barricade which it is mutually forbidden to pass." ** "Under the present circumstances a fight among our troops would be disastrous."

Of another battalion he reports that "sixty-one returned to Paris without leave;" and he also says: "The men for the most part have declined to undertake the service of the defences."

The insubordination is universal, and if it were not so alarming, would be ludicrous. Soldiers shout mock orders to their officers. The other evening I saw and heard a common soldier in full uniform mount the tribune and retail complaints of the officers, for whose misdemeanours he declared that he would take the heads off the officers whose discipline was so severe. The burden of the grievances was having to hear mass. A soldier objected to attending mass. The officer said: "Are you not a Christian, and are you not afraid of being killed in battle?" [Rounds of fierce laughter.] Trochu was complained of for going to church, as well as for not going at the Prussians.

Paris has long been practically the most democratic city in the world. The sentiment of perfect liberty and entire equality has long since undermined the discipline of the family, and all respect for the ancient courtesies of society. Servants, children, clerks, have been gradually attaining the present "superior equality," in which "one man is as good as another," and better in his own esteem.

I am sorry to say that public and commercial honesty does not flourish under this Republic. If contracts are made and broken, there is no authority capable of enforcing justice, and if you are cheated you must abide by it. A fellow who swindled me out of fifty francs justifies himself on the ground that he had been defrauded out of the same amount by a countryman of mine. Drunkenness, however, does not increase in Paris: there is the virtue of ebriety left, at least.

9th December.—I attended the funeral of General Renault, the eminent artist, who was mortally wounded in the last sortie. He had been wounded also in Italy. He had brilliant penetrating eyes, and a face very like a wedge. In dash and mettle he realized one's idea of what some of the chiefs must have been who served under the First Napoleon. Shortly before his death, when he was breathing with difficulty, a Sister of Mercy said to him,—

"Shall we pray for you?"

"Pray for France," was the reply, and they were his last words.

The funeral ceremonies were performed at the Invalides. Gorgeous catafalque; cloudy day; "dim religious light;" green flames in tall urns; black canopy sprinkled with white stars; immense white cross against a black background; mass by the choir, and *Dies Iræ* by a military band; striking tableau of eminents—generals, ministers, ecclesiastics, and statesmen.

Jules Favre led the line. The colour had all gone from his face, and his lips were resolutely closed. The sight of him filled me with sympathy for him. Jules Ferry, Simon, Ernest Picard, and Eugène Pelletan were also in the line; the venerable Governor of the Invalides, General de Martigny, Schmitz of German descent, and the sturdy Clement Thomas, the new commander of the National Guards.

The venerable Archbishop of Paris spoke briefly, but he was not impressive on this occasion, and his words were indistinct. Not a speech or sermon calculated to impress or inspirit the people have we had yet. Nobody speaks the word which everybody is longing to hear. No archbishop, nor priest, nor parson—no Catholic or Protestant! No public utterance is equal to the occasion—all of them are far below the occasion. Great preachers, great orators, great statesmen, great generals—all fail, utterly fail, to say the rousing or inspiring word.

BREAD RAID.

———

12*th December*.—Yesterday there was a Bread panic and a raid on the bakeries. "What has become of the Bread?" was the universal question. It was the first symptom of the ugly possibility that is never absent from our minds. I made a tour of the bakehouses. Every one I found empty, and nearly all closed. As I had very recently seen those same bakeries well supplied, I was startled at this spectacle of dearth. "What does it mean?" said I, to the weary-faced woman who stood at the door of one of the shops. "It means, Monsieur, that our flour is giving out. I am told there is plenty of wheat, but nothing to grind it with."

13*th December*.—The Government has soothed the Bread panic, declaring there was no cause for it. They promise that Bread shall be "at discretion" and not rationed, but to-day there is a line at the bakers', as there is at the butchers'.

The principal topic of conversation just now is —Food! and the universal salutation is, "What do you get to eat?" The worst of it is, the more one talks about eating the more one wants to eat. People are beginning to dream of eating and of good dinners, from which they awaken and find themselves hungry. Oh! the mirages we have of those mutton-chops and large, mealy, well-roasted potatoes which are only found in perfection in London! The poorest class are now provided with "canteens," where, for a few sous, or even for nothing, they obtain an excellent palatable soup. There is comparatively little suffering among this class.

16th December. — Another encouraging pigeon despatch from Gambetta.

The *Temps* speaks sneeringly of the "sonorous incertitudes of Gambetta," and seems to have no confidence in his despatches.

17th December. — The Minister of Agriculture says we still have 10,000,000 kilogrammes of rice, 10,800,000 kilogrammes of split peas and beans, and a large quantity of cheese.

As other articles disappear, Colman's mustard becomes more and more conspicuous. It is in every grocer's window. It is tantalizing and aggravating to see windows full and windows full of these hateful little jars of mustard! They attract the attention of everybody. There is something absurdly horrible in the suggestion of a surfeit of mustard and a famine of meat!

20th December. — General Thomas again complains of the National Guard. The 200th Battalion marched to the front in a state of intoxication. The

201st added profanation to intoxication. They broke into a church, arrayed themselves in such vestments as they could find, passed round the bread and wine, and performed a sham mass.

20th December.—Four thousand eggs were sold at the Halle for 1023 francs. The English baker told me pleasantly to-day, "This is the last loaf you will get during the siege."

21st December.—Madame Jules Simon states, on behalf of a ladies' society for the succour of the victims of the war, that they have kept up five kitchens and disbursed 100,000 portions a day, given meals to the children of two infant asylums, and given employment to 600 women, and distributed food and fuel,—in all expending 32,000 francs a month.

PHRASEOLOGICAL.

M. Favre thought that by "Piously laying crowns at the feet of the statue of Strasbourg our garrison would swear to be worthy of their brethren of Alsace, and to die as they have done."

So many, however, prefer swearing at the statue to fighting at the outposts, that the former is officially discouraged with some sneering, and the latter commanded with some impatience. Possibly M. Favre regrets that other altiloquent oath of his, not to give up one stone of a fortress or inch of territory. His bombast surprises everybody; but nobody is surprised to hear Victor Hugo exclaim, "We draw from the scabbard an idea." At the same time von Moltke draws his Krupp guns into position around Paris.

The French really seem to derive nutriment, inflation at all events, from this gaseous rhetoric. Queen Hortense expressed the French idea of it when she wrote to her son, Napoleon III.:

"Speech is an admirable power for seduction; it colours what one desires to illumine. It is excellent for enveloping skilful projects in calculated obscurity. There is a princely [Frenchly?] art of flashing phrases in such a manner that by an optical phenomenon it makes people see just what they desire to see. One learns to employ a language which has all the diversity of aspect of the chameleon, or that of a harlequin's jacket, which Florian shows us in his fable. Every one sees in it the colour which pleases him most. Thus, your uncle the Emperor was able to establish his authority by giving to all parties that particular hope which amused the vanity of Royalist or Republican, as the case might be.

"You should not disdain the aid of journalists. They are incomparable for rendering misfortune interesting, and I may add that most of them have a mania for resuscitating the vanquished."

This policy of keeping the pen going has been that of every government, provisional and permanent, that France has ever had. The most famous (and infamous) political circular ever addressed to the Prefects was written in the "flashing phrases" of Jules Favre, when he was Secretary-General under the arch Republican Ledru-Rollin, who, upon the fall of Louis Philippe, became Minister of the Interior of the (as usual, Personal) Republic.

ANOTHER SORTIE.

22nd December.—We were up at six and off at seven o'clock. The morning was dark, drizzling, chilling, penetrating. It came down upon you like a weight, and went through you like pins of ice. Here and there a small lot of shivering workpeople. Pass a long line of ambulances—the ambulance of the Press, the Italian, the Swiss, the American, the International, and the rest, rolling along toward the field. That ecclesiastic who goes dashing by on a gay charger is a Hungarian bishop *in partibus*, they say. His regimentals are gorgeous. His ecclesiastical hat is bounded and suspended (behind) with a scarlet scarf. On his breast blazes an enormous star, suggesting the order of the sunflower, to say the least.

The French are evidently making an attack upon Bourget, which they lost with so much discredit about six weeks ago. But there is the usual interminable length of line, and the usual complicacy of strategy. To the right, to the left, far away and near at hand, there is the customary bang, crackle, roar, and thunder.

Here go the Marines, the best fellows in the army. They are soldiers of the past; know no better than to obey orders, stand to their posts, and fall at them. They are going to the extreme front. A dogged, sullen countenance the captain has, which seems to say, "We are going to our doom." They did go to their doom. Out of 600 nearly 300 fell. An hour after they marched past us, they were carried past us on stretchers—among them the captain, with the same dogged, sullen countenance. The little town of Bourget was terrifically alive with batteries. To the right of it, to the left of it, and in front of it, the fire belches and the thunder rolls. The wretches seem to fall to no purpose. 100,000 men gathered about Bourget, where, probably, there are about 20,000 Prussians, none of whom are visible to the naked or assisted eye. There was very little movement of troops, or a change in positions. It was a stationary banging of artillery mainly, from early morning to early in the evening.

That day passed, and this day has passed, without result. The cold is perilous. We hear of several having perished on the field during the night. They become completely benumbed, and cannot be resuscitated; nor have they sufficient animal food to resist the rigour of the weather. Poor fellows! it is very sad to see them suffer and perish in this purposeless way.

None of our leaders have the confidence of their followers and none of our followers have confidence in their leaders. I hear officers dilate upon the impossibility of getting the soldiers to stand, and I hear soldiers affirm that their leaders are a lot of muffs who ought to be shot. Meanwhile both officers and men will ask you if you do not think they are furnishing a sublime spectacle to the world!

CHRISTMAS.

CHRISTMAS in the Siege of Paris! It was the climax of the forlorn. Thermometer at zero, snow dribbling, scowling heavens, slippery pavements, ominous silence all round the city; failure of another sortie; troops ordered in to get .warm; thousands of people lying abed to save food and fuel; long lines taking their turn for hoofs of horses at the butcheries at a franc a pound, and for dirt-coloured bread at the bakeries; a thousand soldiers lost from cold; growing growl of indignation against Trochu, against the Government, against everybody, the Deity not excepted; National Guards protecting the wood-yards from the freezing women; freezing women succeed in a raid, and carry off armloads; at other places National Guards do the carrying off; soldiers denouncing their officers in the clubs; complaints of commissariat department; complaints of every department; wounded dying hourly of cold, of bad food or no food, and of infectious atmosphere, as at the Grand Hotel, where it is said a man can't cut his finger and reach the door alive; smallpox deaths nearly 400 a week; typhoid fever, 220—total, 2,728. Horse-meat getting scarce; hares, forty francs apiece; cats, fifteen; chickens, sixty;

turkeys, 100; dogs, fifty; ducks, eighty; rats, two; wood, a penny a pound, and hard to find; no coal; gas gone, lamps instead; dismal Boulevards in consequence. Such is Christmas in the siege of Vanity Fair!

There was no midnight mass. On Christmas Eve we hurried shivering through the nipping air to the Church of St. Roch. The doors were closed; the gates were closed. The lamps threw à sickly illumination on the sacred mass of revolutionary history. Lonely—lonely! We turned away with a sense of bereavement. It would have been a comfort to have heard the music, and joined in the prayers of the midnight mass, on this gloomy Christmas Eve.

27th December.—The Germans tried the range of our forts to-day. The ground has frozen hard enough to enable von Moltke to order up his Krupp cannon.

Long before the break of day, we arose in our beds, and leaned upon our hands in the biting atmosphere, listening to the unusually lively cannonade. When daylight came, we were up again, and off again. Paris was alert. Everybody was talking about the big racket to the eastward. People stood in groups. Rumour rose and spread. The bombardment had commenced!

With intermissions, the terrific storm goes raging on all day long. As the day closes, and the sky darkens, the storm gradually subsides. There is a lull, then a booming, then a longer lull, then a

shorter din, then a bang and a burst at longer in-
tervals, and then—silence and darkness. The wind
moans on, the gunners rest. Some sit on a bench,
some lean listlessly against their favourite gun,
some roam round chatting over their day's work.
All smoke, and nobody knows, or seems to care,
what it all means, or what will be on the morrow.

If there shall be anything done toward redeeming the fall of this nation, or averting the doom
which impends over this city, you may depend upon
it, it will not be done by the Parisians of any class
or any battalion. It will not be done by the *pro-
létaire* or the *bourgeois*, by the fire-eaters of Belleville or the snobs of the Quartier des Champs Élysées.
It will be done by these steady-headed, straight-
stepping fellows from the South and East of France,
—by the Norman Mobiles, the Alsatian Liners,
or the gendarmerie from the provinces, who have
been picked and assorted for several generations for
military duty. The gendarme is the best-dressed,
best-behaved, best-drilled soldier in the city—if, indeed, he is not the only real soldier in the city.
To see them on guard, or on the street, or in their
quarters, is to be impressed with their appearance,
and to believe in their fidelity. I have never yet
seen one of them lounge, or slouch, or draggle.
They are all and always minding their own business. Their dress is neat, pretty, substantial, and
picturesque; those of them who wear long-tailed,
blue, double-breasted coats, with short sword, and
kepis in keeping, being particularly attractive. The
gendarme becomes his uniform and the uniform be-

comes him, and I shall grieve to see one of these handsome veterans carried by me on the stretcher. But how can we grieve for the loss of those reprobate Parisians who live without an object higher than their own enjoyment, and fight, if they fight at all, with no definite end whatever?

29th December.—The Plateau d'Avron was swept clean to-day by the Krupp guns.

The number of persons detected in giving aid and comfort to the enemy is, I am sure, much larger than the number given by the newspapers. A little boy, of about ten years of age, carried on a traffic in newspapers and tobacco for two months before he was detected. A quarryman, aged fifty-two, has been sentenced by court-martial to twenty-five years' hard labour in the penitentiary, for having given the Prussians the route to the catacombs of Paris. As he was a well-known inhabitant of the vicinity of Châtillon, he went back and forth through the Prussian lines unsuspected. In the course of the trial two respectable citizens, one of them the Mayor of Clamart, were implicated.

In the balloon department, a man who is intimate with several members of the Government is strongly suspected of being in league with the Prussians.

Four women escaped the lively pickets, and even their livelier bullets, and reached the Prussian lines with their information or booty.

We have all taken our turn in being run to earth for spies. The other evening an American banker, a Chicago merchant, and myself were sauntering along the Champs Elysées, on our way home from one of Consul-General Read's rare siege-dinners, when a small Englishwoman stepped up to us from behind, and asked the time of night. The banker replied, "Quarter to ten." In five minutes we were conducted into a *caserne* by a chassepot, and arraigned before a diminutive National, for the crime of having said "Quarter to ten" in German. We denied the charge, and produced our passports. The diminutive National became exasperated at being foiled, and, but for the interference of his associates, would doubtless have sent us into confinement for not being the spies he took us for. My knuckles itched to knock the little tribunal over. However, we prudently held our tongues and our temper, and were soon bowed out of the august presence of the diminutive, with whom we exchanged cards, when, lo and behold! he turned out to be a Dutch chemist! Then we tried, but in vain, to induce him to say "Quarter to ten" in German.

NEW YEAR'S DAY, 1871.

A SAD New Year's Day for Paris! There are no visits exchanged. The presents are pieces of cheese and loaves of bread. The newspapers take the occasion to renew their "No surrender" vows, but there is something deeply pathetic in these words of one of the papers; "Adieu 1870, adieu fatal year! Let all the earth that we cast on our dead accumulate on thy tomb and on thy memory." The bells are ringing. If they only would "ring out the false and ring in the true!"

The Minister of the Interior distributed to-day 104,000 kilogrammes of preserved beef (not horse-meat), 104,000 kilos. of dried beans, 104,000 kilos. of olive-oil, 104,000 kilos. of unroasted coffee, and 52,000 kilos. of chocolate.

There is, and will be to the end, whenever that may be, no deficiency in and no change in the price of coffee, chocolate, wines, liqueurs, and tea.

We have been breathing an atmosphere of zero for a fortnight. Several hundred soldiers have been disabled or killed outright by the cold.

My little pile of wood is diminishing with ominous rapidity, and when it is gone there will be no more to be had!

The Boulevards are a spectacle still. It would require several sieges to rob them of their unexampled interest. At about 9 P.M., notwithstanding the bitterness of the atmosphere and the gloominess of the lamps, which drop but a feeble and circumscribed light, there is the same old languid tide of thoughtless Parisians. Your thoughtless Parisians will stroll and lounge, and sip and smoke and chat, although they curl up and shiver in the nipping air.

As you go hurrying along in your massive overcoat, even trotting to get up a glow, you see the thoughtless Parisian absolutely sitting without gloves on the Boulevard benches, or at the outdoor café tables. He shivers, and sips on, and thinks about nothing.

I sat last evening and watched the panorama of faces that came and went at the café 'Left Centre.' There was a decent-looking family—husband, wife, and two pretty children. One of these children was particularly sweet and pretty. She was dressed in white, which gave her ethereal beauty a still more ethereal appearance. That family have no home but the café—some rooms, doubtless, but cheerless, dismal ones. That family sit in the open café, suffocating with tobacco-smoke, and odorous with unwashed Frenchmen, and buzzing with harlots—what could it mean for the husband's fidelity, the mother's constancy, and the pretty little daughter's future?

The cafés are full, too, of spurs and swords, and red trousers and blue. The tide on the Boulevards contains all the colours of the military rainbow. These are the rearguard of the sortie-ing army. Cafés, boulevards, theatres, all going—these are the signs of the times. The temper of the people in the play-house has its relations to the temper of the army at the front. How can there be health in the right arm of Paris while she is decaying at the heart?

Poor, beautiful, sad, fascinating, detestable, comical, tragical Paris! There is just one thing she can do in order to pull through—nothing. Doing nothing will bring her through, and that she can do. She can go to bed at bed-time, whenever that is; and get up at getting-up-time, whenever that is; and she can browse about, and pick up what she can find to eat, whatever that may be. So she can go on for two months for aught I know. This torpid nothing she can do, and this torpid nothing her poets may call endurance and heroism and all that; but enduring heroism is as pronounced and perceptible a quality as any other, and if Paris had real heroic endurance, and not sham twaddle of that name, in her streets, she would have resolution, pluck, and some measure of success at the front.

3rd January.—No end of glorious rumours from the provinces! Shall we ever have any realities?

6th January.—General Trochu placards all the walls with a denial of the rumour of capitulation. He says—"The Governor of Paris will not capitulate."

The Rothschilds offer to the city, for the poor, clothes sufficient for 48,000 children, 32,000 women, and 12,000 men.

News of a victory by Faidherbe at Bapaume.

The Church of St. Etienne du Mont was quite filled to-day. This is the church of the patron saint of Paris, Ste. Geneviève, whom the crowd were supplicating to-day in behalf of the beautiful capital.

9th January.—A wine-seller near the ramparts of Point du Jour put upon his half-demolished shop, "The rendezvous of the obus."

The Vaugirard omnibus-conductors at the Palais Royal cry, "Here's your 'bus to the bombardment; fine view of the Prussian batteries from the top!"

11th January.—Another hurly-burly. It is over the sortie which did not come off. The "plan Trochu" hung fire, and the newspapers say the reason why there was no sortie is that the enemy heard of it, and prepared for it. Somebody has revealed it, cry the newspapers! The civilization shut up in Paris vibrates between "*trompé*" and "*trahison.*"

There never was in all history such a spectacle of helplessness as Paris during this siege. And the thoughtful Parisians see it themselves occasionally. *La Liberté* says: "After reigning 80 years (not 18 then?) the *bourgeoisie* are exhausted. There remains to it neither an institution, an idea or a man. There is no principle of resistance left in it. Its individual egotism has rendered it so unsocial that it is not even one body. History has nothing to compare with this fall!"

But so incorrigible is this "individual egotism" of Paris that it will repudiate the "fall" when insinuated by a foreigner.

THEORIES PARISIAN AND DARWINIAN.

An old Subscriber writes as follows to the *Figaro:*

"During the siege my numerous acquaintances in Paris were anxious to contribute their best efforts to the defence of our city, and I have the great happiness of informing you that all of them are in perfect health notwithstanding the horrors of the siege. I have a proof that all have done their duty, since all are *décorés*. One of them, indeed, who, although he had volunteered to serve, had not received any arms (having been attached to the correspondence department of a general officer), has only obtained the military medal."

The Editor says in reply that "Common sense has been discarded in Paris. It is a city of madmen, and it is not without cause that it is the gayest city of the universe."

And yet our journals flew into a passion when the rumour came in that General Burnside had said "Paris was a madhouse full of monkeys." But the fact is that such a remark sounds far more like a Frenchman's than a foreigner's comment on this people. I have quoted Voltaire. Napoleon I. said of the Parisians: "I care very little for their opinions.

They are no better than wasps that are always
buzzing. They are no more worthy of attention
than an ape delivering a lecture on metaphysics."

Every day or two we have our government described in our press as monkeys ("*singes*"). The
vehement critic never leaves off until he has cul-
minated in the exclamation, "O, the monkeys!" ("*O,
les singes!*")

One journalist addresses another in these words:
"Listen, Escande, little old man, broken and
withered; thou art a hunchback, morally as well as
physically. Continue to scratch thy miserable brain
with thy owl's talons. Calumniate, howl, bite, if
you can. Lie, since you cannot do otherwise. But
thy days are numbered, my little man. There will
soon remain no one of thy kind but a strange and
deformed skeleton that a descendant of Cuvier one
hundred years from now will take for the remains
of an ugly monkey!"

I thought it noteworthy that there should be
such a concurrence in the way of vituperative
vocabulary. It is manifestly written in the indicative
mood. These people seem to hold the Darwinian
theory wrong end foremost; they believe they are
descending to monkeys. Or perhaps they hold the
theory both ends foremost—they believe not only
that they are descended from, but descending to,
monkeys!

BOMB-GAZING.

13*th January*.—Last night we were a thousand or two strong on the Place de la Concorde, looking at the bombs. Everybody enjoyed it hugely. The little pale woman, leaning on the arm of a littler and paler man, said she wouldn't have missed it for the world. The boys vied with dogs in gamboling ecstacy. The moon sat on her bowl-side in the cloudless sky, pouring her shimmer on monument and river. The Seine furnished us one of her tranquil night-scenes, which, once seen, are never to be forgotten. We missed the lustre of the gas, but miles of lamps, acres of lamps, contributed to the spectacle. Before us a dark mass of columns—the Corps Législatif, mutely eloquent of other days. Behind us a dark mass of columns—the incomparable Madeleine, always picturesque, but particularly so when illuminated into sombre outline by the moonlight through the trees—the Madeleine, pathetically poetical of a better country beyond. To our right, down the Champs Elysées, the Arc de Triomphe, its columns of lies protected from the bombs by planks. Among the victories you will read the town "Weissenburg." To our left, gloomy, silent, dark, the Tuileries; the Empress' birdcage empty, the Prince's apartments dark, the lonely sentinel gone from his beat, the great park covered with sheds for army horses, and some of the mammoth trees lying prostrate. In the midst of the capacious Place the Egyptian obelisk, grim and old—nobody knows how old—a witness of all the tempestuous ages. Near by stands the drooping and forsaken statue of Strasbourg, a faithful symbol at last, telling its "tale of two cities" and their doom.

A black lump with a bright spot makes a vast grand curve, makes a whizzing, howling sound, and drops, with a resounding boom and clang, into the "Latin quarter," into the revelry of vice and the carnival of lascivious pleasure. Another, and another. The boys and dogs scamper, the little girl is afraid her mamma will not see it. The beautiful night passes, the moon sets, the shells cease, the crowd dissolves silently. Heroic Paris goes to bed.

The weather has changed at last, but I fear not for the better. The biting cold has given place to a penetrating damp, and from complaining of being cold we have passed to growling about taking cold. Every man, woman, child, and National Guard of us has a cold, a bad cold, a wretched cold. The wringing wet atmosphere goes through and through you, sinks through your thickest garments, and reaches your remotest joints; you are alternately twitched with the tweezers of rheumatism, and stabbed with the stiletto of neuralgia.

14th January.—I suspect that Jules Favre and

all the rest of the Conservative Republicans here are afraid of their own principles.

The Reds, or Communists proper, have an Idea, or think they have, which amounts to the same thing. Their "Commune" may be but a mirage with most of them, but even that much their compatriots of the Conservative school do not seem to possess.

Our *concierge* has turned Communist. The *concierge*, or the porter who pulls the cord for you when you ring the bell of the street, gate, or door, is not as a general thing a public favourite, since (perhaps by reason of his vocation of night-watchman) he is of an extremely inquiring turn of mind and eye.

But I have just heard of an incident which has somewhat softened my prejudice. A *concierge's* wife, who was very popular with the lodgers on account of her fidelity at the cord, as well as for her amiable demeanour, died the other day. During her last and delirious moments she was deeply concerned lest anyone should be kept waiting at the gate. She must have somebody at the cord perpetually, and her last words were "*Tirez le cordon, Marie.*"

Let us hope that at that moment the door of one of the "many mansions" was opened for the poor soul who in this life was so faithful over her "few things."

16*th January.*—Dinner at the London Tavern. Bill of fare—Ass, mule, larks, fried potatoes, peas, red wine, and coffee—twelve francs.

I prefer dog-meat to horse-meat, but I cannot

say I like it. I suppose, however, it is hardly fair to pass judgment upon these unusual viands until one has tasted them at their best.

Cat is downright good eating. A young one, well-cooked, is better than hare or rabbit. It tastes something like the American grey squirrel, but is even tenderer and sweeter.

I saw a beautiful Angora for sale by a moblot to-day on the Boulevard, stolen probably, price twenty-five francs. I was touched to observe what pity poor Tabby drew from all classes of persons, illustrating the fondness of the French for pet animals. Some of them are hiding their ugly terriers and hateful old scratchers. An old lady tells me she will starve before she will consent to be saved by eating her cat.

Rats, to my surprise, taste somewhat like birds. My restaurateur says he paid a franc-and-a-half for the one he gave me, and I see them occasionally at the Halle selling, or at least for sale, at one franc. But they are extremely scarce.

This is Molière's birthday. Performances at the theatres in honour thereof; at the Théâtre Français, 'Amphitryon' and 'Dépit Amoureux.'

Bakers announce that they can give only 400 grammes, and this only to clients with butchers' cards.

Horrible bread it is. It tastes as if it were made of sawdust, mud, and potato-skins.

17th January.—Watched the bombardment; but it **was** not very lively.

Trochu's throne is tottering; Favre's is trembling. Gambetta's only seems at this moment to be firm. But it will not stand long. "Uneasy lies the head that wears the crown" in France, whether the crown be red or golden.

18*th January*.—Spent the day in watching and dodging shells.

It is very fascinating to see these huge projectiles flying through the air. The crowds who look on share I am sure in my fascination. Old and young, women and little boys, especially the boys, are drawn to the perilous entertainment by an irresistible bewitchery. We are alternately hilarious and terrified. The moment the peculiar whiz and whir of the coming shell is heard, everybody falls face-foremost upon the pavement. Sometimes the Boulevard St. Germain' resembles the thoroughfare of a Mohammedan town when some high ecclesiastic passes that way.

Prostrations such as these, to either God or man, were, I am sure, never seen before on the streets of Paris.

Then one's curiosity is to the last degree keen to see the effect produced by the obus, some of which are as big as the ordinary sugar-loaf, and about the same shape, and weigh about 150 pounds.

THE SERPENTS AT THE HEARTH.

As I sat the other afternoon in a Parisian draw-
ing-room I was attracted, I may say startled, by the
embellishments of the fire-place, or rather of the
hearth-stone.

Hearth-stone is the term. It is a very sacred
term in the English language, is it not? It has a
cherished significance to all English-speaking peoples.
It has a precious and profound meaning in the way
of affection, fidelity, devotion, "hospitality without
grudging," self-sacrifice without murmuring, godly
fear and manly valour. Then it recalls something
about every man's house being his castle, and that
suggests all that is beautiful and chivalric in personal
bravery.

Well, as I was about to say, this Parisian hearth-
stone was profusely decorated with shining brass
fender and shining knobbed hand-irons, et cætera
et cætera, all of the olden time and all very quaint,
therefore, and attractive. But what startled me was
to see, rearing up on either side, a shining brass
serpent, with mouth wide open and a forked tongue
protruding directly toward the hearth! The heads of
these serpents vied with the remainder of the adorn-
ments in brazen shine; and of all the elegant and

elaborate furnishings of the apartment they were the most conspicuous and, of course, the most eloquent. Look where I would, my eyes instinctively returned to these arched and glittering serpents. Listen as I might to the tick of the clock on the mantel, or the roar of the street under the window, or the thunder of the artillery at the fortifications, I could hear over all the "dark sayings" of these serpents at the hearth-stone.

Is there, I thought, no connection between this (let us call it unconscious) treachery in symbolism and the tragedy of errors going on around us? Has this sentiment of the brazen snake in social life nothing to do with the tumbling of this great nation from its high estate of insolent domination? May we not trace all this horrid din and devastation of the splendid city back to its homes—or rather to its want of homes? There is no such word as "home" in the French language, "no place like home" in the French capitol, and nothing like "home" among the much vaunted multitude of French "ideas."

Where there is no such word and no such thing as home there is no such influence or inspiration as emanates therefrom; and where no such influence or inspiration is to be found you look in vain for that stamina and tenacity of character which insures an endurance and resistance equal to any emergency that may overtake a people. Character, like charity, should "begin at home." If it is not cultivated at the hearth-stone it will, sooner or later, fail at the fortifications. Here is the nation's first line of defences.

As I strolled along the streets of the besieged capitol, wondering what in the world could suggest anything so incongruous as a pair of serpents with their tongues out at a hearth-stone, I saw plenty of this species of symbolical furniture in the shop windows. Strange that I had not noticed this French "idea" before. I thought I was "up" in all the French ideas. We live and learn. Where the device was not of this snakine kind it was almost sure to be after our traditional notion of what is familiarly known as "the old serpent." The French take to the *diable* with artistic enthusiasm. He seems to be in all their thoughts of illustration and ornamentation. Their grave and comic literature are both full of him. He is the inspiring genius of their serious and their humorous art. "*Vive le Diable!*" I heard one of them cry at a club meeting.

"Murder will out"—So will character, especially national character. It is expressed in popular devices as well as proclaimed in favourite watch-words. "We are betrayed!" has been the shout from the beginning of the siege of Vanity Fair. "Treason! treason!" shrieks everybody to everybody at the recurrence of every failure to break the "circle of fire." And everybody is right; they are betrayed—self-betrayed. The leaven of treachery has leavened the whole lump at last. "Treason has done its worst" in France. Fidelity and uprightness are impossible in official stations where they are repudiated in private life. The serpent will reign in the councils of the nation if it is enshrined at the hearth-stone of the people.

The nation may be monarchy or republic, the result will be the same. The people may be French or American, it is a question of time. They must decay, root and branch, if they have begun to decay at the heart. Their home-life is their heart-life. When they fail there they fail everywhere. "All was lost except honour" when Francis I. lost the battle of Pavia. Honour and all will go down when Paris falls.

JULES FAVRE.

———

JULES FAVRE declines Lord Granville's invitation to London, and everybody exclaims—"What a fool!"

Instead of jumping at the chance of playing a card which he knows the Prussian Chancellor is afraid he will play, he hesitates and vacillates, calls his Mayors together, asks for their advice and refuses it.

Jules Favre the lion of the London Democracy which escorts him from station to hotel, and from hotel to conference, where he may plead to his heart's content for his country—would not this spectacle be as annoying to Prussia as advantageous to France?

Our distinguished Foreign Minister seems to be completely shorn of his strength, and acts like one in a dream. What has become of the splendid oratory, with which he used to electrify his followers and terrify his foes? It died away with the uproar that ushered in his regime.

Nor is his wisdom any more conspicuous than his eloquence. He thundered at the tribune under the Empire for a municipal government for Paris, and when he was at the head of an Empire of his

own he declined to grant it. He granted nothing
to his old followers which the Emperor refused
them, except the muskets with which they propose to
bayonet the Republic of their choice. He handled
the Parisian Democracy as though he, like his pre-
decessor, were their master; whereas they know, what
his vanity prevents him from knowing, that when
Napoleon III. is out of Paris they are rulers in
Paris. He supposed he could imitate the Emperor
in keeping down Belleville, after departing from
the Emperor's policy of keeping chassepots out of
the hands of Belleville.

And yet there must be strength and will-power
where there is such a protrusion of underlip and
such a shock of wiry hair. There is a gritty tenacity
of purpose in that hair, and vigorous resolution in
those lips. The hands too are indicative of grip,
hold-on, and doggedness. Then as to his intellectu-
ality and culture and elegance of diction there can
be no doubt.

Evidently his order of mind is not for such a
place as he now occupies. He is not a statesman,
or a diplomat, or a ruler, or a leader—except in
opposition. He is made for irresponsible popular
leadership. He is the born leader of the minority
contending for a supremacy which may destroy
them to attain. He excels in the aggressive, in
arraigning an administration, or charging an en-
trenchment of obstructive conservatism.

He is successful as a barrister, but even here
he has a grave defect. He will sometimes spend

his strength in protecting the strongest points of his case, and leave the weakest points exposed.

In short he knows nothing of diplomacy, and has to defend himself against the greatest diplomat in Europe; he is ignorant of the highest forms of statesmanship and has to grapple with the most astute statesman in the world. He is good only for pulling down, and is now expected to build up; his efficiency consists only in criticising Government, and he is now obliged to administer one.

He is a large round man in a very large square hole. No wonder he cannot fill it. But he was tossed into it by a hurricane of public opinion, and therefore it is no fault of his that he is where he is. Public men must do the best they can in the hole they are tossed into, but they should not throw away such an opportunity for getting out of it as Lord Granville has given Jules Favre.

"THE FOG IS THICK."

Midnight, 19*th January*.—We are nearly through now. The end cannot be far off. Paris betrays apprehension. The old woman at the kiosque handed me my evening papers without a word. She is usually very talkative. She did not look me full in the face. Could I be mistaken?—was it my friend in regimentals who gave me a furtive glance, and shrank out of the café door? Poor man! he feels deeply, for he is a Breton, and is ashamed of Paris. The bookseller, who so often predicted the hour of deliverance, stepped out as I stepped in; why in such haste? The shoemaker, who has always been so anxious to fit me, was quite sure he had nothing that would fit me to-day.

The coffee and absinthe sippers under the lamps in the cafés, and the shiverers at the tables on the pavement, the crowd around the crack billiard-player, the silent group around the silent chess-players, the enormous chimney-pot hat in the corner sipping absinthe, the bizarre necktie smoking drearily at the pillar, the middle-aged woman who always comes into the café at 9 P.M. alone, and always goes out alone at 10—all looked, everybody looked to-day, as if the end were near. There can be no doubt of it this time. It is very exciting. It is impossible to sleep. What a day we have had! So let me make note of it hour by hour:—

8 A.M.—"The enemy kills our women and children. He bombards us day and night. He throws obus on our hospitals. A cry to arms escapes from all breasts. Those of us who can give our lives on the field of battle, let us march against the enemy; and those who remain behind, zealous to show themselves worthy of the heroism of their brothers, will accept the most painful sacrifices as another means of serving their country. Let us suffer, and die if need be, but vanquish."

There was something extremely sad in the sound of this. Paris read it on the walls with a shrug; hardly that. "To arms! escaped from all breasts," and into the arms of the Prussians are already gone "those of us who can give their lives on the field of battle." Into the arms of Delilah are gone the remainder, and into the arms of Doom go we all.

10 A.M.—Combat at Montretout. "We are masters. The column Bellemare hold the heights of Buzenval."

10.32 A.M.—Poor Trochu! He says: "Fog intense; observations very difficult."

10.50 A.M.—"Fog absolutely conceals the phases of the battle. Officers carrying orders cannot find the troops. This is very much regretted by me, because it is very difficult to make the combinations I had intended!"

9.50 P.M.—"Our day, happily commenced, has

not had the issue we hoped for. The enemy having borne down on our position with enormous masses of artillery and reserves of infantry, our columns were obliged to retire from the heights which they had taken in the morning.

"A pigeon arrived yesterday evening with despatches, which we could not decipher before the publication of the official journal."

21st January.—Bread is now rationed 300 grammes for two sous for each adult, and 150 at one sou for each child.

Poor Paris! The political fog is indeed intense, and "observations are difficult." Nobody knows our latitude. But the foggy, drizzly day has been followed by a beautiful night. I spread apart the curtains just now, and saw the stars. The guns boom, but the streets are silent. An occasional footfall only. The fire is almost out. In the mass of expiring embers I see the doomed capital with its glorious churches and noble trees. I never felt so sad in all my life: and with this is mingled a strange feeling of shame and humiliation.

One cannot help feeling ashamed of a people who are not ashamed of themselves. The bravest army and the manliest nation have to submit to the conqueror sometimes, but the fall of Paris is the fall of all that goes to constitute heroism and patriotism. In all history there never was so humiliating a disaster. It is the wreck of a national manhood.

It is not easy to keep down the spirit which

would thank God that one is not of this people, who will not make a heroic failure of it even; or to repress the pride with which one recollects the two Fatherlands, the one over the Channel, the other over the sea.

I seriously doubt whether an Anglo-Saxon, ever so well-grounded in the homely virtues of our forefathers, can for any considerable time keep his manhood in the social atmosphere of Paris. Certainly it is not an atmosphere in which heroes can breathe and live. It is fatal to the moral sense. And if that be valuable to the youth who visits Paris, I would advise him to imitate Pilgrim, put his fingers in his ears, turn his back upon this "City of Destruction," and take to his heels.

Some small idea may be formed of the cost of the war, in one fraction of one department only, when we read: "The calculation of the newspapers is, that in five days the forts received 25,000 projectiles, each weighing 50 kilogrammes, total 1,250,000 kilogrammes—to throw which cost 1,500,000 francs. Damage, nil."

9.30 A.M.—Trochu tells us again that "The fog is thick. The enemy does not attack. We have asked for an armistice for two days, for the purpose of relieving the wounded and burying the dead."

The despatch from Gambetta has been deciphered. Chanzy, after two days of brilliant battles, near Le Mans, has retreated behind the Mayenne.

Furious hurricane of shells. The enemy pressing in on all sides. Two forts seriously damaged.

The irreconcilables are restless. The hungry are
pillaging the markets and shops. A long, long,
anxious day.

Some noteworthy names are on the roll of losses
in the "foggy" sortie of the 19th. Regnault, a pro-
mising young artist, was killed. When the order
came to retire from the Buzenval wall, he remained,
and shouted that he would not return until he had
killed a Prussian. He did not return until he was
brought back killed himself.

Among the lost are Count D'Estournel, who fell
at the head of his battalion, and was therefore one
of the "leaders" so loudly demanded, but never
followed, by our garrison; and Lambert, who was
captain in an expedition to the North Pole; and
Topin, author of a History of the Fronde; and
Peloux, a barrister of note; and Tavernier, an
eminent polytechnician; and De Brancion, mathema-
tician; and Perilli, one of the greatest pianists in
the world; and the Marquis D'Espinouze, who fell
dead in the ranks; and the Vicomte de Murat; and
Lereste, a young actor of the Théâtre Français; and
the Count de Montbrian colonel of Mobiles; and
the Vicomte de Charsonville; and Kaiser, a frigate
captain; and the Count de Langle, of Trochu's staff;
and Bernard, a distinguished musician of the Con-
servatoire; and two women *cantinières*, Madame
Massey and Madame Phillipos, who seized the
chassepots of fallen soldiers, and fell themselves in
the very first rank.

EXIT TROCHU.

TROCHU has resigned, and General Vinoy has succeeded him—so ends the "plan Trochu," which, together with his will, he informed us the other day, was left with a notary. How "the plan Trochu" reads I do not know: the only one I ever saw in operation consisted of two revolutions of the President-General's army—one on its axis and the other around Paris. "The Governor will not capitulate," but will turn the capitulation over to another whose superior wisdom he always spurned! What greater indignity could he put upon a fellow soldier than to offer him the supreme command at the moment of his own, his army's and his country's supreme humiliation? When the position was an honour, it was greedily retained in the face of a unanimous demand for his resignation; when it had become a disgrace, it was not only forsaken, but proffered to a soldier who, up to that moment, carried an unblemished sword.

The only conditions upon which General Trochu would consent to save his country was that he should be put at the head of it. So Napoleon I. said, and Napoleon III., and Robespierre and Gam-

betta. This is the French idea of "self-government,"
—the *plan Francais.*

Trochu is a combination of Micawber, Captain
Cuttle, Podsnap and the Artful Dodger. He was
always waiting for something to turn up, he winks as
a vent for his superfluous sagacity, he depends upon
Providence, which invariably means what Trochu
means, and he endeavours to divert attention from
his treacheries by shifting their consequences to
other people. His military failure is bad enough,
but his skulking is worse.

In the midst of famine and dearth of most
things, with horseflesh and black bread for our chief
food when we can procure it, there remains the
solitary luxury of chocolate! We have even chocolate queues! There is apparently abundance of
chocolate left, which is sold at the ordinary price.

Quantities of potatoes have suddenly made their
appearance, to the surprise of everybody, and we
hope there are more where these came from. The
bread which we receive in rations is very black, and
very unwholesome.

Stepping to-day into a church where there was
a funeral service, I observed that there were five
coffins of little children lying on the bier. I stopped
to question the old man in the skullcap at the door,
who held the brush which protruded with a dozen
fingers, made of bristles, and saturated with holy
water. Anything less suggestive of the beauty of
holiness than one of these brushes, I cannot imagine.
It is ugly, slovenly, greasy; in short, filthy, like the
sour-looking and sour-smelling old *citoyen* who holds

it. He told me, with a flashing eye, that these little ones were killed by Bismarck's "Obus." Bismarck has the credit of all the casualties and calamities of this war. The coffins were spread all over with pretty flowers, and I heard the sobs of the parents, amidst the chanting of the priests and the responses of the boys. Poor little children! or rather happy children, to be safe in the Arms where no war, nor any hunger, or pain, or sorrow, will ever reach them more. The pity should be given to those left behind!

As I repassed the old man with the holy-water brush, he said, "Bismarck will have to answer for this!"

As I was going out of the church-gate, a French lady said, bitterly, "And this is your Protestant King! Oh, he is so good, and so pious!" I could not find it in my heart to remind her that French rulers and French armies have done the same sort of things in their wars. I do not know how it may be in other cities under bombardment, but for the damage done to real estate in the city by the obus, it requires, to my certain knowledge, a prolonged, elaborate, and scientific search to see it with the naked eye. The space shelled does not comprise more than one-tenth of the city, so that it is absurd to call it a "bombardment of Paris."

THE FREAKS OF THE SHELLS.

A CURIOUS and even impressive chapter might be written on the effects of the projectiles by which von Moltke "begs to remain" disrespectfully ours. Their disposition is as inscrutable as their arrival is startling. Their jagged fragments are distributed with, shall I say a careful regard for, or shall I say, a reckless disregard of consequences? (This is a philosophical, not a strategical reference.) If they are hurled about with destructive intent, why are they not more destructive? If they are dropped here and there with a discriminating purpose, why not with more discrimination? If "nothing walks with aimless feet," perhaps nothing flies with aimless wing. Suppose our "evolution" theorists try their theory upon these bombs. Some boys who seemed to be doing that on an unexploded one, were suddenly dispersed by the hissing of the fuse. They reached the corner none too soon.

A shell burst in a room where an old woman was knitting, and a little girl was frolicking. It broke the big toe of the old lady and the little finger of the little girl. Two women were grinding at a chocolate mill, the one was taken, the other left. I had no sooner dodged around the corner

of a small house at the suburbs than I saw a fragment of an obus knock the piece out of a wagon-
wheel which extends from spoke to spoke, and then
dart into the window of the kitchen, where, as I
was afterward informed, it split the ear of the
woman at the wash-tub. An American student had
his leg broken while in the act of getting into bed,
and he died of the wound, notwithstanding a skilful
amputation. The poor fellow, whose name I believe was Swager, from Louisville, Ky., was of German descent and sympathies, and, as if to make
"the irony of fate" still more conspicuous, he had
fought unharmed from beginning to end of our
civil war as a common soldier. A shell comes
crashing into a bogus hospital, or one of our deserted five houses with the Geneva flag on the top
and the word "ambulance" over the door; another
takes the corner off a genuine place of resort and
succour for the wounded—a convent where, as one
of the sweet faces in the white bonnet told me,
"women who are pursued by the world go to get
away from it." Far inside was a wee chapel as
pretty and tidy and secluded as it could be. A
tall candle was burning on either side of the altar,
and in front of which hung a little lamp, which, in
both the feebleness and the tenacity of its red
flame, seemed to typify the falling nation.

After a flight of five miles, a shell exploded in
the *Bal Bullier*, the notorious licentious resort of
the students of the *Quartier Latin*. But, alas for
"the irony of fate" again. The place deserved just
now no such visitation. The dancing-hall had been

converted into a hospital. The nurses crouched to the floor, and the wounded started up in their beds with a terror heightened, as some of the terrified have confessed, by the recollection of the tableaux to which that hall had long been familiar. Nobody was seriously wounded, but there was no disposition to repeat the risk, and the place was soon deserted, and has been watched ever since by the crowd as a spot marked for doom.

One of these long-winded or long-fired projectiles came crashing down into close proximity to the lecture-room of Prof. Levasseur, who paused and remarked to his class: "Messieurs, if this incident does not annoy you any more than it does me, we will proceed with the lecture." The students cried "Bravo," and the lecture proceeded without further interruption.

No sooner does a shell burst in the streets than its pieces are snapped up by the gamins who drive a lively trade in them as mementoes of the siege.

It is astonishing with what composure, even indifference, we stroll about in the bombarded district which, by the way, does not comprise more than about one-tenth of the city, not including the vicinity of the fortifications, of course, which may be called a perpetual battle field. I suppose if it did really rain pitchforks for any length of time, we should finally abandon the iron-clad umbrellas with which we at first fortified ourselves. Dodging shells, which was for a while a rare adventure, and then an exhilarating pastime, has now come to be a dull routine.

THE SISTER OF CHARITY.

A Sister of Charity, whom I conversed with to-day, spoke with great simplicity and earnestness of the present state of things. I have written down our conversation as well as I could recollect it. She said, pointing through the window at the huge hole the shell had made in the wall on the opposite side of the street—"That is a messenger from heaven to remind us of our wickedness and sin."

I felt my whole nature startle at the words "wickedness and sin," coming from a face so eloquent of purity and devotion.

"Yes, yes; God is displeased with us. I know it—oh! I know it. He has borne long with us, and now He is chastising us. Have you not observed, Monsieur, how everything has been against us, and favourable to our enemy? We have noticed it in the convent, and have spoken of it often and often. It has made us very, very sad. The weather, the clouds, the winds—everything, everything against poor France! Such a winter as it has been—we have never had such a winter! The sun refused to shine on us, and the moonlight was so queer and uncertain. Oh! I have thought of it over and over, as I have watched through the night by the bedside of the wounded, and heard the awful crash of the bombs."

"And were you not afraid?"

"Oh no, no, Monsieur. Are you ever afraid of anything that happens in this world? Surely it is not the child of God who should be afraid of his Father. No, it was not that. I felt so for my dear country, to think that God should visit it in such wrath. I know it is all for our sins. For years Paris has been doing wickedly. Our churches are not as well attended as they used to be, nor the confessional, nor the early prayers. Neglect of the holy ordinances, infidelity, luxury, idleness—these have eaten up the soul of Paris. A judgment is on her, and that is what that means" (pointing to the handwriting on the opposite wall).

"Will the judgment benefit Paris? Will the sinful lay it to heart?"

"I sometimes fear they will not, but some I know will. They have already done so. Some who have wandered have returned. Only to-day I saw a youth who has been lost to us for a long time, come back, driven back by the conviction which so many of us have, that God is making His power felt in France. And yesterday a young woman, whose brother, who was her all, had been killed, threw herself upon my neck, and sobbed, as if her heart would break, over the sins of Paris, and begged to be received back into the fold of the Blessed Shepherd."

"THE BLOODLESS REVOLUTION."

22nd January (Midnight).—The fog is thicker than ever. Last night Flourens was released from prison by the Reds, who to-day (22nd) pillaged 20,000 rations from the 20th Mairie, made an attack on the Hôtel de Ville, and "the bloodless revolution" posts up about twenty-five persons killed and wounded. The Government, as usual, speaks with great contempt of the *petit* number of the *émeutes;* and declares, as usual, that it "will not fail to do its duty."

The Hôtel de Ville becomes, for the hundredth time, the theatre of a bloody "manifestation." Again that extraordinary spectacle, a Paris mob—thousands of people of all ages, from aged men to infants in arms. Little children laughed and frolicked; dogs scampered; babes crowed or slept in their mothers' arms; well-dressed gentlemen strolled leisurely through the angry turbulent mass, with their wives upon their arms, and leading fancifully-dressed children by the hand. Some of the multitude cry, "We want bread;" others, "*A bas Trochu!*" others, "We are betrayed;" others, "War to the death!" others, "No capitulation!" others, "*Vive la République Rouge!*"

Some of the faces are the faces of ourang-outangs, others of gentle youths, and others of pretty, gentle-looking women; but there was a terrible look of insanity in the eyes of the whole mob. Sounds of rollicking laughter are to be heard amid the fiendish cries for murder and revenge.

Some one at the door of the Hôtel de Ville tries to appease the armed crowd of Nationals, who surge up against the iron railing. Muskets are pointed at the windows of the palace—muskets are pointed at the crowd from the windows. A shot is fired—a scream—a headlong rush and tumble. Shouts of "Provocation!" "Provocation!" "They fire on the people!" "Oh, my poor babe!" "Citizens!" (implores a tall old gentleman) "for God's sake stop; you will overturn the Republic and restore the Bonapartists." A wild-looking woman is fired by this suggestion, and flies about, shouting, "The Bonapartists are doing this; they are in the Hôtel de Ville. Let us storm the palace!"

Bullets rattle through the window-panes, and chip the grey stone of the old revolutionary pile. The confusion and uproar is now positively frightful. Men can be seen rushing hither and thither, making frantic efforts to stop the firing. A lull. Another shot—two shots—a dozen! A women shrieks, throws up her hands, and tumbles. As is always the case on such occasions, most of the bullets fly too high to be fatal; or else the loss of life would be prodigious.

A band of what looks very like women, in the costume of the National Guard, is led by a veritable woman in the costume of a student of Saint-Cyr. She orders her troop to fire at the palace, which they do. A captain of the National Guard falls. The fiends yell; the women scream; the dogs bark; well-dressed men stand on the outskirts of the crowd, looking on and smoking. A child is shot. "They kill our women and children!" Bullets whiz high and low, far and near; a man falls in the doorway of a café; those on the outskirts of the crowd make off. The crash of the windows, the whiz of the cartridges, the maniacal shrieks of the women, the shouts of the men, the shrill terror in the voices of children, the stampede of the terrified, the chiming of the clock over the palace-door, mingling with the rapid clap of the closing of the shop window-shutters; above all, the rattle of the musketry, and the boom from the cannon at the forts, can be heard. What scenes!—what sounds!

Suddenly a compact body of troops appear, as if out of the ground. They are Bretons; they hate the Parisians. They turn the corner of the palace with fixed bayonets, and fire a few shots.

The Red Nationals turn instantly upon their heels and run, tumbling over one another. In three minutes the great square is cleared, the palace is surrounded by troops, which come in on the double-quick from the front, and all is still.

The statues in their niches on the walls of the palace have been well peppered with cartridges. The statue of St. Vincent de Paul has lost the stretched-out hand; the mantle of St. Landry is torn; the niche of Sully is chipped; a ball rebounds

from the stony breast of Juvenal; Le Rollin loses
his right arm; Colbert, Catinet, and Condorcet are
more or less mutilated; Lafayette is wounded;
while in the midst of the fight (as ever), proudly
and unharmed on his fiery charger, sits King Henry
of Navarre; and while a ball bites a piece out
of his horse's thigh, one recalls his words:—
"Where you see my white plume, there, my children, will you find victory and your King!"
Henry IV. lived in stormy times; and as it was then,
so it is now.

Such is the record of this day, the 22nd of
January; what will the next bring forth? What will
come of it all? What sort of a Government of
France had one better pray for? In any event may
she (and the rest of us) be delivered from an un-
limited Republic with the hydra monarch in the Red
crown!

23rd January.—Paris is as tranquil as any rural village. Who would ever suspect her of being the insane asylum that she is? The Hôtel de Ville is completely surrounded with troops and artillery; mitrailleuses decorate the streets of Belleville. The frantic mob of yesterday gaze on them with indolent curiosity—torpid, smoking, chatting, sipping coffee or absinthe.

Victor Hugo is quite right: "To Paris all transformations are possible." The consequence is that the most contradictory statements may be made of this city, every one of which shall be correct, since nothing can be said of Paris but what is as true as it is improbable. It is everything delightful and everything abominable. It is a volcano on which flowers may be plucked and children may gambol, and it is a political Vesuvius whose crater may at any moment open itself precisely where you reside. You might live a long life—thousands I know do live long lives in Paris—without seeing an eruption. There are plenty of people here who never read the papers, and never go near the crater. Nor does the crater ever come near them. Indeed, a newspaper correspondent might, would have to indeed, run the whole gamut of description from heaven to hell, in order to compass this capital, subject to all "transformations," a prey to all moods, and "checkered with all complexions of mankind."

The clubs are silenced, one of them having informed M. Favre that if he went to London his house would be torn down. Two of the Red papers are suppressed, and no more of that sort will be tolerated. Force reigns as it has for twenty years past, and our prison is perfectly quiet—quiet within, noisy enough without. The thunderous cannonade goes on. It is like the tramp of the feet of a rescuing army, not an army of invaders and usurpers. Hist! comrades, deliverance is near. Paris in her deepest heart prays for it.

23rd January. — The official report of the victims of the bombardment yesterday is—killed, one child, two women, and three men; wounded, two children, six women, and fourteen men—total, twenty-eight.

The victims of the *émeute* of this same day were —killed, one child, one woman, and seven men; wounded, two women and fifteen men — total, twenty-six.

24th January.—"A pigeon has arrived, but it brings no despatches. It has lost five feathers, from which we infer that it has dropped its messages."

A newspaper says: "With that fatality which follows everything we do, a pigeon comes in without despatches." Another newspaper says: "Why are the forts so silent to-day?"

I met the Count; he simply lifted his hat and passed. I am afraid he does not think, as he used to, that "all goes beautifully." Neither does boulevard or café. They think that Jules Favre has gone to Versailles. They suspect that all is over, but they do not care. There was the old crowd this evening about the crack billiard-player, and the silent group round the silent chess-players. Everybody sipping and everybody shrugging; but very little is said. I met a friend of one of the members of the Government, and asked him if he knew anything?

He only knew it was all up with us; that the food is nearly all gone, that the army is used up, and that Jules Favre was at that moment at Versailles talking with Bismarck over the terms of capitulation!

This is something like news; and enough for one day.

THE DEATH OF THE SAXON SOLDIER.

I SHALL never forget the death of a young Saxon soldier in one of the tents of the American Ambulance.

He was only one of the rank and file of the great German army; but he had the intelligence and mettle that marked him for the promotion which he would undoubtedly have received if he had not been cut down by a French bullet in the fulness of his youth. I never saw a more attractive face on man or woman—or, rather, on boy or girl —for he was quite young. He had the Saxon's eye of kindly blue, and the Saxon's flaxen hair and fair complexion. His complexion was as transparent and beautiful as any English girl's, and his countenance as open, genial and ingenuous as that of any home-bred boy you ever saw. He bore the impress of a powerful maternal influence, and must have been, as Cicero said of Cornelia's sons, "brought up in the very breath and speech of the mother."

His whole appearance and behaviour return to me vividly. I can see the look he gave me as I looked upon him, lying there on his tidy cot, so patient and cheery; for cheerful he was in spite of the torture he was obliged to endure. The tent was lit with the sunshine of his countenance, which contrasted strongly with the more southern faces of his prostrate "enemies."

Enemies!—What a mocking sound the word has here! What did these wretched creatures, whom we had picked up on the battlefield, know of personal enmity? What could they know of the causes of the conflict in which each had fallen by the other's hand?

But to return to the dying soldier. It is an affecting scene, and goes to all hearts. The surgeon, a skilful and humane man, declares with quivering lip that "nothing can be done," and the brave boy reads his fate in the cloud that settles on all faces but his own. Tears come to the dark eyes of the gallant fellows all around, when they learn that the blue eyes must presently close forever, and their sunshine disappear from the tent. Those who can, lean upon their elbows, and every wounded man shares in the tender anxiety of nurses and visitors. The tent is silent. The wind ceases to lift the canvas. He is dying. In his delirium he fumbles his breast with his right hand and mutters in German:

"Oh, I did want it! I did want it. I thought I deserved it! I thought I deserved it!"

"What is it you thought you deserved, my good fellow?"

"Oh, the Iron Cross! the Iron Cross! I wanted to get that. It would have been glorious, would it not, to take the Iron Cross from the king's hand?

How it would have pleased my dear father and mother. When will father and mother come? Oh, when will they come.

"Yes, yes, you say they will soon be here. And my dear brothers and sisters—yes, they will soon be here."

In a rational interval he asked some one to write, and these are the words that he dictated:

"DEAR FATHER AND MOTHER:—I fell in the battle of the 31st, before Paris. I hope my wound is not serious, but I am in God's hands. I send my love to all my brothers and sisters, and pray God to take care of you all. Everything has been done for me, and I am very thankful for the kindness of these good people. Farewell.

"Your affectionate

"GUSTAVE."

The delirium returns. He is very feeble now. His voice falters, his bright eyes grow dim, and the colour fades from his cheeks. He whispers, "God's will be done! God's will be done! No Iron Cross for me."

"But there is another cross for you, my dear boy. Do you understand what I mean?"

After a pause, "Yes, I understand. You mean the other cross."

"Yes, I mean the cross of the other King—the King of us all. You have his cross?"

"Oh, yes. I have his cross, and it is better than—"

Then suddenly he exclaims: "How beautiful the spring time! Oh, the flowers! the flowers! how beautiful they are! I should like some!"

Some are brought, and all the soul of the young soldier seems to come to his eyes as he gazes upon the flowers. Sobs are heard in all parts of the tent. He repeats: "How beautiful they are!" and the hand that holds the bouquet drops upon the bed. The light of the eyes goes out, the surgeon lays his fingers on the wrist, and says "He is gone!"

So dies the simple hearted Saxon soldier, babbling of the spring time and the flowers, in the midst of the bitter winter of the siege. And his soul passes out of our sight to where the flowers never wither, and where winter never comes, or war, and where there is but one season, and "that one season an eternal spring."

THE FOG LIFTS A LITTLE.

25th January.—The dense fog which has enveloped the Government and their doings is beginning to lift. . The rumour of negotiations is well-founded. Favre is negotiating. Other rumours:—Provincial armies smashed; Gambetta and Bourbaki have committed suicide; two Governments in the provinces.

Nothing definite. Oppressive suspense. Boulevards crowded and silent. Cafés full and silent all the evening. The crack billiard-player draws his usual audience; the silent chess-players have their usual group of silent lookers-on; the tall hat in the corner sips his absinthe; the flaring necktie smokes dreamily against the pillar; the middle-aged woman comes at 9 and goes at 10, as usual, alone; the gaudy French "girl of the period" caresses her curls, and makes herself fascinating to her "young man." The everlasting sipping goes on, and Paris is about to capitulate!

26th January.—The Government is silent, to everybody's surprise, but the German batteries are not silent. "The bombardment goes on with implacable regularity," says my paper. "The anxiety

is more lively and poignant than ever. It is said
that Bourbaki is beaten, and Chanzy is beaten, and
Faidherbe is beaten, and that our armies of succour
are in full retreat."

Jules Favre is said to have returned from Versailles. Cannonade subsides during the evening.
Groups on the Boulevards discuss the situation. One
man cries, "Oh, for a Gambetta!"

Another replies: "Why, citizen, he is a lawyer,
and you have been complaining of the Paris Government for being lawyers. Besides, Gambetta's armies
are beaten."

"Yes," added another, "He wished to ape
(singeur) '92, and he has spoiled everything."

"Thou art a capitulard!" screamed Gambetta's
champion.

"Ah, citizen," said a little round-shouldered old
fellow, weeping. "What can we do? We cannot
make a *trouée.* Our armies in the provinces cannot
get to us. *O! mon Dieu! mon Dieu!* Poor France!
—poor France!"

The cafés are full as usual. What incorrigible
sippers these French are! Perhaps their sipping
disposition has something to do with their fall.
They sip cognac, sip coffee, sip wine, sip absinthe,
sip books, sip women. They sip with their knives
and forks, sip with their chassepots, and sip with
their swords. They take a little sip of a stroll, a
little sip of sleep, and a little sip of manual labour
—a very little sip of manual labour. This sip, sip,
sipping race have been devoured by a race which
does nothing by sips, but everything by craunches.

In my tour of the bombarded district I stumbled on the old Huguenot. He had one child in his arms, and led another by the hand. Upon these his eyes were looking with loving tenderness, while his mouth was muttering—I well knew what.

"What ho! good friend," I exclaimed; "what does all this mean?"

"It means that we have been given to pleasures, and have dwelt carelessly, and Paris has said, 'I shall not sit as a widow, or know the loss of children.' But these things have come upon her in a moment."

We huddled into a doorway to get out of the whirring crashing shells. The old man's eyes looked pityingly on the children, but he smiled grimly, as he ran on about the doom and the punishment of Paris.

"It is all, I tell thee, on account of the revocation of the Edict of Nantes. My forefathers will have joy if they are allowed to look down upon this. These people are not the Lord's people. Their Bishop at Orleans is quite right, 'they have almost all of them ceased to speak the truth.' They trust in vanity, and speak lies. We wait for light, but behold obscurity—for brightness, but we walk in darkness. We grope for the wall like the blind, and are groping as if we had no eyes; we stumble at noonday."

The voice of the old man and his words terrified the children, but he had only to turn his eyes upon them to compose them. Lowering his tones, he bent over me and whispered, or rather hissed:

"Stand fast in the truth of the Lord God of battles, my son, and thou shalt have peace in the midst of war. Remember what I tell thee. War is a mighty worker for truth in the earth. Armies are the flail of the Lord, and with them He thrasheth the nations out of the north. Out of the north an evil shall break forth. They shall come and set everyone his throne at the entering of the gates of Paris.—But I must get the poor children away from this. I knew their mother, poor thing! Wretched life, more wretched death. Father's life a wretched death. O Paris—Paris! Adieu!"

The old Huguenot was soon out of sight, hurrying away with his charge from the perilous streets.

NAPOLEON III. DISCUSSED AT THE HUNGRY CLUB.

AT a meeting of "The Hungry Club," the other evening, the Count, who was one of the Emperor's intimate friends, suddenly exclaimed: "By the way, I have a curiosity for you;" and took from his pocket a bit of paper with these words upon it:

"reseived of the Prince Louis Napoleon too Bills of £1,000 each, the money or Bills to be returnd on Wensday next.
(Signed)   "POLLARD."

"There! (resumed the Count) that is a copy of what Louis Napoleon wrote in London about, I think, the year 1847—a *verbatim* copy."

"But I thought the Emperor was a good English scholar."

"He was, in the ordinary sense. He spoke English very well; almost as well as he spoke German; but the niceties and felicities of the language he never mastered. He rarely wrote it, and as rarely as possible spoke it."

"Preferring the French?"

"Yes."

"He was up in that, was he not?"

"Perfectly. Few Frenchmen could write it with more elegance or ease. His proclamations prove that. Better French was never penned than some which he has left in his public documents and books."

"Are you sure he wrote them?"

"Perfectly sure. I have known him intimately for thirty years, and know him to be wonderfully clever with his pen. I do not mean that he could deliver an elaborate oration equal to those of Ollivier, Thiers, or Rouher, but in the matter of terse sentences, and rhetoric of the real French snap and flavour, for producing an immediate effect, he surpassed every one of his contemporaries."

"Better in words than deeds—aye?"

"Well, he has deeds too. For that matter, he will average about as the rest of them—on the throne and off of it. He ruled France and governed Paris for nearly twenty years—that is something. He failed in Mexico, succeeded in Italy, accomplished his object in the Crimea, and lost his throne at Sedan."

"He was no general, was he?"

"Just enough of one to be the sport of chance —like MacMahon, Vinoy, Trochu, and lots of them. Good luck sends them up like a rocket, bad luck brings them down like a stick. The happy accident that wins the battle crowns them; the unhappy accident that loses them the battle damns them beyond all depths. If they die on one of their lucky days they are renowned in history as great captains. If the day of their death is one of their unlucky ones, they are precipitated into oblivion."

"Then the Emperor has gone there?"

"His military reputation has, but not his name

as the ruler of the most unruly population in the world. He performed the most difficult task in the way of government that has ever fallen to the lot of a king or queen, and he performed it better than any monarch now living could have performed it."

"Or any other of the present aspirants for the French throne?"

"Most certainly. Not one of them was equal to the task which he performed."

"Then you really regard him as a great monarch?"

"The best monarch for France. He knew the French people better than they knew themselves, and governed them better than they can govern themselves; but if he could have had his way he would really have made his words good that the Empire was peace."

"You have no doubt then of his having been forced into this war?"

"Nobody doubts it. The difference of opinion is not upon that point, but upon the question whether he should or should not have been better informed respecting the condition of his army. And there I think he was deficient in the days of his comparative health and strength. He never was a perfectly sound man physically, and for the last five years, of course, he was an utterly broken man. But he always would depend upon others for information which he should have obtained at first hand. This was all well enough, perhaps, while he had men about him upon whom he could depend, and who had a genuine personal devotion to his dynasty—Niel and De Morny for example, and several others of lesser note, but quite their equals as crafty scouts or resolute staff officers. But their very efficiency which served him so well while they lived, left him all the more imperilled and exposed when they died. They ministered to both his elevation and his fall.

"Singularly enough, with all his adventures, and intrigues, he never learned perfect self-reliance. Somebody to stick to, and to stick to him was a necessity with him. In fact he was an extraordinary compound of vacillation and obstinacy. He would exhaust the patience of his friends by a series of nibbles, and then alarm them by the suddenness of his bite. He was provokingly long in making up his mind, but when his mind was made up, his body soon followed, and followed vigorously."

"You think his fame will rest on his civil policy then?"

"I do. No ruler, or leader of France has done for her what he has. The Reds are forever abusing him for adding to the taxes, but the property-owners know very well that for every franc he took from them he returned to them three. He increased the taxation on real estate, but he added correspondingly to its value. He gave employment and wages to thousands who must themselves have been a burden to the tax-payers, but for his reconstruction of Paris. He built the finest city of our modern world. He gave this volatile people a relish for commerce that they never knew before, and by his policy of approximate freedom of trade he doubled the foreign trade of France. The material prosperity of the country during his reign was without a parallel in its history. Nor is it fair to say the prosperity was inevitable, a mere natural order of things, for, if France had not prospered, who would have had the blame but the Emperor? Personal government must be credited with national prosperity if it can be justly charged with national decay. It's a poor 'Personal' rule that does not work both ways."

"You spoke of his sticking to his friends. He was rather noted for that, was he not?"

"He was. He never forgot a favour or a face. I never knew a man so scrupulously magnanimous. I can tell you a good anecdote of him to illustrate this point. A wealthy New York gentleman (a sort of Franco-American, I think) used to loan him money while he was in that city, in the days of his Micawberism. The Prince never received one of these loans without saying with his well-known moody gravity, 'When I get to be Emperor of France I will refund it.' Whereupon the American would smile and say: 'O never mind, Prince; don't trouble yourself about that.' Well, when the Prince became the monarch, the sum had grown to considerable proportions. Not long after, the American being in Paris, a request came from the Tuileries, by an *aide*, that he should make the Emperor a call. He did so, and received a cordial greeting, the loaned sum with compound interest for, I think, about seven years, and an offer of a carriage during his stay in Paris. There are plenty of similar anecdotes, some of them quite touching."

"Do you know anything trustworthy of his parentage?"

"Oh, I presume there is no doubt of his being the son of the Dutch Admiral Verheul and Queen Hortense."

"Hence his phlegm—aye?"

"Yes; and the other qualities I have named—they say. The Admiral (so runs the gossip of the courts) was endowed with the vacillation and obstinacy for which the Emperor was distinguished."

"I never could detect any Bonaparte in his face, could you?"

"No. You remember what the French commander said when Napoleon took an attitude before them, hoping to bewitch them out of their loyalty—'Look at him, men! Do you see a single mark of the Bonaparte in his face?' but they did not, and they acted accordingly. What would he not have given for the face of 'Plon-Plon,' or that of Jerome, of Baltimore, at that juncture? They both have the Bonaparte face, and the Baltimore Bonaparte had even the shrug of the great Emperor, and never appeared on the street or in a public assembly without attracting attention."

As we dispersed, the bells in the towers of Notre Dame were chiming a quarter to two, and the guns of Mount Valerien were filling the city with their melancholy reverberations.

Boom, boom, boom! Doom, doom, doom! So runs the siege away.

BREAKING THE NEWS.

27th January.—The news at last—the dreadful news—is broken gently this morning in the official journal:

"The Government, not being able longer to count on an army of succour, do not feel it their duty to prolong the defence of Paris. Armies in the provinces are overwhelmed; subsistence in the city nearly ended. In this situation we are forced to negotiate. German army will not enter Paris during the armistice. National Guard to preserve their arms. Assembly to be called. More details to-morrow."

The destruction of three great armies, and the capitulation of Paris! It is useless to write or speak of events of such magnitude.

Last night, at precisely fifteen minutes past twelve, the reverberation of the last shot died away. The first gun was fired at Saarbrück by the French on the 2nd of August, 1870, and the last was fired from Mont Valerien at midnight on the 26th of January, 1871. What a history in less than six months!

In the course of a conversation with the Swiss

gentleman, he called my attention to these words of Wolfgang Menzel:—

"The French owe all their earlier successes in Germany to the mutually destructive conflicts of popular parties among the Germans, or to the reciprocal enmity of the various cabinets. When the Germans ranged themselves as Guelfs and Ghibelines (partisans of the Pope and the Emperor), the French wrested Artois and Burgundy from the German Empire. Again, when the Germans were divided into Leaguers and Reformers, the French laid hold of Alsace, secured the friendship of the Swiss, and obtained a commanding influence in Italy, where the enfeebled Emperors redeemed their authority only by permitting Lorraine to revert to France." .... "Prussia was cajoled at the Treaty of Basle, and immediately after France achieved boundless success, gaining possession of Holland and the Netherlands, the whole left bank of the Rhine, and Switzerland."

"ALL IS LOST EXCEPT"—VANITY.

28th January.—Government to-day gives us another glimpse into the abyss:

"The convention is not yet signed, but you may count upon the enemy not entering Paris during the armistice. The enemy recognise your bravery and energy."

And so, with these sugar-plums, it is hoped that the people will swallow the bitter draught of humiliation quietly, or at least without another "manifestation." An order of the day from General Thomas puts the number of the National Guard killed in the late sortie at two hundred. Two hundred killed out of an army of 300,000 men during a siege of four months!

These two hundred, says the General, have had a grand funeral, and the sixty who were not recognised by friends have been photographed. It seems hard to "point a moral" with these brave dead; but I cannot refrain from the remark, that this absurd partiality of the military authorities for a section of the army, which was notoriously its most mischievous portion, is just one of those inexcusable blunders which have fomented jealousies, and sown discord and insubordination in the garrison.

Some of these Nationals have been, and are, as brave and true soldiers as ever carried musket or sword; but a faithful and detailed report of the part they have, as a body, played in this siege would be simply incredible, which is reason enough, perhaps, for leaving it unwritten.

Upon calling the attention of a kiosque woman, as I bought a paper, to our blue sky and sunshine, she said: "Yes, citizen, yes—it is very strange. God has been against us. We have never known such a winter. One sortie was prevented by the freshet, another by the cold, another by the rain, another by the fog. Then look at the sickness and death! Oh! it is dreadful the way our poor children are dying. Oh, Monsieur, if I can only save my poor boy! He is very ill, Monsieur. Have you seen the new caricature, Monsieur?" (getting it). "Ha! ha! Isn't that a good one, now?"

It was a "good one" in the French sense, but a detestable one in every civilized, decent sense.

29th January.—The weather is dismally chill, and the air is saturated with moisture. A dull sunless sky reigns over all.

On my way to breakfast I try in vain to get the *Journal Officiel*, which is to tell the worst and all of it. Not out yet, although it is eleven o'clock. Read some other papers over my *ragout de chat*. They all growl over the delay of the final revelation.

The *Siècle* says, "Paris has compelled the respect of Europe," which is explained by what the

Journal des Débats says: "For six months we have lived on illusions, and the last of our illusions is death." The *Soir* says, "France is dead!—*vive la France!*" But the *Temps* says, "It is time to have an end of the charlatanism of rhetoric, which is one of our chief plagues." But Edmond About is still smitten with it, and writes, "France is going to renew a lease with history;" but perhaps history will reply that the "lease" is "taken" by a better-behaved tenant, very properly.

The *Rappel* says, "It is not an armistice, it is a capitulation," and cries "Away with illusions—away with sophisms!" But it retains one or two for its own consumption, for it says: "Paris is trembling with anger, admired of Europe, and feared by Prussia. It is the Senate that capitulates in the person of Vinoy, and the Corps Législatif in the person of Thiers, and the sword of Bazaine in the hand of Trochu.

"France will be saved by the Republic, which will merit, after having been called by our fathers the Government of Terror, to be called by our grateful children the Government of Revenge."

This theatrical panacea, for all the ills that France is heir to, is quite inexhaustible.

When we stupid Anglo Saxons are licked, we are the first to acknowledge it, although we are the first too to pick our flint and try it again; but these dramatic people always find a reason for their misfortunes in the necromantic regions of the mind, or in the mystic pages of the book of fate.

I would as soon expect to see a camel go through

the eye of a needle as to hear a French man or woman say, "We are beaten in this war."

But perhaps happy is the disposition

"That can translate the stubbornness of fortune
Into so quiet and so sweet a style!"

On my return to my fourth-storey cell, I find the *Journal Officiel* has arrived. I set fire to the last three sticks of my precious pile, and read the text of the convention between M. le Comte de Bismarck, chancellor, stipulating in the name of His Majesty the Emperor of Germany, King of Prussia, and M. Jules Favre, Minister of Foreign Affairs of the Government of National Defence, furnished with regular powers.

The Government, in their preface to the announcement, resort to the usual "charlatanism of Rhetoric." Paris, say they, is not vanquished by von Moltke. She could have held out against him, but Paris succumbs to hunger, and capitulates to famine. If we surrender to famine and not to von Moltke, it is the bread, and not Paris, that deserves the credit of these heroic four months!

The fog lifts entirely, and reveals France, with her armies and her people, her fortresses and her territory, her commercial centres and her munitions of war, all at the feet of Germany.

I watched the people read "the hand-writing on the wall" signed "Jules Favre" and "Bismarck." There was here and there a shrug, and now and then a brief ejaculation like "betrayed," "treason," or something more profane. One genteelly-dressed woman hurried away sobbing, and one gendarme merely glanced, passed on, and wept, muttering something to himself. The mass of readers read it all over, word for word, with torpid indifference. Of course there are people who make manifestations of emotion. The irreconcilables are effervescent. They fly about with protests and remonstrances, calling quiet people "*Capitulards.*"

I saw a lot of wild National Guard officers gesticulating and smoking in the court of the Grand Hôtel. Presently two of them, young and fleet of foot, ran out, one of them carrying a roll of paper, which I was told was a remonstrance against capitulation. It was taken to General Thomas, who sarcastically commended the eleventh hour zeal of the protestants, but begged them to lay it by for some future opportunity. He also publicly reproved the delegation, and expressed the fear that these "illusions" might compromise the armistice.

Among these indignant uniforms, that of the Garde Nationale *Sédentaire* figure excitedly. It is the first time they have figured excitedly during the siege.

DEAD ON HIS GUN.

THREE captains of frigates have been killed in the battles around Paris, nine lieutenants of fleet, and three ensigns. In all, fifteen marine officers, of whom three were superior officers.

The losses in the rank and file of these faithful gunners are comparatively enormous. When Trochu was remonstrated with for so often putting them at the front, he replied: "How in God's name am I to help it? I must have some men at the guns who will not run away from them at the first round." Like the gendarmerie, the marines were always prompt, obedient, and energetic, and were never known to disobey.

I shall never forget the appearance and the conduct of these gallant gunners.

They were the personification of fidelity. They looked as they behaved, and always compelled respect wherever they appeared.

When the capitulation came it was difficult to restrain them from blowing up their guns, they declaring they had as much right to do so as to blow up a ship. Some of them blew out their brains—Captain de Lamalgini for example, who commanded at Mont Rouge.

I must record the name of another of these
staunch gunners, a Breton nearly seventy years
of age. He had the Breton's sturdiness of face.
He had nothing of that skinniness and angularity
which you find in the visage of the Parisian French.
And there was an honestness in his eye and an
openness in his brow which you never see in a
typical Parisian. Really there was an expression
of sweetness on the old man's countenance. He
was erect, and in stature, too, he was conspicuously unlike the short-legged lot who inhabit these
parts.

Well, the good old marine from Brittany was
pointeur of a good old gun from Brittany. It was
diverting in the extreme to see the old man's affection for the old 24-pounder. The gunner loved his
gun as an engine driver will his locomotive or a
farmer his favourite plough. There the old Breton
has stood for all these four months at his place in
the Batterie de Nanterre. Few of the young eyes
at the ramparts could point a gun better than those
of this venerable marine. Many an unwelcome shot
he has sent into the Prussian defences. Better than
eating, better than sleeping, was his employment
liked by old François Deldroux. When there was
no firing to do he could be seen scouring or rub-
bing, or leaning against the earthwork, smoking his
pipe and gazing affectionately on his gun. He
would take his great coat off and put it on his gun.
He robbed himself of clothing to shelter his gun
from the rain, and was jealous of the sunshine that
smiled upon it.

The day of doom came for France at last. The old man leaned against his gun for support as he listened to the horrid news. He leaned upon his gun and wept. The order was for him to join his comrades and leave the ramparts.

"But my gun?"

"Oh, that will be taken care of."

"But I can't leave my gun."

"Then you will be guilty of disobedience."

"I cannot go. I would prefer dying on my gun to seeing it carried away by the enemy."

There was a report of a pistol. The poor old marine sank senseless against his gun—he was not quite dead, but he expired in less than an hour.

Among the names of gentle memory which occasionally occur on the roll-call of the dead at Paris, write the name of old François Deldroux—dead on his gun.

"DRUNKEN BUT NOT WITH WINE."

THE Prefect of Police has published an order which would make an admirable feature of a temperance law. It was issued early in the siege and is as follows:

"Any retailer convicted of having supplied with drinks gratuitously, or on payment, any drunken man armed, or unarmed, will have his establishment immediately closed, and proceedings taken against him, according to law."

Recurring again to the drinking question, which being one of the most interesting that engages the attention of England and America, is certainly exceedingly interesting under such circumstances as these, when one would naturally expect the craving for stimulants to be greatly intensified. But after a daily (and nightly) observation from the beginning of the investment, I am bound to express my surprise at the scarcity of drunken men. You may go all over the city at any hour of day or night without seeing enough intoxicated persons to attract the attention of either stranger or police.

In a tour of the *cafés*, one evening, I found about three thousand persons drinking something. Of these I found—

Sipping Coffee, about . .	1,000
„ Beer, about . .	850
„ Cognac and coffee, about	550
„ Cognac alone, about .	250
„ Common wine, about .	250
„ Absinthe, about . .	70
„ Whisky, about . .	20
„ Expensive wines, about	10

The Americans and English were among the
cognac and whiskey-drinkers. The women—and
there was about one woman to every three men—
were generally drinking coffee. Of the three thousand,
only four could be said to be noisy from intoxication, and they were Americans; and only a half
dozen more could be described as even boozy. A
noisy French restaurant, where only French are
present, is extremely rare. The uproar is almost
sure to proceed from Americans, English, or Irish.

Putting together, then, my observation during
this time of extraordinary excitement and demoralization, and my observation in the provinces of France,
in Italy, in Germany, in Great Britain and in the
United States, I must conclude that the difference
in the number of drunkards to which I have alluded
is owing to the difference in beverage.

The English, Scotch, Irish and Americans drink
whisky, and the lower classes of them drink an
adulterated, quality of whisky. The Italians and
French drink wine and beer, the Germans drink
beer and wine—wine being the principal beverage
of the common people in France and Italy, and
beer in Germany. You are no more certain to find
bread in one fist of the working man in France or
Italy than you are certain to see wine in the other.

A sight which has often reminded me of the words of the Bible whose similes are so largely drawn from the social customs of these countries— "Wine that maketh glad the heart of man, and bread that strengtheneth man's heart."

But behind this cause there is another—climate. We have more drunkards than the Europeans, because our people drink a more intoxicating beverage. But why do they drink a more intoxicating beverage? Because the climate suggests it, if it does not cause the craving for it. And to our debilitating climate we must add our exhausting manner of life, which, however, is probably another effect of the climate. Driven by climate and mode of living, the Americans resort to whisky for both stimulation and obliveration. They obtain from their "liquid fire" the buoyancy which tides them over the obstacle and the stupor which renders them oblivious to it.

But here is another fact: The Germans of this country have so far withstood the American climate and abstained from the American beverage, while doing as much work of the most laborious kind as (if not more than) any other race in the country. They may be said to have literally erected an industrial civilization in the Western and North-western States. They were as poor as the poorest of the emigrants when they left their native land; they are now, as a community, distinguished for their wealth, industry, intelligence and sobriety. Their history in America will, if ever written, be one of the most impressive and encouraging chapters in the annals of material progress. The criminal statistics bear as

strong testimony to their law-abiding disposition
as their houses and lands do to their energy, thrift,
tact and perseverance.

But through all these years of toil and hardship,
of manual labour and public service, they have taken
their lager beer with all the regularity with which
they have gone forth to their labour until the evening.

Is it not fair, then, to conclude that we are somewhat indebted to their abstinence from spirits for
their orderliness and pertinacity, and that they are
indebted to their beer for their superiority in adipose
to the original (and aboriginal) American? The
American, whether native, Anglo, Celtic or Scottish,
whether addicted to the use of spirits, or totally
abstaining from every kind of drink (except ice
water), passes through a process of physical shrinkage.
The tendency to attenuation and emaciation is one
of the national features. The Irish girl loses her
colour, and the Briton his brawn. All races succumb
to the same process of muscular impoverishment
except the Teutonic. Is not this because they are
the only people who discard spirits as an habitual
beverage, and restrict their diet, as respects both
what they eat and what they drink, to what they ate
and drank in the Fatherland?

So that when we take into consideration their
mode of living, which, like that of their fathers, is
quiet, however busy; and their musical and social
diversions which break the routine of grinding labour;
and the kind of nutriment and stimulant which they
use, we need not be at a loss, I think, for an explanation of their prosperity, physical and financial.

Instead, therefore, of prohibiting all kinds of drink, would it not be wiser to at least make the experiment of prescribing that which is found to be comparatively harmless, if not positively advantageous, and proscribing that which is unquestionably deleterious. Instead of depriving the German of his beer, suppose the American substitutes it for his whisky. Let the American, whether of the tea-total school or of the whisky-total school at least give the experiment a trial of, say, ten years, so that we may see whether it is, or is not, the lager beer that saves the German-American from our gaunt and pallid appearance in the flesh, and makes him so much the superior of other foreigners in good nature and good order. It would make a far more conclusive experiment of it, for the Americans to change habits with the Germans, we taking their lager, and they taking our whisky, ice-water and hot bread. In ten years they would be as lean, dyspeptic, nervous, angular and acrid as we are.

So while the "total abstinence" Americans are being consumed by dyspepsia, for the want of some nutritious beverage like the German beer or the French wine, the drinking Americans are being devoured by whisky and "mixed drinks." And nature, as though to set her seal of impartial reprobation upon the irrational behaviour of both parties, makes them look so much alike that you cannot tell one from the other. They have the same cadaverous physiognomy, and the same irascible temper.

GATHERING THE FRAGMENTS.

30th January.—Already the troops which Bismarck had allowed to retain their arms for "interior service," have occasion to use their chassepots. This morning the Halle was attacked, and not without reason, by a mob of hungry wretches, who declared they were tired of seeing food kept from them by the cupidity of (not the rich but) their fellow-working people. The poor have no crueller enemy than the poor.

Sure enough, there stood the long row of large dames with their pigeons, hares, ducks, and chickens, which have now fallen 50 per cent. in price, that I have seen from day to day ever since the commencement of the siege. It is funny enough to see the old woman pick up her old hens and trundle off back to her cottage at the suburbs, "conquered by famine." She had "held out" nobly, she and her hens, and now that she is starved out, will she eat her hens? Another woman waddled away with her duck under her arm, and the girl followed with her box of rabbits, as the crowd came pouring in from all the streets.

"They have been making money out of our distress," growled the young woman in the faded blue dress. "Some have got rich during the siege, while the rest of us have been starving," shouted a well-kept, burly fellow, in Mobile uniform, as he tapped his pipe against the lamp-post, and then shouted to a slovenly youth who was making for a pile of potatoes, "Jean, Jean, where is the tobacco?" But the slovenly youth was too intent upon the potatoes to hear, and exclaimed, "We are entitled to all we can lay our hands on, while we are charged such prices, citoyenne." The citoyenne was of the usual diameter, with a face on fire with excitement, and the whole of her vast physique in a tremendous state of perspiration. She screamed her orders to a much thinner but no less perturbated associate, "Don't let them carry off the Baron's cabbage." This injudicious remark did away with the Baron's cabbage immediately. "*Sacré!*" cried the fellow who snatched it, "the citoyenne dares to preserve cabbages for barons under a Republic!"

The potato baskets were overturned, and the contents scrambled for with shouts of laughter. "To the cellars!" they cried. The cellars were supposed to be full of vegetables. The new police began, according to venerable custom, to arrest spectators, while the mob continued to appropriate the potatoes. A body of National Guard cleared the market at last, and the pillagers dispersed, "having attained their object," as General Trochu would say. The slovenly youth made strides with his pockets full of potatoes, and a bunch of celery under his arm, followed by a yelling lot of *gamins*, and the fat Mobile shouting for tobacco.

"THE DEEDS OF MERCY."

AMONG the names which Paris cannot "let die,"
are those of the committee of the British Charitable
Fund:—

> Charles Shrimpton—*Chairman.*
> Richard Wallace.
> John Rose Cormack.
> J. W. Smyth, D.D.
> •H. Herbert—*Treasurer.*

The number of English supported by this fund,
rose from about 300 to nearly 1600. The committee had not only the disbursement, but the creation of the fund; Mr. Wallace's subscriptions amount-
ing to about 30,000 francs.

Dr. J. W. Smyth endured all the privations that
he helped others to endure, and thus fulfilled the
Apostle's injunction, to remember them that are in
"bonds as bound with them," and to feel for those
that suffer adversity "as being yourself also in the
body."

The English Ambulance, established by Mr.
Richard Wallace, contained fifty beds, and was
under the care of the English surgeons, Herbert,

Cormack, and Shrimpton, who deserve commendation for their gratuitous and skilful services.

The American Ambulance was one of the most conspicuous features of the siege. Its neat and tasteful grounds, its ample and well ventilated hospital tents, and above all, the skill of Surgeon Swinburne, and the energy and fidelity of his fellow-workers on the field and at the bedside, must ever be remembered in Paris with gratitude and delight.

The Ambulance was founded by Thomas W. Evans, M.D., Ph.D. The committee of superintendence during the siege were, Dr. E. A. Crane, Rev. W. O. Lamson, and Mr. Albert Lee Ward. Surgeon, John Swinburne, M.D., Physician; W. E. Johnston, M.D. The volunteer aids comprised fourteen ladies and twenty-three gentlemen.

Among the foremost of those who laboured amongst the poor were the Sisters of Charity. I have seen so much of their usefulness, that I could never forgive myself if I were to neglect to speak of them here.

It is a fact worth noticing and remembering that, amid all this wreck of faith in God, and reverence for woman, there is an exceptional and remarkable feeling of respect shown to these Sisters. This respect is like the feeble flame of a lamp left alive in some mysterious and deserted fane. It will not long survive alone, and when it expires, the darkness will be such "as may be felt."

Thirty or forty Sisters died of smallpox, contracted in the hospitals. They never hesitated when called upon, and the places of those who fell were

instantly filled. In one hospital where a dozen sisters
died one after the other very rapidly, a call was
made for others to fill the vacant places, and about
forty responded.

At the head of the Ladies Ambulance Committee
was the Countess de Flavigny, who, with a score of
other ladies of the highest rank and of great distinction in fashionable circles, devoted her money
and her hands to the care of the wounded. Several
noble ladies filled their houses with wounded.

A leader among the devoted women was Madame
Jules Simon, whose Fair realized a large amount of
money for the wounded.

The Rothschilds gave away clothes to the value
of 200,000 francs. But I do not pretend to give
all the good deeds that were done, or the names of
all the good people who dwelt in Paris during the
siege. I have only wished to say a word on a topic
upon which much more could be said—the good
influences that were at work during the siege of
Vanity Fair.

Well for this world, that in the midst of all its
iniquity and corruption, there is always to be found
this incorruptible salt of human goodness. O! Paris,
"Well for thee that salt preserves!"

31st January.—I visited the ruins of St. Cloud,
I know of no more pathetic or suggestive picture
left by the war than the church of St. Cloud, standing
solitary and alone among the "ruinous heap." One
obus did indeed fall through the roof, but I looked
in and saw that no harm had come to the altar;

the lamp had gone out, but the tower is intact. It guided us to the scene of desolation, and there pointed us to the tranquil skies. The churches and cathedrals have been wonderfully preserved during the war. He seems to have given His angels charge concerning them; for as the battle clouds dissolve and drift away, we behold unharmed the splendid spire at Strasbourg, the Gothic mass at Metz, the stately pile at Rheims, the glorious Notre Dame, the charming Madeleine, and the weird old cathedral of St. Denis.

I have wondered, as I saw the poor souls in peasant's gown or blouse, crouching under the pillars, and muttering before the altar, with its solitary lamp burning dreamily in the shadow, whether they were not a little safer there than anywhere else, and whether the god of battles would not turn away the bomb from these hallowed places, which are as a shadow of a great rock in a weary land.

The palace of St. Cloud is completely destroyed, scarcely a dwelling of the town is left; the church alone survives. It is impossible to ramble over these ruins without recalling the history of the illustrious chateau. French shells destroyed the apartment in which the first Napoleon subscribed the declaration of his abdication, and the Third Napoleon signed the declaration of this "long and painful" war now come to an end.

"KING'S EVIDENCE."

LET us look through the medium of the judicial press—*Le Droit* and *Gazette des Tribunaux*, official police reports—upon the *morale* of the people during the siege of Vanity Fair. They are not mere detached crimes and offences; they illustrate the condition of the whole body, social and politic, and especially administrative.

Le Droit of the 11th November, 1870, says:— "The Francs-Tireurs are a thousand times more formidable than the Prussians for the unhappy villages situated between our walls and the enemy's lines. On the Prussian side the harvests are still standing; on ours all is devastated and ravaged. The pillagers not only steal, they waste and destroy. The wine they cannot drink, they spill; they leave the spiggots in the casks running. The answer to the question, 'Who has done these things?' is invariably, 'The Francs-Tireurs; who tell us it is better than keeping things for the Prussians.' The Francs-Tireurs begin the work of devastation, which is subsequently finished by the common marauders, who roam about like wolves, and who sometimes give *largesse* out of the booty which has cost them so little to obtain. The example of the Francs-Tireurs develops the cupidity of all who covet the things that belong to their neighbours."

Here is what a magistrate, M. Alexandre Sorel, says of the normal state of the *Corps de Garde* of besieged Paris:—

"If any one had ever doubted the pernicious influence of drunkenness, he would be convinced by the sights of daily occurrence in the terrible period we are traversing. At the time when all hearts should be animated with one thought, when all the physical and moral energies ought to be braced up, and when the prospect of privation and endurance ought to excite the sentiment of self-sacrifice and self-denial, there is the spectacle of men drinking beyond measure, and forgetting, in the fumes of wine, all self-respect and all power of action. Sometimes it is the soldier-citizens, whose only idea seems to be to search out the canteens where they may spend the pay intended for their maintenance; sometimes it is the regular soldiers, who are scarcely installed in their encampments in the Banlieu of Paris before they break into the wine cellars of houses that have been abandoned, and become too drunk to shoulder their arms or to recognize the patrols when they approach."

Amongst the wretches who made a harvest in robbing and stripping the dead on the field of battle, the *Droit* of the 10th of November mentions "a child of twelve years old." "When any wounded man attempted to retain either the money or the watch which he might have about him, he was at once dispatched," or, as they called it, in their cynical slang, "they made him cold," *ils le refroi-dissent.*

"The soldiers billeted on private houses," says *Le Droit* of January 5th, 1871, "fancy themselves masters of all they see in the houses in which they are received. They not only dispose of everything as they please, but they wantonly destroy. There are some who do not destroy, but steal instead whatever pleases them. One householder, when he abandoned his house, had left in it a portion of his furniture. Two men in one battalion were interrupted in the act of loading this furniture on a cart to take it to a store for such goods, established in Paris. One of the men, on being brought before the permanent court-martial of the National Guard for that section, declared naively enough his own principles of economy and morals: 'It is necessary to know how to make a fortune. All means are good which enable one to do that; but for myself, I wish to make a large fortune.' Occasionally a National Guard of a war company calmly collects a quantity of furniture belonging to some householder in the Banlieu, and carts it away to his own dwelling. Some members of the Garde Mobile have openly offered for sale whole cases of books found in a house which they said had been abandoned—the only pretext they offered. In the suburban districts the civil portion of the community is not behind the military in appropriating the goods of their neighbours, always on the plea of not allowing them to fall into the hands of the Prussians. The simple process is to carry the furniture bodily out of the

house where it has been left into some other house.
Some proprietors, even, have no scruple to furnish
their own places with the goods of their neighbours.
The intervention of municipal authority is needed
to convince those who have become possessed of
other people's goods that they have no right to
keep them!"

The *Droit* of January 9 and 10, says, "Not a
day passes without prisoners being brought before
the *tribunaux correctionels* for stealing wood in
whatever shape they could find it. In houses in
process of building, the beams are taken away,
flooring broken up, and wooden partitions torn
down. In houses that have been abandoned, doors,
window-frames, panels, cupboards, floors, every
morsel of woodwork is sacked, broken, and carried
off."

"In the latter end of the month of December,
raids upon the stores of timber merchants, as well
as on the woodwork of empty houses, were particularly frequent. On one occasion as many as 1,500
or 2,000 persons joined in an attack on the timber-
yard of a large contractor for public works. They
demolished the gates, and carried off all the wood
stored in the enclosure. Amongst those arrested in
the act of aiding in this wholesale robbery was a
manufacturer in easy circumstances, who gave, as
his excuse, that he 'only did what everybody else
was doing.'

"Another time, a National Guard, reasonably
honest in other respects, but who complained that
he had 'too much sensibility,' finding himself near

a palisading, set the example to a crowd of men,
women, and children, who were gathered together,
by giving the first blow to the planking with the
butt end of his rifle; and then he helped, with the
rifle still on his shoulder, to finish breaking down
the enclosure and distributing the broken wood."

"Things did not always pass off so quietly; but
the proprietor always ran great personal risk who
ventured to offer any opposition to the destruction
of his property."

"On the banks of the Bievre, in the enceinte of
Paris, some hundred men, women, and children
entered into private grounds of some extent, with
hatchets, scythes, and waggons; they broke down
the palings, and took possession of 1,500 fine trees.
The proprietor was threatened and maltreated because he remonstrated. Fortunately, a scholar from
the 'Ecole Polytechnique' and a detachment of
National Guards arrived in time to rescue the proprietor, and save the property thus audaciously
threatened. The marauders could not be made to
understand why they should be thus prohibited.
One of them said, 'This tree is mine, because I
cut it down.'" "Curious," adds the journal, "to
see how tenacious is the idea of property. It no
sooner is destroyed under the form of 'Yours,'
than it revives under that of 'Mine!'"

The utter absence of safety was not confined to
property. The *Gazette des Tribunaux* of January
24th, 1871, gives an instance where "a dealer in
vegetables in the Banlieu, who had come to Paris

for refuge, found himself arrested as a spy, after a domiciliary visit from the concierge of the house where he lived, who was also a National Guard. The too zealous patriot, who had a grudge against the poor man, could find nothing better to say in his own defence than, 'This citizen was suspected by me. The proprietor had accepted him without consulting me. Subaltern officer as I am, charged with the duty of defending the country, as an auxiliary of justice I did not consider his conduct natural, and I used the rights which the people had conferred in electing me their serjeant, to use my vigilance to verify my suspicions.'"

Here is a specimen of contracts for the army:—

"A merchant draper of Foix, who, besides having furnished both capotes and shoes for the Mobiles of Arrières, was also on the point of sending a supply of mitrailleuses, when he was brought before the Correctional Police. When the president of the tribunal asked, 'What had been the contract between Government and himself. What conditions had been imposed, and what samples had been sent for his guidance?' He replied, 'that no contract or agreement had been signed; no sample had been sent to him; it had been simply and verbally agreed upon that he was to supply so many pairs of shoes for a certain sum.' Now, the soles of the shoes were mostly of cardboard. Yet this fraud was set down to score of negligence and extreme haste, and no punishment followed!"

"The waste by the soldiery—by the National

Guards, by the Mobiles—by robbery, by pillage, were as nothing when compared with the ever flowing tide of wasteful expenditure caused by the creation of the national military workshops. The measures taken on behalf of the necessitous classes did not profit them exclusively, for many received the allowance of a National Guard, 1 franc 50 centimes a day, with 75 centimes for the wife of the said National Guard, who had no claim whatever to this daily premium upon idleness. This goes far to explain how this premium has swelled the budget of the siege of Paris by four or even five hundred thousand francs a day."

"The history of the regimental chests would be curious. There was one notable military chest, in which the commandant of a battalion of the 'Garde Nationale Sédentaire' had been in the habit of dipping his hands, to provide for his own personal expenses; he, however, was brought before a council of war, in company with the Adjutant-Major and the Captain-Treasurer."

"Some officers in one battalion of the National Guard wished to give a testimonial to their commandant, for his care and skill in organizing his battalion. They accordingly voted him 500 francs out of the military chest, as a 'mark of their esteem and sympathy.' The commander accepted the present, and neither party seemed to see the least peculiarity in the proceeding."

This is only a fraction of the testimony which could be gathered from Parisian sources upon the demoralization of Paris during the siege. But it is eminently French for these newspapers to vent their indignation upon the helpless poor.

I am bound to testify, as an eye-witness, that the pilfering of timber and "pieces of unfinished houses" was marvellously rare, considering the necessities of the people and the imbecility of their Government. The old fence that surrounded the unfinished Academy remained throughout untouched. So did miles and miles of other useless fences, and piles on piles of timber, which should have been requisitioned and distributed. Then all round the city there were acres and acres of prostrate and gigantic trees, which might have been cut up and brought in. In this way employment might have been given to a few thousands of idle soldiers, and warmth to a multitude of the perishing.

To say the truth, the administration of subsistence was conducted with such imbecility that the poor were quite justified in carrying away "houses in process of building," and even in cutting down splendid trees on the Champs Elysées. These so-called depredations might have been regulated by the Government, which could have saved the trees and given away the old fences and new timber.

As for the peculation, chicanery, venality, and robbery—highway and byeway—which rouses the wrath of these newspapers, such sins were not (and are not) confined to any class in Paris, and, most assuredly, did not originate with the lowest class.

However, this is not the place, and perhaps this is not the time, for writing an elaborate history of the Government of Paris during the siege. It will be a narrative of the liveliest interest when it is written.

"How long shall weary nations toil in blood,
  How often roll the still returning stone
  Up the sharp painful height—ere they will own
  That on the base of individual good,
  Of virtues, manners, and pure homes endued
  With household graces—that on this alone
  Shall social freedom stand?   Where these are gone
  There is a nation doomed to servitude.
  Oh, suffering, toiling France, thy toil is vain !
  Where men are selfish, covetous of gloire,
  Heady and fierce, unholy and impure,
  Their toil is lost, and fruitless all their pain ;
  They cannot build a work which shall endure."

THE UNITED STATES LEGATION.

THE relations of the United States Legation to the Germans who were expelled from, and to the Germans, the Americans, the English, and even the French, who were shut up in Paris, have become an historical incident of the late war.

But first of all, to prevent any misunderstanding, let me say, that what I shall say has no reference, directly or indirectly, positively or negatively, to the absence, during a portion of the siege, of the British Embassy. That is none of my business, and I have no opinion upon it. But certainly the sequel has abundantly proved that, as far as Lord Lyons is personally concerned, he was more useful to his Government and to the cause of peace outside than he could possibly have been inside of Paris. This suggests an opinion which I hold firmly, and will express strongly. The attitude of the British Government during the war has been not only unexceptionable, but glorious.

England did her utmost, which was far more than the utmost of any other nation could have been, to prevent the war, and her failure to do so, as any fair-minded reader of the official facts will concede, is one of the strongest possible proofs that no human intervention could have kept the belligerents apart.

England took the initiative, and led the great Powers in the armistice which was proposed by Count Bismarck through M. Thiers and rejected by the Favre Government; and England revictualled Paris in three days after peace was declared.

This is an outline of facts which, when given in detail, will reflect the highest credit upon the statesmanship, the diplomacy, and the humanity of the English Government during the Franco-Prussian War.

Nor can I refrain from resenting with some spirit the croak of those who see, in the absence of an enormous and burdensome standing army, the decline of a nation's prestige, and the decay of its "military spirit."

My resentment comes of the fact that two nations are subjected to this unmanly and unpatriotic criticism.

A free people do not always plume themselves on being "ready" for a stupendous war, but they do not object to being considered perfectly willing and able to get ready upon the shortest possible notice.

Their normal condition and their general preference is peace, nevertheless they have succeeded, now and then, in adapting themselves, with tolerable speed and success, to a time of war. As the "time" for going to war may be "ill-chosen" by "the greatest military nation in the world," so the taunt of the loss of military prestige may be ill-judged when applied to a people who talk about everything except fighting, but who can fight about everything worth talking about.

The man who whines over loss of prestige, takes counsel of his own state of health rather than that of his country.

To pass to the topic of which this is not, I think, an inopportune introduction.

The United States Legation, during the siege, was composed of——

Hon. E. B. Washburne, Minister Plenipotentiary.

Col. Wickham Hoffman, Secretary of Legation.

Albert Lee Ward, Esq., Private Secretary to the Minister.

On the 15th of July, 1870, Count Solms, *Chargé d'Affaires* of the North German Confederation, asked Colonel Wickham Hoffman, *Chargé d'Affaires* of the United States (the Minister, Mr. Washburne, being ill at Carlsbad), if the United States Government would take under its protection the subjects of the Confederation.

Colonel Hoffman immediately obtained the necessary consent from Washington by telegraph, and in person from the French Government on the 18th. On the 19th, Mr. Washburne returned to his post, where he has remained ever since.

On the 23rd, the subjects of Hesse Ducal, and on the 26th those of Saxe-Coburg Gotha, were taken under the protection of the United States Minister.

The Olivier Government gave permission for

German subjects to remain in France "so long as their conduct does not give any legitimate cause of complaint," and forbade the departure of "Confederate Prussians" liable to military duty.

The American Minister opposed this prohibition in an able and conclusive letter to the Duke de Gramont, in the preparation of which he had the benefit of the counsel of the eminent international lawyer George Bemis, Esq., of Boston, U.S.

The Palikao Government, "with a view of both relieving itself from the presence, in the heart of the capital, of some 40,000 Germans, and at the same time protecting them from the excited population of Paris," ordered the Germans to "leave the country."

Mr. Washburne and M. Kern (the Swiss Minister) entreated M. Cheverau to modify the order of expulsion, as it would involve the Germans in great hardships, and the protecting embassies in great embarrassments. The French Minister replied that Prussia had banished the French.

The statement was promptly called in question, and has never since been made good, for I believe French subjects have remained undisturbed in Germany throughout the war.

Failing to obtain a revocation or any modification of the order of expulsion, nothing was left for Mr. Washburne but to carry it out with all the humanity possible under such circumstances. He declared to me that it was the most painful duty he ever had to perform, and that some of the scenes in his apartments cut him to the heart. It was indeed fortunate for these wretched exiles that they had for protector a man who has not been long enough in the petrifying atmosphere of diplomatic circles to have his heart transformed into stone.

About 30,000 persons were sent away by the American Minister, who was careful to provide the most efficient superintendence for the work.

Some of the incidents at the station and the hotel of the Legation were peculiarly distressing.

In the crowd were women in all stages of pregnancy—literally all; for one woman was taken with labour pains on the steps, and carried away in a cab.

So the company contained every age and every condition, from babes just come into this unfortunate country only to be driven out of it for spies, to decrepid old people staggering on the brink of the grave.

For the comfortable and expeditious transit of this mass of helpless outcasts, much is due to the United States Consuls of the towns through which they passed. The Consuls were obliged to appeal more than once to the French Government for protection for the Germans against the infuriate mob. And the American Minister, in his official despatches, describes their flocking to him for shelter from the fraternal ferocity of Republican Paris.

The exiles were met on the frontier by German officers, and their wants were supplied by the society founded by the Queen of Prussia for the assistance of refugees.

The women and children who were unable to get away gradually increased from 200 to 2,300. A large number were put under arrest, and kept in comfortable concealment from the ferocious spy hunters. Many were kindly cared for in Catholic and Protestant asylums, where their board—from one to three francs per day—was paid by Mr. Washburne.

Those in prison and in the asylums were periodically visited by a messenger from the Legation, and provided with money, food, and clothing. Still a great many were left out in the cold (literally).

For these Mr. Washburne fitted up the ground floor of the Legation apartments, and there the poor creatures were fed with such food as could be picked up during the famishing days of the siege. They were allowed besides, one and a half francs a day. A credit was opened with the Rothschilds, at first for 50,000 thalers, and subsequently for 50,000 francs.

When the war broke out there were in Paris about 10,000 Germans liable to military duty, and about 100,000 in France.

The English residents have joined the Americans in testifying, in a marked way, their gratitude for the services rendered by the United States Legation. There was a friendliness between the English and Americans during the siege which cannot be forgotten by either party.

The services done the French by the American Minister were far from inconsiderable. All the official communications which passed between the belligerents (those on the exchange of prisoners being especially voluminous) passed through his hands,

and all were carefully copied in the office. So were
the broadsides of "personals" in the *Times*, which
were sent to the Paris papers for publication, much
to the rejoicing of thousands, who thus heard, for
the first time for months, from their relatives and
friends. The gratitude of many was expressed in
money, that of others in vituperation. While tears
of gratitude were falling in the Minister's apartments,
his name was held up to execration in the columns
of *La France*.

I have the best reason for believing that the
Legation was at one time in danger of a hostile
"manifestation." At the same time it was seriously
debated in Belleville circles whether the entire population of Anglo-Saxons should not be ordered to
quit the city. At another time it was resolved to
get rid of the newspaper correspondents. But neither
project came to a practical result, although much
nearer to it than was generally supposed. There
were scores of "denounced" English and American
names on the files of the Prefect of Police.

All the letters from "out in the world," which
were like angels' visits in more than the proverbial
sense, came through the "American bag;" and the
most inspiring tidings we could receive was, "The
bag is in! the bag is in!" We were indebted for
an occasional London newspaper, a fortnight old,
to the same channel.

The history of this "bag" itself would furnish
some curious and entertaining reading. Several times
it was nearly strangled in the military department at
Versailles, where it was looked upon with, perhaps,

excusable suspicion, which put the Legations in London and Paris in possession of several copies of the great Chancellor's autograph.

In London the duty of "making up" a bag was performed, and well performed, by the United States *Chargé d'Affaires*, Benjamin Moran, Esq. What with distracted siege widows of his own country, importunate French refugees, and the watchful warriors around Paris, Mr. Moran's position was one of rare perplexity and peril.

The besieged Anglo-Saxons will not forget the services of the urbane and obliging Secretary of Legation, Colonel Wickham Hoffman. We had a most generous and indefatigable friend also in the United States Consul-General, John Meredith Read, who kept open house and hand.

It will, I am sure, always be very pleasant for the Anglo-Saxon community, in looking back upon the siege, to remember that we were shut up in Paris with the United States Legation.

APPENDIX.

DEATHS.

17th Sept. to 24th Sept.—First week of siege:—

Small-pox	158
Typhoid fever	45
Bronchitis	61
Pneumonia	62
Other causes	940
Total	1266

24th Sept. to 1st Oct.—Second week of siege:—

Small-pox	210
Typhoid fever	56
Bronchitis	36
Pneumonia	46
Other causes	854
Total	1202

1st Oct. to 8th Oct.—Third week of siege:—

Small-pox	212
Typhoid fever	50
Bronchitis	53
Pneumonia	60
Other causes	1008
Total	1383

8th Oct. to 15th Oct.—Fourth week of siege:—

Small-pox	311
Typhoid fever	51
Bronchitis	55
Pneumonia	64
Other causes	1129
Total	1610

15th Oct. to 22nd Oct.—Fifth week of siege:—

Small-pox	360
Typhoid fever	55
Bronchitis	70
Pneumonia	66
Other causes	1195
Total	1746

22nd Oct. to 29th Oct.—Sixth week of siege:—

Small-pox	378
Typhoid fever	62
Bronchitis	77
Pneumonia	72
Other causes	1289
Total	1878

29th Oct. to 5th Nov.—Seventh week of siege:—

Small-pox	380
Typhoid fever	61
Bronchitis	72
Pneumonia	69
Other causes	1180
Total	1762

5th Nov. to 12th Nov.—Eighth week of siege:—

Small-pox	419
Typhoid fever	62
Bronchitis	82
Pneumonia	79
Other causes	1213
Total	1855

12th Nov. to 19th Nov.—Ninth week of siege:—

Small-pox	431
Typhoid fever	94
Bronchitis	92
Pneumonia	73
Other causes	1374
Total	2064

19th Nov. to 26th Nov.—Tenth week of siege:—

Small-pox	386
Typhoid fever	103
Bronchitis	89
Pneumonia	81
Other causes	1468
Total	1927

26th Nov. to 3rd Dec.—Eleventh week of siege:—

Small-pox	370
Typhoid fever	155
Bronchitis	183
Pneumonia	124
Other causes	1950
Total	2782

3rd Dec. to 10th Dec.—Twelfth week of siege:—

Small-pox	381
Typhoid fever	170
Bronchitis	191
Pneumonia	130
Other causes	1812
Total	2684

10th Dec. to 17th Dec.—Thirteenth week of siege:—

Small-pox	391
Typhoid fever	173
Bronchitis	190
Pneumonia	131
Other causes	1843
Total	2728

17th Dec. to 24th Dec.—Fourteenth week of siege:—

Small-pox	388
Typhoid fever	221
Bronchitis	172
Pneumonia	147
Other causes	1800
Total	2728

24th Dec. to 31st Dec.—Fifteenth week of siege:—

Small-pox	454
Typhoid fever	250
Bronchitis	258
Pneumonia	201
Other causes	2117
Total	3280

31st Dec. to 7th Jan.—Sixteenth week of siege:—

Small-pox	329
Typhoid fever	251
Bronchitis	343
Pneumonia	262
Diarrhœa	151
Scarlatina	13
Measles	31
Other causes	2300
Total	3680

7th Jan. to 14th Jan.—Seventeenth week of siege:—

Small-pox	339
Typhoid fever	350
Bronchitis	457
Pneumonia	396
Diarrhœa	143
Scarlatina	15
Measles	40
Other causes	2236
Total	3976

14th Jan. to 21st Jan.—Eighteenth week of siege:—

Small-pox	380
Typhoid fever	375
Bronchitis	598
Pneumonia	486
Diarrhœa	136
Dysentery	42
Croup	27
Measles	44
Other causes	2356
Total	4444

21st Jan. to 28th Jan.—Nineteenth week of siege:—

Small-pox	327
Typhoid fever	313
Bronchitis	548
Pneumonia·	478
Diarrhœa	134
Scarlatina	9
Measles	39
Other causes	2538
Total	4386

Totals from 17th Sept. to 28th Jan. :—

Small-pox	6604
Typhoid fever	2897
Bronchitis	3627
Pneumonia	3027
Diarrhœa	564
Scarlatina	37
Measles	154
Dysentery	42
Croup	27
Other causes	30,402
Killed in battle	3000
Died in hospital	10,000
Killed in émeutes	15
Murders and assassinations	6
Suicides	10
Deaths by accident	40
Deaths from excitement	13
Spies and deserters shot	20
Total	60,485

Persons who fell dead, apparently from want of food . . .	6
Infirm, aged, and sick persons, whose death may be said to have been hastened by want of food or by bad food	1800
Deaths of infants from the same cause	3000
	4,806
	60,485
Total . . .	65,291

GASTRONOMIC.

Horses eaten	65,000
Donkeys	1000
Mules	2000
Dogs	1200
Cats	5000
Rats	300
Mice	200
Elephants (three sold for 27,000 francs)	3
Camel	1
Ostriches	3
Porcupines	2
Bears	2
Kangaroos	3
Wild boars	1
Stags	2
Deer	5
Antelopes	6
Dromedaries	1
Tropical birds	25

PRICES.

17th Sept. to 24th Sept.—First week of siege:—

<table>
<tr><td></td><td colspan="2">fr. c.</td></tr>
<tr><td>Butter</td><td>4 00</td><td>the demi kil.</td></tr>
<tr><td>Fresh butter</td><td>2 80</td><td></td></tr>
<tr><td>Codfish</td><td>1 20</td><td></td></tr>
<tr><td>Salt mackerel</td><td>0 75</td><td></td></tr>
<tr><td>Cabbage</td><td>0 75</td><td></td></tr>
<tr><td>Cauliflower</td><td>0 75</td><td></td></tr>
<tr><td>Eggs</td><td>1 80</td><td>per doz.</td></tr>
<tr><td>French beans</td><td>1 75</td><td>per pound.</td></tr>
<tr><td>White beans</td><td>1 25</td><td>per litre.</td></tr>
<tr><td>Ham</td><td>3 00</td><td>per pound.</td></tr>
<tr><td>Bacon</td><td>2 00</td><td>,,   ,,</td></tr>
<tr><td>Sausage</td><td>4 00</td><td>,,   ,,</td></tr>
<tr><td>Fowl</td><td>6 00</td><td></td></tr>
<tr><td>Rabbit</td><td>8 00</td><td></td></tr>
<tr><td>Cheese</td><td>2 00</td><td>per pound.</td></tr>
</table>

24th Sept. to 1st Oct.—Second week of siege:—

<table>
<tr><td></td><td colspan="2">fr. c.</td></tr>
<tr><td>Fresh pork</td><td>2 30</td><td>per kil.</td></tr>
<tr><td>Bacon</td><td>2 50</td><td>per pound.</td></tr>
<tr><td>Potatoes</td><td>2 75</td><td>per bushel.</td></tr>
<tr><td>Cauliflower</td><td>1 00</td><td></td></tr>
<tr><td>Carrots</td><td>1 20</td><td>per box.</td></tr>
<tr><td>Mushrooms</td><td>0 80</td><td>per pound.</td></tr>
<tr><td>French beans</td><td>1 00</td><td>,,   ,,</td></tr>
<tr><td>Ham</td><td>3 00</td><td>,,   ,,</td></tr>
<tr><td>Sausages</td><td>5.50</td><td>,,   ,,</td></tr>
<tr><td>Salt beef</td><td>2.25</td><td>,,   ,,</td></tr>
<tr><td>Salt butter</td><td>5.00</td><td>,,   ,,</td></tr>
<tr><td>Eggs</td><td>1.80</td><td>per doz.</td></tr>
</table>

					fr.	c.	
Fowl	.	.	.	.	6	50	
Goose	.	.	.	.	20	00	
Small rabbit	.	.	.	7	00	
Fish	.	.	.	.	7	00	
Small plate of fried fish	.	1	00	
Fresh butter	.	.	.	4	00	per pound.
Lard	.	.	.	.	2	25	,, ,,

Flour is requisitioned.

1st Oct. to 8th Oct.—Third week of siege:—

				fr.	c.	
Mutton liver	.	.	.	1	00	per pound.
Mutton head	.	.	.	1	00	,, ,,
Mutton feet	.	.	.	2	00	per bundle.
Sausage of beef	.	.	3	00	per pound.
Butter	.	.	.	.	6	00	,, ,,
Cabbage	.	.	.	1	50	
Cauliflower	.	.	.	1	40	
Carrots	.	.	.	.	0	60	per box.
Small hen	.	.	.	6	00	
Chicken	.	.	.	12	00	
Pike	.	.	.	.	10	00	
Carp	.	.	.	.	12	00	
Ass	.	.	.	.	0	80	per pound.

8th Oct. to 15th Oct.—Fourth week of siege:—

			fr.	c.	
Mutton kidney	.	.	0	50	
Beef kidney	.	.	.	2	50	
Mutton feet	.	.	.	2	50	the bundle.
Ham	.	.	.	.	8	00	per pound.
Sausages	.	.	.	10	00	,, ,,

		fr c.	
Bacon	10	00	per pound.
Butter	12	00	,,
Eggs	2	40	per dozen.
Potatoes . . .	4	00	per bushel.
Carrots . . .	2	20	per box
Cabbage . . .	2	00	
Peas	8	00	per litre.
Onions . . .	0	75	,,
Fowl	12	00	
Rabbit	9	00	
Fish	12	00	
A golden pheasant was sold for . . .	40	00	

15th Oct. to 22nd Oct.—Fifth week of siege:—

		fr. c.	
Ass	3	00	per pound.
Fillet of horse . .	5	00	,,
Eggs	3	20	per dozen.
Cabbage . . .	2	00	
Cauliflower . . .	1	50	
French beans . .	2	00	per pound.
Artichokes . . .	0	75	
Beef dripping . .	2	50	per pound.
Ham	4	00	,,
Bacon	6	00	,,
Potatoes . . .	4	00	per bushel.
Mutton kidney . .	0	60	
Sausages . . .	6	00	per pound.
Fowl	10	00	
Goose	15	00	
Mutton sold privately .	5	00	per pound.

22nd Oct. to 29th Oct.—Sixth week of siege:—

		fr. c.	
Eggs		2 40	per dozen.
Butter		12 00	per pound.
Ass		4 00	,,
Mule		4 00	,,
Fillet of beef		8 00	,,
Ham		5 00	,,
Bacon		5 00	,,
Beef dripping		2 50	,,
Fowl		10 00	
Small goose		15 00	
Sausages of beef or pork		3 00	per pound.
Cabbage		2 50	

Vegetables are very scarce. The merchants are beginning to sell preserved fruits.

29th Oct. to 5th Nov.—Seventh week of siege:—

		fr. c.	
Eggs		0 60	each.
Fresh eggs		1 00	,,
Milk		1 00	per litre.
Potatoes		4 00	per bushel.
Rice		0 80	per pound.
Fowl		18 00	
Rabbit		15 00	
Salad		0 15	per head.
Salsify		2 00	
Cauliflower		3 00	per head.
Cabbage		4 00	,,
Carrots		2 50	per box.
Butter		18 00	per pound.

Olive oil has disappeared.

5th Nov. to 12th Nov.—Eighth week of siege:—

	fr.	*c.*	
Eggs	1	00	each.
Butter	25	00	per pound.
A ham	215	00	
Small fowl . . .	20	00	
Cabbage . . .	5	00	

It is said that bread will be requisitioned.

12th Nov. to 19th Nov.—Ninth week of siege:—

	fr.	*c.*	
Celery	0	50	
Potatoes . . .	10	00	per bushel.
Rabbit	25	00	
An old hen . . .	18	00	
A pigeon . . .	6	00	
Butter	25	00	per pound.
A goose . . .	70	00	
Bear	10	00	per pound.
Lard—very scarce . .	5	00	
A few cauliflowers at .	4	00	
A few cabbages at . .	5	00	

Dog, cat, and rat, are sold more or less openly.
The markets are deserted.

19th Nov. to 26th Nov.—Tenth week of siege:—

	fr.	*c.*	
Butter	20	00	per pound.
Rabbit	18	00	
Fowl	18	00	
Cabbage . . .	3	00	
Cauliflower . . .	3	50	
Salsify	1	80	per box.
Fat of fowls . . .	4	00	per box.

The potatoes are requisitioned at seven francs per bushel. This causes great excitement.

The merchants have an abundance of provisions of all sorts at very high prices.

26th Nov. to 3rd Dec.—Eleventh week of siege:—

	fr.	c.	
Butter	25	00	
Rabbit	30	00	
Fowl	25	00	
Fresh eggs	2	00	each
Fillet of horse	10	00	per pound.
A turkey	90	00	
A pigeon	6	00	
Ham sold by stealth	15	00	per pound.
Salad	0	40	per head.
Carrots	7	00	per box.

There is an abundance of *conserves*.

3rd Dec. to 10th Dec.—Twelfth week of siege:—

	fr.	c.	
Butter	28	00	per pound.
A fowl	25	00	
A goose	70	00	
A turkey	80	00	
A pigeon	8	00	
A rabbit	30	00	
Fillet of horse	14	00	per pound.
Small cauliflower	3	50	
Corn salad	2	50	per pound.
Fish	10	00	,,
Olive oil	7	00	
Coals	1	50	per bushel.
Wood	70	00	per 1000 kilos.

Two peacocks have been sold for 110 francs.

The English butchers sell deer and antelope at eight francs per pound.

10th Dec. to 17th Dec.—Thirteenth week of siege:—

		fr. c.	
Dog	. . . .	1 00	per pound.
Cat	. . . .	6 00	
Rat	. . . .	0 50	
Fillet of horse	. .	16 00	per pound.
Wild boar	. . .	15 00	,,
Butter	. . . .	30 00	,,
Rabbit	. . . .	30 00	
Fowl	. . . .	25 00	
A pigeon	. . .	7 00	
Codfish	. . . .	5 00	per pound.
A lark	. . . .	2 00	
Eggs	. . . .	1 50	each.
A goose	. . .	75 00	
A turkey	. . .	95 00	

17th Dec. to 24th Dec.—Fourteenth week of siege:—

		fr. c.	
Butter	. . . .	35 00	per pound.
Fowl	. . . .	26 00	
Goose	. . . .	80 00	
Duck	. . . .	36 00	
Turkey	. . . .	100 00	
Pigeon	. . . .	8 00	
Rabbit	. . . .	40 00	
Carrots	. . . .	2 80	per pound.
Onions	. . . .	37 00	per litre.
Eggs	. . . .	2 00	each.
Olive oil	. . .	9 00	

		fr.	*c.*	
Sugar	. . . .	0	90	
A sheep sold for	. .	1164	00	
Potatoes	. . .	15	00	per bushel.

The fruit stalls are empty, and the markets are deserted.

24th Dec. to 31st Dec.—Fifteenth week of siege:—

		fr.	*c.*	
Corn salad	. . .	3	00	per pound.
Rabbit .	. . .	40	00	
A turkey	. . .	180	00	
A leg of mutton	. ..	175	00	
Potatoes	. . ..	28	00	per bushel.
Bear	. . . .	15	00	per pound.
Goat	. . . .	15	00	,,
Elephant	. . .	15	00	,,
The elephant's trunk	.	40	00	
Cheese .	. . .	30	00	per pound.
Butter .	. . .'	40	00	,,
Eggs	. . . .	3	00	each.

31st Dec. to 7th Jan.—Sixteenth week of siege:—

		fr.	*c.*	
Butter	. . . ..	35	00	per pound.
Eggs	. . . ..	3	50	each.
A turkey	. . .	180	00	
Fowl	. . . .	35	00	
Rabbit .	. . .	40	00	
A lark .	. . .	3	50	
Cat	. . . ..	12	00	
Potatoes	. . ..	35	00	per bushel.
Onions .	. . .	7	00	per litre.
Dog	. . . ..	3	00	per pound.
Rat	. . . ..	0	75	

The English butchers are selling elephant, ass, and bear, from 8 to 20 francs per pound.

7th Jan. to 14th Jan.—Seventeenth week of siege:—

	fr. c.	
Butter	35 00	per pound.
Elephant . . .	15 00	„
Bear	15 00	„
Onions	7 00	per litre.
Potatoes, very scarce .	25 00	per bushel.
Salad	5 00	per pound.

The bread is very poor.

It is almost impossible to get chocolate.

Sugar has been taxed at 1 franc the pound. This causes a loss of two millions and a half to the grocers, who negotiated at 1 fr. 40 c., and even at 1 fr. 70 c.

14th Jan. to 21st Jan.—Eighteenth week of siege:—

	fr. c.	
Ham	25 00	per pound.
Crane	18 00	
Butter	25 00	per pound.
A hen	40 00	
A rabbit . . .	55 00	
Turkey	180 00	
Goose	140 00	
Onions	1 00	each.
Fish	10 00	per pound.
Dog	3 00	
Cat	12 00	
Coals	3 00	per bushel.
Wood	15 00	per hundred kil.

Bread is rationed at 300 grammes for an adult, and at 150 grammes for a child under five years of age.

Potatoes are requisitioned at 25 fr. the bushel.

21st Jan. to 28th Jan.—Nineteenth week of siege:—

Prices remained the same until Friday of this week, when they suddenly fell.

		fr. c.	
Potatoes	. . .	12 00	per bushel.
Carrots .	. . .	3 00	per pound.
Salad .	. . .	3 00	
Onions .	. . .	5 00	per litre.
Butter .	. . .	25 00	per pound.
Cheese .	. . .	18 00	,,
Salt butter	. . .	12 00	,,
Small quantities of rice at	. . . .	1 20	,,

A chemist has analyzed the bread which we were reduced to when we were "conquered by famine." Its constituent parts were as follows: One-eighth wheat, 4-8 melange of potatoes, beans, peas, oats, and rye, 2-8 water, and 1-8 straw and the hulls of grain, and the skins of vegetables.

THE BOURSE DURING THE SIEGE.

Saturday, 24th Sept.—First week of siege:—

3%: 52·50; 4½%: 80·25.—*Banque*, 2055.—*Société générale*, 445.—*Crédit foncier*, 985.—*Crédit mobilier*, 93·75.—*Orléans*, 820.—*Nord*, 990.—*Est*, 428·75.—*Lyon*, 832·50.—*Midi*, 550. —*Ouest*, 535.—*Suez*, 250.

Saturday, 1st Oct.—Second week of siege:—

3%: 53·60; 4½%: 79.—*Banque*, 2275.—*Crédit foncier*, 935·40.—*Crédit mobilier*, 95.—*Société générale*, 449·35.—*Est*, 440.—*Lyon*, 855·50.—*Midi*, 550.—*Nord*, 975.—*Orléans*, 810.—*Ouest*, 480.—*Suez*, 245.

Saturday, 8th Oct.—Third week of siege:—

3%: 51·90; 4½%: 77·50.—*Banque*, 2300.—*Société générale*, 437·50.—*Est*, 420.—*Lyon*, 835.—*Midi*, 530.—*Nord*, 780.— *Orléans*, 795.—*Ouest*, 475.—*Suez*, 245.

Saturday, 15th Oct.—Fourth week of siege:—

3%: 52·90; 4½%: 77·50.—*Banque*, 2270.—*Crédit foncier*, 895.—*Crédit mobilier*, 95.—*Est*, 405.—*Lyon*, 835.—*Midi*, 315. —*Nord* 980.—*Orléans*, 881·50.—*Ouest*, 478.—*Suez*, 245....

Saturday, 22nd Oct.—Fifth week of siege:—

3%: 52·80; 4½%: 79·50.—*Emprunt*, 53·90.—*Banque*, 2376.—*Société générale*, 436.—*Crédit foncier*, 861.—*Crédit mobilier*, 120.—*Orléans*, 776.—*Nord*, 965.—*Est*, 401.—*Lyon*, 845.—*Midi*, 521.—*Ouest*, 460.

Saturday, 29th Oct.—Sixth week of siege:—

3%: 52·74; 4½%: 79.—*Emprunt*, 53·85.—*Banque*, 2375.—*Société générale*, 436.—*Crédit foncier*, 860.—*Crédit mobilier*, 102.—*Orléans*, 775.—*Nord*, 965.—*Est*, 400.—*Lyon*, 845.—*Midi*, 520.—*Ouest*, 460.—*Suez*, 242.

Saturday, 5th Nov.—Seventh week of siege:—

3%: 51·30; 4½%: 77.—*Emprunt*, 52·50.—*Banque*, 2370.—*Crédit foncier*, 955.—*Est*, 415.—*Lyon*, 860.—*Nord*, 990.—*Orléans*, 772.—*Ouest*, 505.—*Suez*, 242.

Saturday, 12th Nov.—Eighth week of siege:—

3%: 51·20: 4½%: 77.—*Emprunt*, 52·25.—*Banque*, 2369.—*Crédit foncier*, 954.—*Est*, 415.—*Lyon*, 859.—*Midi*, 515.—*Nord*, 989.—*Orléans*, 771.—*Ouest*, 506.—*Suez*, 241.

Saturday, 19th Nov.—Ninth week of siege:—

3%: 53·85; 4½%: 79.—*Emprunt*, 55.—*Crédit foncier*, 970.—*Crédit mobilier*, 132.—*Société générale*, 485.—*Est*, 415.—*Lyon*, 862.—*Nord*, 985.—*Orléans*, 802·50.—*Ouest*, 505.—*Suez*, 240.

Saturday, 26th Nov.—Tenth week of siege:—

3%: 53·50; 4½%: 80.—*Banque*, 2700.—*Société générale*, 480.—*Crédit foncier*, 950.—*Crédit mobilier*, 128.—*Est*, 415.—*Lyon*, 860.—*Nord*, 995.—*Orléans*, 800.—*Ouest*, 505.—*Suez*, 236.

. Saturday, 3rd Dec.—Eleventh week of siege:—

3%: 53·80; 4½%: 80.—*Emprunt*, 55.—*Banque*, 2695.—*Crédit mobilier*, 130.—*Crédit foncier*, 950.—*Société générale*, 380.—*Est*, 420.—*Lyon*, 850.—*Midi*, 575.—*Nord*, 977.—*Orléans*, 800.—*Ouest*, 500.—*Suez*, 237·50.

Saturday, 10th Dec.—Twelfth week of siege:—

3%: 53·65; 4½%: 80.—*Banque*, 2689.—*Crédit foncier*, 955.—*Crédit mobilier*, 125.—*Société générale*, 472·50.—*Lyon*, 845.—*Midi*, 585.—*Nord*, 985.—*Orléans*, 797.—*Ouest*, 520.—*Suez*, 225.

Saturday, 17th Dec.—Thirteenth week of siege:—

3%: 52·45; 4½%: 81.—*Emprunt*, 54·40.—*Banque*, 2395.—*Société générale*, 470.—*Crédit foncier*, 940.—*Crédit mobilier*, 127·50.—*Est*, 415.—*Lyon*, 830.—*Midi*, 580.—*Nord*, 980.—*Orléans*, 775.—*Ouest*, 491.—*Suez*, 227·50.

Saturday, 24th Dec.—Fourteenth week of siege:—

3%: 52·75; 4½%: 79·75.—*Banque*, 2395.—*Société générale*, 470·50.—*Crédit foncier*, 937·50.—*Lyon*, 822·50.—*Nord*, 980.—*Orléans*, 762·50.—*Ouest*, 490.—*Suez*, 230.

Saturday, 31st Dec.—Fifteenth week of siege:—

3%: 51·80; 4½%: 81.—*Emprunt*, 52·80.—*Banque*, 2396.—*Société générale*, 470·50.—*Crédit mobilier*, 120.—*Crédit foncier*, 890.—*Est*, 380.—*Lyon*, 780.—*Midi*, 550.—*Nord*, 950.—*Orléans*, 737·50.—*Ouest*, 480.—*Suez*, 220.

Saturday, 7th Jan.—Sixteenth week of siege:—

3%: 51·80; 4½%: 76·50.—*Emprunt*, 52.60.—*Banque*, 2399.—*Société générale*, 450.—*Crédit foncier*, 860.—*Crédit mobilier*, 112·50.—*Est*, 395.—*Lyon*, 747·50.—*Midi*, 515.—

Nord, 900.—*Orléans*, 715.—*Ouest*, 465.—*Suez*, 230.—*Cette bourse est significative après quatre jours de bombardement ; toutes les valeurs, moins le Crédit mobilier, sont en hausse.*

Saturday, 14th Jan.—Seventeenth week of siege:—
3%: 51·50; 4½%: 76.—*Banque*, 2325.—*Société générale*, 450.—*Emprunt*, 52·62.—*Crédit foncier*, 850.—*Crédit mobilier*, 115.—*Est*, 337·50.—*Lyon*, 742·50.—*Midi*, 510.—*Nord*, 882.—*Orléans*, 717.—*Ouest*, 480.—*Suez*, 227.

Saturday, 21st Jan.—Eighteenth week of siege:—
3%: 50·75; 4½%: 78.—*Emprunt*, 51·70.—*Banque*, 2325.—*Société générale*, 450.—*Crédit foncier*, 862·50.—*Crédit mobilier*, 105.—*Est*, 390.—*Lyon*, 763.—*Midi*, 535.—*Nord*, 880.—*Orléans*, 720.—*Ouest*, 480.—*Suez*, 227.

Saturday, 28th Jan.—Nineteenth week of siege:—
3%: 52.50; 4½%: 77·75.—*Emprunt*, 58·80.—*Société générale*, 500.—*Est*, 430.—*Lyon*, 832·50.—*Midi*, 590.—*Nord*, 952·50.—*Orléans*, 840.—*Ouest*, 500.—*Suez*, 227·50.

THE END.

PRINTING OFFICE OF THE PUBLISHER.

September 1882.

TAUCHNITZ EDITION.

Each volume 1 Mark 60 Pf. or 2 Francs.

This Collection of British Authors, Tauchnitz Edition, will contain the new works of the most admired English and American Writers, immediately on their appearance, with copyright for continental circulation.

Contents:

Latest Volumes:

Flip and other Stories. By *Bret Harte*, 1 vol.
Schloss and Town. By *Frances Mary Peard*, 2 vols.
A Ballroom Repentance. By *Annie Edwardes*, 2 vols.
In Trust. By *M. O. W. Oliphant*, 2 vols.
A Woman-Hater. By *Charles Reade*, 2 vols.
The Stolen White Elephant, etc. By *Mark Twain*, 1 v.
Lady Alice. By *Emma Marshall*, 1 vol.
Plain Speaking. By the Author of "John Halifax," 1 v.
Unknown to History. By Miss *Yonge*, 2 vols.
For Cash Only. By *James Payn*, 2 vols.

Collection of British Authors.

Rev. W. Adams: Sacred Allegories 1 v.

Miss Aguilar: Home Influence 2 v. The Mother's Recompense 2 v.

Hamilton Aïdé: Rita 1 v. Carr of Carrlyon 2 v. The Marstons 2 v. In that State of Life 1 v. Morals and Mysteries 1 v. Penruddocke 2 v. "A nine Days' Wonder" 1 v. Poet and Peer 2 v.

W. Harrison Ainsworth: Windsor Castle 1 v. Saint James's 1 v. Jack Sheppard (w. portrait) 1 v. The Lancashire Witches 2 v. The Star-Chamber 2 v. The Flitch of Bacon 1 v. The Spendthrift 1 v. Mervyn Clitheroe 2 v. Ovingdean Grange 1 v. The Constable of the Tower 1 v. The Lord Mayor of London 2 v. Cardinal Pole 2 v. John Law 2 v. The Spanish Match 2 v. The Constable de Bourbon 2 v. Old Court 2 v. Myddleton Pomfret 2 v. The South-Sea Bubble 2 v. Hilary St. Ives 2 v. Talbot Harland 1 v. Tower Hill 1 v. Boscobel; or, the Royal Oak 2 v. The Good Old Times 2 v. Merry England 2 v. The Goldsmith's Wife 2 v. Preston Fight 2 v. Chetwynd Calverley 2 v. The Leaguer of Lathom 2 v. The Fall of Somerset 2 v. Beatrice Tyldesley 2 v. Beau Nash 2 v. Stanley Brereton 2 v.

L. M. Alcott: Little Women 2 v. Little Men 1 v.

"All for Greed," Author of— All for Greed 1 v. Love the Avenger 2 v.

Thomas Bailey Aldrich: Marjorie Daw and other Tales 1 v. The Stillwater Tragedy 1 v.

L. Alldridge: By Love and Law 2 v. The World she Awoke in 2 v.

Miss Austen: Sense and Sensibility 1 v. Mansfield Park 1 v. Pride and Prejudice 1 v. Northanger Abbey, and Persuasion 1 v. Emma 1 v.

Lady Barker: Station Life in New Zealand 1 v. Station Amusements in New Zealand 1 v. A Year's Housekeeping in South Africa 1 v.

Rev. R. H. Baynes: Lyra Anglicana, Hymns & Sacred Songs 1 v.

Lord Beaconsfield: *vide* Disraeli.

Averil Beaumont: Thornicroft's Model 2 v.

Currer Bell (Charlotte Brontë): Jane Eyre 2 v. Shirley 2 v. Villette 2 v. The Professor 1 v.

Ellis & Acton Bell: Wuthering Heights, and Agnes Grey 2 v.

Frank Lee Benedict: St. Simon's Niece 2 v.

William Black: A Daughter of Heth 2 v. In Silk Attire 2 v. The strange Adventures of a Phaeton 2 v. A Princess of Thule 2 v. Kilmeny 1 v. The Maid of Killeena 1 v. Three Feathers 2 v. Lady Silverdale's Sweetheart 1 v. Madcap Violet 2 v. Green Pastures and Piccadilly 2 v. Macleod of Dare 2 v. White Wings 2 v. Sunrise 2 v. The Beautiful Wretch 1 v. Mr. Pisistratus Brown, M.P., etc. 1 v.

R. D. Blackmore: Alice Lorraine 2 v. Mary Anerley 3 v. Christowell 2 v.

"Blackwood," Tales from— 1 v. *Second Series* 1 v.

Isa Blagden: The Woman I loved, and the Woman who loved me; A Tuscan Wedding 1 v.

Lady Blessington: Meredith 1 v. Strathern 2 v. Memoirs of a Femme de Chambre 1 v. Marmaduke Herbert 2 v. Country Quarters (w. portrait) 2 v.

Miss Braddon: Lady Audley's Secret 2 v. Aurora Floyd 2 v. Eleanor's Victory 2 v. John Marchmont's Legacy 2 v. Henry Dunbar 2 v. The Doctor's Wife 2 v. Only a Clod 2 v. Sir Jasper's Tenant 2 v. The Lady's Mile 2 v. Rupert Godwin 2 v. Dead-Sea Fruit 2 v. Run to Earth 2 v. Fenton's Quest 2 v. The Lovels of Arden 2 v. Strangers and Pilgrims 2 v. Lucius Davoren 3 v. Taken at the Flood 3 v. Lost for Love 2 v. A Strange World 2 v. Hostages to Fortune 2 v. Dead Men's Shoes 2 v. Joshua Haggard's Daughter 2 v. Weavers and Weft 1 v. In Great Waters 1 v. An Open Verdict 3 v. Vixen 3 v. The Cloven Foot 3 v. The Story of Barbara 2 v. Just as I am 2 v. Asphodel 3 v. Mount Royal 2 v.

Lady Brassey: A Voyage in the "Sunbeam" 2 v. Sunshine and Storm in the East 2 v.

Shirley Brooks. The Silver Cord 3 v. Sooner or Later 3 v.

Miss Rhoda Broughton: Cometh up as a Flower 1 v. Not wisely, but too well 2 v. Red as a Rose is She 2 v. Tales for Christmas Eve 1 v. Nancy 2 v. Joan 2 v. Second Thoughts 2 v.

John Brown: Rab and his Friends, and other Tales 1 v.

Eliz. Barrett Browning: A Selection from her Poetry (w. portrait) 1 v. Aurora Leigh 1 v.

Robert Browning: Poetical Works (with portrait) 2 v.

Bulwer (Lord Lytton): Pelham (with portrait) 1 v. Eugene Aram 1 v. Paul Clifford 1 v. Zanoni 1 v. The Last Days of Pompeii 1 v. The Disowned 1 v. Ernest Maltravers 1 v. Alice 1 v. Eva, and the Pilgrims of the Rhine 1 v. Devereux 1 v. Godolphin, and Falkland 1 v. Rienzi 1 v. Night and Morning 1 v. The Last of the Barons 2 v. Athens 2 v. The Poems and Ballads of Schiller 1 v. Lucretia 2 v. Harold 2 v. King Arthur 2 v. The new Timon; St Stephen's 1 v. The Caxtons 2 v. My Novel 4 v. What will he do with it? 4 v. The Dramatic Works 2 v. A

Strange Story 2 v. Caxtoniana 2 v. The Lost Tales of Miletus 1 v. Miscellaneous Prose Works 4 v. The Odes and Epodes of Horace 2 v. Kenelm Chillingly 4 v. The Coming Race 1 v. The Parisians 4 v. Pausanias 1 v.

Henry Lytton Bulwer (Lord Dalling): Historical Characters 2 v. The Life of Henry John Temple, Viscount Palmerston 3 v.

John Bunyan: The Pilgrim's Progress 1 v.

Buried Alone 1 v.

Miss Burney: Evelina 1 v.

Robert Burns: Poetical Works (w. portrait) 1 v.

Richard F. Burton: Mecca and Medina 3 v.

Mrs. B. H. Buxton: "Jennie of 'the Prince's'" 2 v. Won! 2 v. Great Grenfell Gardens 2 v. Nell—on and off the Stage 2 v. From the Wings 2 v.

Lord Byron: Poetical Works (w. portrait) 5 v.

Cameron: Across Africa 2 v.

Thomas Carlyle: The French Revolution 3 v. Frederick the Great 13 v. Oliver Cromwell's Letters and Speeches 4 v. The Life of Friedrich Schiller 1 v.

Maria Louisa Charlesworth: Oliver of the Mill 1 v.

"Chronicles of the Schönberg-Cotta Family," Author of— Chronicles of the Schönberg-Cotta Family 2 v. The Draytons and the Davenants 2 v. On Both Sides of the Sea 2 v. Winifred Bertram 1 v. Diary of Mrs. Kitty Trevylyan 1 v. The Victory of the Vanquished 1 v. The Cottage by the Cathedral 1 v. Against the Stream 2 v. The Bertram Family 2 v. Conquering and to Conquer 1 v. Lapsed, but not Lost 1 v.

Frances Power Cobbe: Re-Echoes 1 v.

Coleridge: The Poems 1 v.

Chas. A. Collins: A Cruise upon Wheels 2 v.

Mortimer Collins: Sweet and Twenty 2 v. A Fight with Fortune 2 v.

Wilkie Collins: After Dark 1 v. Hide and Seek 2 v. A Plot in Private Life 1 v. The Woman in White 2 v. Basil 1 v. No Name 3 v. The Dead Secret 2 v. Antonina 2 v. Armadale 3 v. The Moonstone 2 v. Man and Wife 3 v. Poor Miss Finch 2 v. Miss or Mrs.? 1 v. The New Magdalen 2 v. The Frozen Deep 1 v. The Law and the Lady 2 v. The Two Destinies 1 v. My Lady's Money & Percy and the Prophet 1 v. The Haunted Hotel 1 v. Fallen Leaves 2 v. Jezebel's Daughter 2 v. The Black Robe 2 v.

"Cometh up as a Flower," Author of— *vide* Broughton.

Fenimore Cooper: The Spy (w. portrait) 1 v. The two Admirals 1 v. The Jack O'Lantern 1 v.

George L. Craik: Manual of English Literature & Language 2 v.

Mrs. Craik (Miss Mulock): John Halifax, Gentleman 2 v. The Head of the Family 2 v. A Life for a Life 2 v. A Woman's Thoughts about Women 1 v. Agatha's Husband 1 v. Romantic Tales 1 v. Domestic Stories 1 v. Mistress and Maid 1 v. The Ogilvies 1 v. Lord Erlistoun 1 v. Christian's Mistake 1 v. Bread upon the Waters 1 v. A Noble Life 1 v. Olive 2 v. Two Marriages 1 v. Studies from Life 1 v. Poems 1 v. The Woman's Kingdom 2 v. The Unkind Word 2 v. A Brave Lady 2 v. Hannah 2 v. Fair France 1 v. My Mother and I 1 v. The Little Lame Prince 1 v. Sermons out of Church 1 v. The Laurel Bush 1 v. A Legacy 2 v.

Young Mrs. Jardine 2 v. His Little Mother 1 v. Plain Speaking 1 v.

Miss Georgiana Craik: Lost and Won 1 v. Faith Unwin's Ordeal 1 v. Leslie Tyrrell 1 v. Winifred's Wooing, and other Tales 1 v. Mildred 1 v. Esther Hill's Secret 2 v. Hero Trevelyan 1 v. Without Kith or Kin 2 v. Only a Butterfly 1 v. Sylvia's Choice; Theresa 2 v. Anne Warwick 1 v. Two Tales of Married Life 2 v. (Vol. I. Hard to Bear, Vol. II. *vide* M. C. Stirling.) Dorcas 2 v. Two Women 2 v.

Miss Cummins: The Lamplighter 1 v. Mabel Vaughan 1 v. El Fureidîs 1 v. Haunted Hearts 1 v.

"Daily News," War Correspondence 1877 by A. Forbes etc. 3 v.

De-Foe: Robinson Crusoe 1 v.

Charles Dickens: The Posthumous Papers of the Pickwick Club (w. portrait) 2 v. American Notes 1 v. Oliver Twist 1 v. The Life and Adventures of Nicholas Nickleby 2 v. Sketches 1 v. The Life and Adventures of Martin Chuzzlewit 2 v. A Christmas Carol; the Chimes; the Cricket on the Hearth 1 v. Master Humphrey's Clock (Old Curiosity Shop, Barnaby Rudge, and other Tales) 3 v. Pictures from Italy 1 v. The Battle of Life; the Haunted Man 1 v. Dombey and Son 3 v. David Copperfield 3 v. Bleak House 4 v. A Child's History of England (2 v. 8° M. 2,70.) Hard Times 1 v. Little Dorrit 4 v. A Tale of two Cities 2 v. Hunted Down; The Uncommercial Traveller 1 v. Great Expectations 2 v. Christmas Stories 1 v. Our Mutual Friend 4 v. Somebody's Luggage; Mrs. Lirriper's Lodgings; Mrs. Lirriper's Legacy 1 v. Doctor Marigold's Prescriptions; Mugby Junction 1 v. No

Thoroughfare 1 v. The Mystery of Edwin Drood 2 v. The Mudfog Papers 1 v. *Vide* Household Words, Novels and Tales, and John Forster.

Charles Dickens: The Letters of Charles Dickens edited by his Sister-in-law and his eldest Daughter 4 v.

B. Disraeli (Lord Beaconsfield): Coningsby 1 v. Sybil 1 v. Contarini Fleming (w. port.) 1 v. Alroy 1 v. Tancred 2 v. Venetia 2 v. Vivian Grey 2 v. Henrietta Temple 1 v. Lothair 2 v. Endymion 2 v.

W. Hepworth Dixon: Personal History of Lord Bacon 1 v. The Holy Land, 2 v. New America 2 v. Spiritual Wives 2 v. Her Majesty's Tower 4 v. Free Russia 2 v. History of two Queens 6 v. White Conquest 2 v. Diana, Lady Lyle 2 v.

The Earl and the Doctor: South Sea Bubbles 1 v.

Mrs. Edwardes: Archie Lovell 2 v. Steven Lawrence, Yeoman 2 v. Ought we to Visit her? 2 v. A Vagabond Heroine 1 v. Leah: A Woman of Fashion 2 v. A Blue-Stocking 1 v. Jet: Her Face or Her Fortune? 1 v. Vivian the Beauty 1 v. A Ballroom Repentance 2 v.

Miss Amelia B. Edwards: Barbara's History 2 v. Miss Carew 2 v. Hand and Glove 1 v. Half a Million of Money 2 v. Debenham's Vow 2 v. In the Days of my Youth 2 v. Untrodden Peaks and unfrequented Valleys 1 v. Monsieur Maurice 1 v. Black Forest 1 v. A Poetry-Book of Elder Poets 1 v. A Thousand Miles up the Nile 2 v. A Poetry-Book of Modern Poets 1 v. Lord Brackenbury 2 v.

Miss M. Betham-Edwards: The Sylvestres 1 v. Felicia 2 v. Brother Gabriel 2 v. Forestalled 1 v.

George Eliot: Scenes of Clerical Life 2 v. Adam Bede 2 v. The Mill on the Floss 2 v. Silas Marner 1 v. Romola 2 v. Felix Holt 2 v. Daniel Deronda 4 v. The Lifted Veil and Brother Jacob 1 v. Impressions of Theophrastus Such 1 v.

Mrs. Elliot: Diary of an Idle Woman in Italy 2 v. Old Court Life in France 2 v. The Italians 2 v. The Diary of an Idle Woman in Sicily 1 v. Pictures of Old Rome 1 v.

Essays and Reviews 1 v.

Estelle Russell 2 v.

Expiated 2 v.

G. M. Fenn: The Parson o' Dumford 2 v. The Clerk of Portwick 2 v.

Fielding: The History of Tom Jones 2 v.

Five Centuries of the English Language and Literature 1 v.

A. Forbes: My Experiences of the War between France and Germany 2 v. Soldiering and Scribbling 1 v. See also "Daily News," War Correspondence.

Mrs. Forrester: Viva 2 v. Rhona 2 v. Roy and Viola 2 v. My Lord and My Lady 2 v.

John Forster: Life of Charles Dickens 6 v. Life and Times of Oliver Goldsmith 2 v.

Jessie Fothergill: The First Violin 2 v. Probation 2 v. Made or Marred and "One of Three" 1 v. Kith and Kin 2 v.

"Found Dead," Author of— *vide* James Payn.

Caroline Fox: Memories of Old Friends from her Journals, edited by Horace N. Pym 2 v.

Frank Fairlegh 2 v.

E. A. Freeman: The Growth of the English Constitution 1 v. Select Historical Essays 1 v.

Lady G. Fullerton: Ellen Middleton 1 v. Grantley Manor 2 v. Lady-Bird 2 v. Too Strange not to be True 2 v. Constance Sherwood 2 v. A stormy Life 2 v. Mrs. Gerald's Niece 2 v. The Notary's Daughter 1 v. The Lilies of the Valley 1 v. The Countess de Bonneval 1 v. Rose Leblanc 1 v. Seven Stories 1 v. The Life of Luisa de Carvajal 1 v. A Will and a Way 2 v.

Mrs. Gaskell: Mary Barton 1 v. Ruth 2 v. North and South 1 v. Lizzie Leigh 1 v. The Life of Charlotte Brontë 2 v. Lois the Witch 1 v. Sylvia's Lovers 2 v. A Dark Night's Work 1 v. Wives and Daughters 3 v. Cranford 1 v. Cousin Phillis, and other Tales 1 v.

Right Hon. W. E. Gladstone: Rome and the newest Fashions in Religion 1 v. Bulgarian Horrors; Russia in Turkistan 1 v. The Hellenic Factor in the Eastern Problem 1 v.

Goldsmith: Select Works: The Vicar of Wakefield; Poems; Dramas (w. portrait) 1 v.

Mrs. Gore: Castles in the Air 1 v. The Dean's Daughter 2 v. Progress and Prejudice 2 v. Mammon 2 v. A Life's Lessons 2 v. The two Aristocracies 2 v. Heckington 2 v.

Miss Grant: Victor Lescar 2 v. The Sun-Maid 2 v. My Heart's in the Highlands 2 v. Artiste 2 v.

W. A. Baillie Grohman: Tyrol and the Tyrolese 1 v.

"Guy Livingstone," Author of—Guy Livingstone 1 v. Sword and Gown 1 v. Barren Honour 1 v. Border and Bastille 1 v. Maurice Dering 1 v. Sans Merci 2 v. Breaking a Butterfly 2 v. Anteros 2 v. Hagarene 2 v.

J. Habberton: Helen's Babies & Other People's Children 1 v.

Mrs. S. C. Hall: Can Wrong be Right? 1 v. Marian 2 v.

Thomas Hardy: The Hand of Ethelberta 2 v. Far from the Madding Crowd 2 v. The Return of the Native 2 v. The Trumpet-Major 2 v. A Laodicean 2 v.

Agnes Harrison: Martin's Vineyard 1 v.

Bret Harte: Prose and Poetry (Tales of the Argonauts; Spanish and American Legends; Condensed Novels; Civic and Character Sketches; Poems) 2 v. Idyls of the Foothills 1 v. Gabriel Conroy 2 v. Two Men of Sandy Bar 1 v. Thankful Blossom 1 v. The Story of a Mine 1 v. Drift from Two Shores 1 v. An Heiress of Red Dog 1 v. The Twins of Table Mountain, etc. 1 v. Jeff Briggs's Love Story, etc. 1 v. Flip, etc. 1 v.

Sir H. Havelock, by the Rev. W. Brock, 1 v.

Nathaniel Hawthorne: The Scarlet Letter 1 v. Transformation 2 v. Passages from the English Note-Books 2 v.

"Heir of Redclyffe," Author of— *vide* Yonge.

Sir Arthur Helps: Friends in Council 2 v. Ivan de Biron 2 v.

Mrs. Hemans: The Select Poetical Works 1 v.

Mrs. Cashel Hoey: A Golden Sorrow 2 v. Out of Court 2 v.

Household Words conducted by Ch. Dickens. 1851-56. 36 v. Novels and Tales reprinted from Households Words by Ch. Dickens. 1856-59. 11 v.

Miss Howard: One Summer 1 v. Aunt Serena 1 v.

W. D. Howells: A Foregone Conclusion 1 v. The Lady of the Aroostook 1 v.

Thos. Hughes: Tom Brown's School Days 1 v.

Jean Ingelow: Off the Skelligs 3 v. Poems 2 v. Fated to be Free 2 v. Sarah de Berenger 2 v. Don John 2 v.

Washington Irving: Sketch Book (w. portrait) 1 v. Life of Mahomet 1 v. Successors of Mahomet 1 v. Oliver Goldsmith 1 v. Chronicles of Wolfert's Roost 1 v. Life of George Washington 5 v.

G. P. R. James: Morley Ernstein (w. portrait) 1 v. Forest Days 1 v. The False Heir 1 v. Arabella Stuart 1 v. Rose d'Albret 1 v. Arrah Neil 1 v.

Agincourt 1 v. The Smuggler 1 v. The Step-Mother 2 v. Beauchamp 1 v. Heidelberg 1 v. The Gipsy 1 v. The Castle of Ehrenstein 1 v. Darnley 1 v. Russell 2 v. The Convict 2 v. Sir Theodore Broughton 2 v.

Henry James, Jr.: The American 2 v. The Europeans 1 v. Daisy Miller 1 v. Roderick Hudson 2 v. The Madonna of the Future, etc. 1 v. Eugene Pickering, etc. 1 v. Confidence 1 v. Washington Square 2 v. The Portrait of a Lady 3 v.

J. Cordy Jeaffreson: A Book about Doctors 2 v. A Woman in Spite of herself 2 v.

Mrs. Jenkin: "Who Breaks—Pays" 1 v. Skirmishing 1 v. Once and Again 2 v. Two French Marriages 2 v. Within an Ace 1 v. Jupiter's Daughters 1 v.

Edward Jenkins: Ginx's Baby; Lord Bantam 2 v.

"Jennie of 'the Prince's,'" Author of— *vide* Mrs. Buxton.

Douglas Jerrold: The History of St. Giles and St. James 2 v. Men of Character 2 v.

"John Halifax," Author of— *vide* Mrs. Craik.

"Johnny Ludlow," Author of— *vide* Mrs. Wood.

Johnson: The Lives of the English Poets 2 v.

Emily Jolly: Colonel Dacre 2 v.

"Joshua Davidson, "Author of— *vide* E. Lynn Linton.

Miss Kavanagh: Nathalie 2 v. Daisy Burns 2 v. Grace Lee 2 v. Rachel Gray 1 v. Adèle 3 v. A Summer and Winter in the Two Sicilies 2 v. Seven Years 2 v. French Women of Letters 1 v. English Women of Letters 1 v. Queen Mab 2 v. Beatrice 2 v. Sybil's Second Love 2 v. Dora 2 v. Silvia 2 v. Bessie 2 v. John Dorrien 3 v. Two Lilies 2 v. Forget-me-nots 2 v.

Annie Keary: Oldbury 2 v. Castle Daly 2 v.

Kempis: *vide* Thomas a Kempis.

R. B. Kimball: Saint Leger 1 v. Romance of Student Life abroad 1 v. Undercurrents 1 v. Was he Successful? 1 v. To-Day in New-York 1 v.

A. W. Kinglake: Eothen 1 v. Invasion of the Crimea v. 1-10.

Charles Kingsley: Yeast 1 v. Westward ho! 2 v. Two Years ago 2 v. Hypatia 2 v. Alton Locke 1 v. Hereward the Wake 2 v. At Last 2 v.

Charles Kingsley: His Letters and Memories of his Life edited by his Wife 2 v.

Henry Kingsley: Ravenshoe 2 v. Austin Elliot 1 v. The Recollections of Geoffry Hamlyn 2 v. The Hillyars and the Burtons 2 v. Leighton Court 1 v. Valentin 1 v. Oakshott Castle 1 v. Reginald Hetherege 2 v. The Grange Garden 2 v.

May Laffan: Flitters, Tatters, and the Counsellor, etc. 1 v.

Charles Lamb: The Essays of Elia and Eliana 1 v.

Mary Langdon: Ida May 1 v.

"Last of the Cavaliers," Author of— Last of the Cavaliers 2 v. The Gain of a Loss 2 v.

Holme Lee: *vide* Miss Parr.

S. Le Fanu: Uncle Silas 2 v. Guy Deverell 2 v.

Mark Lemon: Wait for the End 2 v. Loved at Last 2 v. Falkner Lyle 2 v. Leyton Hall 2 v. Golden Fetters 2 v.

Charles Lever: The O'Donoghue 1 v. The Knight of Gwynne 3 v. Arthur O'Leary 2 v. The Confessions of Harry Lorrequer 2 v. Charles O'Malley 3 v. Tom Burke of "Ours" 3 v. Jack Hinton 2 v. The Daltons 4 v. The Dodd Family abroad 3 v. The Martins of Cro' Martin 3 v. The Fortunes of Glencore 2 v. Roland Cashel 3 v. Davenport Dunn 3 v. Con Cregan 2 v. One of Them 2 v. Maurice Tiernay 2 v. Sir Jasper Carew 2 v. Barrington 2 v. A Day's Ride: a Life's Romance 2 v. Luttrell of Arran 2 v. Tony Butler 2 v. Sir Brook Fossbrooke 2 v. The Bramleighs of Bishop's Folly 2 v. A Rent in a Cloud 1 v. That Boy of Norcott's 1 v. St. Patrick's Eve; Paul Gosslett's Confessions 1 v. Lord Kilgobbin 2 v.

G. H. Lewes: Ranthorpe 1 v. Physiology of Common Life 2 v. On Actors and the Art of Acting 1 v.

E. Lynn Linton: Joshua Davidson 1 v. Patricia Kemball 2 v. Atonement of Leam Dundas 2 v. The World well Lost 2 v. Under which Lord? 2 v. With a Silken Thread etc. 1 v. Todhunters' at Loanin' Head etc. 1 v. "My Love!" 2 v.

Laurence W. M. Lockhart: Mine is Thine 2 v.

Longfellow: Poetical Works (w. portrait) 3 v. The Divine Comedy of Dante Alighieri 3 v. The New-England Tragedies 1 v. The Divine Tragedy 1 v. Three Books of Song 1 v. The Masque of Pandora 1 v.

M. Lonsdale: Sister Dora 1 v. A Lost Battle 2 v.

Lutfullah: Autobiography of Lutfullah, by Eastwick 1 v.

Lord Lytton: *vide* Bulwer.

Robert Lord Lytton (Owen Meredith): Poems 2 v. Fables in Song 2 v.

Lord Macaulay: History of England (w. portrait) 10 v. Critical and Historical Essays 5 v. Lays of Ancient Rome 1 v. Speeches 2 v. Biographical Essays 1 v. William Pitt, Atterbury 1 v. (See also Trevelyan).

Justin McCarthy: Waterdale Neighbours 2 v. Lady Disdain 2 v. Miss Misanthrope 2 v. A History of our own Times 5 v. Donna Quixote 2 v.

George MacDonald: Alec Forbes of Howglen 2 v. Annals of a Quiet Neighbourhood 2 v. David Elginbrod 2 v. The Vicar's Daughter 2 v. Malcolm 2 v. St. George and St. Michael 2 v. The Marquis of Lossie 2 v. Sir Gibbie 2 v. Mary Marston 2 v.

Mrs. Mackarness: Sunbeam Stories 1 v. A Peerless Wife 2 v. A Mingled Yarn 2 v.

Charles McKnight: Old Fort Duquesne 2 v.

Norman Macleod: The old Lieutenant and his Son 1 v.

Mrs. Macquoid: Patty 2 v. Miriam's Marriage 2 v. Pictures across the Channel 2 v. Too Soon 1 v. My Story 2 v. Diane 2 v. Beside the River 2 v.

"Mademoiselle Mori," Author of— Mademoiselle Mori 2 v. Denise 1 v. Madame Fontenoy 1 v. On the Edge of the Storm 1 v. The Atelier du Lys 2 v.

Lord Mahon: *vide* Stanhope.

E. S. Maine: Scarscliff Rocks 2 v.

R. Blachford Mansfield: The Log of the Water Lily 1 v. Marmorne 1 v.

Capt. Marryat: Jacob Faithful (w. portrait) 1 v. Percival Keene 1 v. Peter Simple 1 v. Japhet 1 v. Monsieur Violet 1 v. The Settlers 1 v. The Mission

1 v. The Privateer's-Man 1 v. The Children of the New-Forest 1 v. Valerie 1 v. Mr. Midshipman Easy 1 v. The King's Own 1 v.

Florence Marryat: Love's Conflict 2 v. For Ever and Ever 2 v. The Confessions of Gerald Estcourt 2 v. Nelly Brooke 2 v. Véronique 2 v. Petronel 2 v. Her Lord and Master 2 v. The Prey of the Gods 1 v. Life of Captain Marryat 1 v. Mad Dumaresq 2 v. No Intentions 2 v. Fighting the Air 2 v. A Star and a Heart 1 v. The Poison of Asps 1 v. A Lucky Disappointment 1 v. My own Child 2 v. Her Father's Name 2 v. A Harvest of Wild Oats 2 v. A Little Stepson 1 v. Written in Fire 2 v. Her World against a Lie 2 v. A Broken Blossom 2 v. The Root of all Evil 2 v. The Fair-haired Alda 2 v. With Cupid's Eyes 2 v. My Sister the Actress 2 v. Phyllida 2 v.

Mrs. Marsh: Ravenscliffe 2 v. Emilia Wyndham 2 v. Castle Avon 2 v. Aubrey 2 v. The Heiress of Haughton 2 v. Evelyn Marston 2 v. The Rose of Ashurst 2 v.

Emma Marshall: Mrs. Mainwaring's Journal 1 v. Benvenuta 1 v. Lady Alice 1 v.

Helen Mathers: "Cherry Ripe!" 2 v. "Land o' the Leal" 1 v. My Lady Green Sleeves 2 v. As he comes up the Stair, etc. 1 v.

Mehalah 1 v.

Whyte Melville: Kate Coventry 1 v. Holmby House 2 v. Digby Grand 1 v. Good for Nothing 2 v. The Queen's Maries 2 v. The Gladiators 2 v. The Brookes of Bridlemere 2 v. Cerise 2 v. The Interpreter 2 v. The White Rose 2 v. M. or N. 1 v. Contraband; or A Losing Hazard 1 v. Sarchedon 2 v. Uncle John 2 v. Katerfelto 1 v. Sister Louise 1 v. Rosine 1 v. Roy's Wife 2 v. Black but Comely 2 v. Riding Recollections 1 v.

George Meredith: The Ordeal of Feverel 2 v. Beauchamp's Career 2 v. The Tragic Comedians 1 v.

Owen Meredith: *vide* Robert Lord Lytton.

Milton: Poetical Works 1 v.

Miss Florence Montgomery: Misunderstood 1 v. Thrown Together 2 v. Thwarted 1 v. Wild Mike 1 v. Seaforth 2 v.

"Molly Bawn," Author of— Molly Bawn 2 v. Mrs. Geoffrey 2 v. Faith and Unfaith 2 v.

Moore: Poetical Works (w. portrait) 5 v.

Lady Morgan's Memoirs 3 v.

Henry Morley: Of English Literature in the Reign of Victoria. With Facsimiles of the Signatures of Authors in the Tauchnitz Edition [v. 2000].

E. C. Grenville: Murray: The Member for Paris 2 v. Young Brown 2 v. The Boudoir Cabal 3 v. French Pictures in English Chalk (1st Series) 2 v. The Russians of To-day 1 v. French Pictures in English Chalk (2nd Series) 2 v. Strange Tales 1 v. That Artful Vicar 2 v. Six Months in the Ranks 1 v.

"My little Lady," Author of— *vide* E. Frances Poynter.

New Testament [v. 1000].

Mrs. Newby: Common Sense 2 v.

Dr. J. H. Newman: Callista 1 v.

Nina Balatka 1 v.

"No Church," Author of—No Church 2 v. Owen:—a Waif 2 v.

Lady Augusta Noel: From Generation to Generation 1 v.

Hon. Mrs. Norton: Stuart of Dunleath 2 v. Lost and Saved 2 v. Old Sir Douglas 2 v.

Novels and Tales *vide* Household Words.

Not Easily Jealous 2 v.

Mrs. Oliphant: Passages in the Life of Mrs. Margaret Maitland of Sunnyside 1 v. The Last of the Mortimers 2 v. Agnes 2 v. Madonna Mary 2 v. The Minister's Wife 2 v. The Rector, and the Doctor's Family 1 v. Salem Chapel 2 v. The Perpetual Curate 2 v. Miss Marjoribanks 2 v. Ombra 2 v. Memoir of Count de Montalembert 2 v. May 2 v. Innocent 2 v. For Love and Life 2 v. A Rose in June 1 v. The Story of Valentine and his Brother 2 v. Whiteladies 2 v. The Curate in Charge 1 v. Phœbe, Junior 2 v. Mrs. Arthur 2 v. Carità 2 v. Young Musgrave 2 v. The Primrose Path 2 v. Within the Precincts 3 v. The greatest Heiress in England 2 v. He that will not when he may 2 v. Harry Joscelyn 2 v. In Trust 2 v.

Ossian: Poems 1 v.

Ouida: Idalia 2 v. Tricotrin 2 v. Puck 2 v. Chandos 2 v. Strathmore 2 v. Under two Flags 2 v. Folle-Farine 2 v. A Leaf in the Storm; A Dog of Flanders & other Stories 1 v. Cecil Castlemaine's Gage 1 v. Madame la Marquise 1 v. Pascarèl 2 v. Held in Bondage 2 v. Two little Wooden Shoes 1 v. Signa (w. portrait) 3 v. In a Winter City 1 v. Ariadnê 2 v. Friendship 2 v. Moths 3 v. Pipistrello 1 v. A Village Commune 2 v. In Maremma 3 v. Bimbi 1 v.

Miss Parr (Holme Lee): Basil Godfrey's Caprice 2 v. For Richer, for Poorer 2 v. The Beautiful Miss Barrington 2 v. Her Title of Honour 1 v. Echoes of a Famous Year 1 v. Katherine's Trial 1 v. Bessie Fairfax 2 v. Ben Milner's Wooing 1 v. Straightforward 2 v. Mrs. Denys of Cote 2 v.

Mrs. Parr: Dorothy Fox 1 v. The Prescotts of Pamphillon 2 v. Gosau Smithy 1 v.

"Paul Ferroll," Author of— Paul Ferroll 1 v. Year after Year 1 v. Why Paul Ferroll killed his Wife 1 v.

James Payn: Found Dead 1 v. Gwendoline's Harvest 1 v.

Like Father, like Son 2 v. Not Wooed, but Won 2 v. Cecil's Tryst 1 v. A Woman's Vengeance 2 v. Murphy's Master 1 v. In the Heart of a Hill 1 v. At Her Mercy 2 v. The Best of Husbands 2 v. Walter's Word 2 v. Halves 2 v. Fallen Fortunes 2 v. What He cost Her 2 v. By Proxy 2 v. Less Black than we're Painted 2 v. Under one Roof 2 v. High Spirits 1 v. High Spirits (Second Series) 1 v. A Confidential Agent 2 v. From Exile 2 v. A Grape from a Thorn 2 v. Some Private Views 1 v. For Cash Only 2 v.

Miss Fr. M. Peard: One Year 2 v. The Rose-Garden 1 v. Unawares 1 v. Thorpe Regis 1 v. A Winter Story 1 v. A Madrigal 1 v. Cartouche 1 v. Mother Molly 1 v. Schloss and Town 2 v.

Bishop Percy: Reliques of Ancient English Poetry 3 v.

Pope: Select Poetical Works (w. portrait) 1 v.

E. Frances Poynter: My little Lady 2 v. Ersilia 2 v. Among the Hills 1 v.

Mrs. E. Prentiss: Stepping Heavenward 1 v.

The Prince Consort's Speeches and Addresses 1 v.

Horace N. Pym: *vide* C. Fox.

W. F. Rae: Westward by Rail 1 v.

Charles Reade: "It is never too late to mend" 2 v. "Love me little, love me long" 1 v. The Cloister and the Hearth 2 v. Hard Cash 3 v. Put Yourself in his Place 2 v. A Terrible Temptation 2 v. Peg Woffington 1 v. Christie Johnstone 1 v. A Simpleton 2 v. The Wandering Heir 1 v. A Woman-Hater 2 v.

"Recommended to Mercy," Author of—Recommended to Mercy 2 v. Zoe's 'Brand' 2 v.

Alfred Bate Richards: So very Human 3 v.

Richardson: Clarissa Harlowe 4 v.

Mrs. Riddell (F. G. Trafford): George Geith of Fen Court 2 v. Maxwell Drewitt 2 v. The Race for Wealth 2 v. Far above Rubies 2 v. The Earl's Promise 2 v. Mortomley's Estate 2 v.

Rev. W. Robertson: Sermons 4 v.

Charles H. Ross: The Pretty Widow 1 v. A London Romance 2 v.

Dante Gabriel Rossetti: Poems 1 v.

J. Ruffini: Lavinia 2 v. Doctor Antonio 1 v. Lorenzo Benoni 1 v. Vincenzo 2 v. A Quiet Nook 1 v. The Paragreens on a Visit to Paris 1 v. Carlino and other Stories 1 v.

W. Clark Russell: A Sailor's Sweetheart 2 v.

G. A. Sala: The Seven Sons of Mammon 2 v.

John Saunders: Israel Mort, Overman 2 v. The Shipowner's Daughter 2 v.

Katherine Saunders: Joan Merryweather and other Tales 1 v. Gideon's Rock 1 v. The High Mills 2 v. Sebastian 1 v.

Sir Walter Scott: Waverley (w. portrait) 1 v. The Antiquary 1 v. Ivanhoe 1 v. Kenilworth 1 v. Quentin Durward 1 v. Old Mortality 1 v. Guy Mannering 1 v. Rob Roy 1 v. The Pirate 1 v. The Fortunes of Nigel 1 v. The Black Dwarf; A Legend of Montrose 1 v. The Bride of Lammermoor 1 v. The Heart of Mid-Lothian 2 v. The Monastery 1 v. The Abbot 1 v. Peveril of the Peak 2 v. The Poetical Works 2 v. Woodstock 1 v. The Fair Maid of Perth 1 v. Anne of Geierstein 1 v.

Professor Seeley: Life and Times of Stein 4 vols.

Miss Sewell: Amy Herbert 2 v. Ursula 2 v. A Glimpse of the World 2 v. The Journal of a Home Life 2 v. After Life 2 v. The Experience of Life; or, Aunt Sarah 2 v.

Shakespeare: Plays and Poems (w. portrait) *(Second Edition)* compl. 7 v.

Shakespeare's Plays may also be had in 37 numbers, at M. 0,30. each number.

Doubtful Plays 1 v.

Shelley: A Selection from his Poems 1 v.

Nathan Sheppard: Shut up in Paris *(Second Edition, enlarged)* 1 v.

Sheridan: Dramatic Works 1 v.

J. Henry Shorthouse: John Inglesant 2 v.

Smollett: The Adventures of Roderick Random 1 v. The Expedition of Humphry Clinker 1 v. The Adventures of Peregrine Pickle 2 v.

Earl Stanhope (Lord Mahon): History of England 7 v. The Reign of Queen Anne 2 v.

Sterne: The Life and Opinions of Tristram Shandy 1 v. A Sentimental Journey (w. portrait) 1 v.

"Still Waters," Author of— Still Waters 1 v. Dorothy 1 v. De Cressy 1 v. Uncle Ralph 1 v. Maiden Sisters 1 v. Martha Brown 1 v. Vanessa 1 v.

M. C. Stirling: Two Tales of Married Life 2 v. Vol. II, A True Man, Vol. I. *vide* G. M. Craik.

"The Story of Elizabeth," Author of—*v.* Miss Thackeray.

Mrs. H. Beecher Stowe: Uncle Tom's Cabin (w. portrait)

2 v. A Key to Uncle Tom's Cabin 2 v. Dred 2 v. The Minister's Wooing 1 v. Oldtown Folks 2 v.

"Sunbeam Stories," Author of— *vide* Mackarness.

Swift: Gulliver's Travels 1 v.

Baroness Tautphoeus: Cyrilla 2 v. The Initials 2 v. Quits 2 v. At Odds 2 v.

Colonel Meadows Taylor: Tara: a Mahratta Tale 3 v.

Templeton: Diary & Notes 1 v.

Tennyson: Poetical Works 7 v. Queen Mary 1 v. Harold 1 v. Ballads and other Poems 1 v.

W. M. Thackeray: Vanity Fair 3 v. The History of Pendennis 3 v. Miscellanies 8 v. The History of Henry Esmond 2 v. The English Humourists 1 v. The Newcomes 4 v. The Virginians 4 v. The Four Georges; Lovel the Widower 1 v. The Adventures of Philip 2 v. Denis Duval 1 v. Roundabout Papers 2 v. Catherine 1 v. The Irish Sketch Book 2 v. The Paris Sketch Book (w. portrait) 2 v.

Miss Thackeray: The Story of Elizabeth 1 v. The Village on the Cliff 1 v. Old Kensington 2 v. Bluebeard's Keys 1 v. Five Old Friends 1 v. Miss Angel 1 v. Out of the World 1 v. Fulham Lawn 1 v. From an Island 1 v. Da Capo 1 v. Madame de Sévigné 1 v.

Thomas a Kempis: The Imitation of Christ 1 v.

A. Thomas: Denis Donne 2 v. On Guard 2 v. Walter Goring 2 v. Played out 2 v. Called to Account 2 v. Only Herself 2 v. A narrow Escape 2 v.

Thomson: Poetical Works (with portrait) 1 v.

F. G. Trafford: *vide* Mrs. Riddell.

G. O. Trevelyan: The Life and Letters of Lord Macaulay (w. portrait) 4 v. Selections from the Writings of Lord Macaulay 2 v.

Trois-Etoiles: *vide* Murray.

Anthony Trollope: Doctor Thorne 2 v. The Bertrams 2 v. The Warden 1 v. Barchester Towers 2 v. Castle Richmond 2 v. The West Indies 1 v. Framley Parsonage 2 v. North America 3 v. Orley Farm 3 v. Rachel Ray 2 v. The Small House at Allington 3 v. Can you forgive her? 3 v. The Belton Estate 2 v. The Last Chronicle of Barset 3 v. The Claverings 2 v. Phineas Finn 3 v. He knew he was Right 3 v. The Vicar of Bullhampton 2 v. Sir Harry Hotspur of Humblethwaite 1 v. Ralph the Heir 2 v. The Golden Lion of Granpere 1 v. Australia and New Zealand 3 v. Lady Anna 2 v. Harry Heathcote of Gangoil 1 v. The Way we live now 4 v. The Prime Minister 4 v. The American Senator 3 v. South Africa 2 v. Is he Popenjoy? 3 v. An Eye for an Eye 1 v. John Caldigate 3 v. Cousin Henry 1 v. The Duke's Children 3 v. Dr. Wortle's School 1 v. Ayala's Angel 3 v. The Fixed Period 1 v.

T. Adolphus Trollope: The Garstangs of Garstang Grange 2 v. A Siren 2 v.

Mark Twain: The Adventures of Tom Sawyer 1 v. The Innocents Abroad; or, the New Pilgrims' Progress 2 v. A Tramp Abroad 2 v. "Roughing it" 1 v. The Innocents at Home 1 v. The Prince and the Pauper 2 v. The Stolen White Elephant, etc. 1 v.

The Two Cosmos 1 v.
"Véra," Author of— Véra 1 v.
The Hôtel du Petit St. Jean 1 v.
Blue Roses 2 v. Within Sound
of the Sea 2 v.

Virginia 1 v.

L. B. Walford: Mr. Smith 2 v.
Pauline 2 v. Cousins 2 v. Trouble-
some Daughters 2 v.

Mackenzie Wallace: Russia
3 v.

Eliot Warburton: The Cres-
cent and the Cross 2 v. Darien 2 v.

S. Warren: Passages from the
Diary of a late Physician 2 v. Ten
Thousand a-Year 3 v. Now and
Then 1 v. The Lily and the Bee 1 v.

"Waterdale Neighbours,"
Author of— *vide* J. McCarthy.

Miss Wetherell: The wide,
wide World 1 v. Queechy 2 v. The
Hills of the Shatemuc 2 v. Say
and Seal 2 v. The Old Helmet 2 v.
A Whim and its Consequences
1 v.

Walter White: Holidays in
Tyrol 1 v.

"Who Breaks—Pays," Au-
thor of— *vide* Mrs. Jenkin.

Mrs. Henry Wood: East
Lynne 3 v. The Channings
2 v. Mrs. Halliburton's Troubles
2 v. Verner's Pride 3 v. The
Shadow of Ashlydyat 3 v. Trevlyn
Hold 2 v. Lord Oakburn's Daugh-
ters 2 v. Oswald Cray 2 v. Mildred
Arkell 2 v. St. Martin's Eve 2 v.
Elster's Folly 2 v. Lady Adelaide's
Oath 2 v. Orville College 1 v. A
Life's Secret 1 v. The Red Court
Farm 2 v. Anne Hereford 2 v.
Roland Yorke 2 v. George Canter-
bury's Will 2 v. Bessy Rane 2 v.
Dene Hollow 2 v. The Foggy
Night at Offord etc. 1 v. Within
the Maze 2 v. The Master of
Greylands 2 v. Johnny Ludlow (*First
Series*) 2 v. Told in the Twilight
2 v. Adam Grainger 1 v. Edina 2 v.
Pomeroy Abbey 2 v. Lost in the Post
etc. By Johnny Ludlow 1 v. A Tale
of Sin etc. By Johnny Ludlow 1 v.
Anne etc. By Johnny Ludlow 1 v.
Court Netherleigh 2 v.

Wordsworth: Select Poetical
Works 2 v.

Lascelles Wraxall: Wild
Oats 1 v.

Edm. Yates: Land at Last
2 v. Broken to Harness 2 v.
The Forlorn Hope 2 v. Black
Sheep 2 v. The Rock Ahead
2 v. Wrecked in Port 2 v. Dr.
Wainwright's Patient 2 v. Nobody's Fortune 2 v. Castaway 2 v.
A Waiting Race 2 v. The Yellow Flag
2 v. The Impending Sword 2 v. Two,
by Tricks 1 v. A Silent Witness 2 v.

Miss Yonge: The Heir of
Redclyffe 2 v. Heartsease 2 v.
The Daisy Chain 2 v. Dynevor
Terrace 2 v. Hopes and Fears
2 v. The Young Step-Mother
2 v. The Trial 2 v. The Clever
Woman of the Family 2 v. The
Dove in the Eagle's Nest 2 v.
The Danvers Papers; the Prince and
the Page 1 v. The Chaplet of Pearls
2 v. The two Guardians 1 v. The
Caged Lion 2 v. The Pillars of the
House 5 v. Lady Hester 1 v. My
Young Alcides 2 v. The Three Brides
2 v. Womankind 2 v. Magnum Bonum
2 v. Love and Life 1 v. Unknown
to History 2 v.

Collection of German Authors.

B. Auerbach: On the Heights. Transl. by F. E. Bunnett. Second Authorized Edition, thoroughly revised, 3 v. Brigitta. From the German by C. Bell, 1 v. Spinoza. From the German by Nicholson, 2 v.

G. Ebers: An Egyptian Princess. Translated by E. Grove, 2 v. Uarda. From the German by Bell, 2 v. Homo Sum. From the German by Bell, 2 v. The Sisters. From the German by Bell, 2 v.

Fouqué: Undine, Sintram, etc. Translated by F. E. Bunnett, 1 v.

Ferdinand Freiligrath: Poems. From the German. Edited by his Daughter. Second Copyright Edition, enlarged, 1 v.

W. Görlach: Prince Bismarck (with Portrait). From the German by Miss M. E. von Glehn, 1 v.

Goethe: Faust. From the German by John Anster, LL. D. 1 v. Wilhelm Meister's Apprenticeship. From the German by Eleanor Grove, 2 v.

K. Gutzkow: Through Night to Light. From the German by M. A. Faber, 1 v.

F. W. Hackländer: Behind the Counter [Handel u. Wandel]. From the German by Howitt, 1 v.

W. Hauff: Three Tales. From the German by M. A. Faber, 1 v.

P. Heyse: L'Arrabiata and other Tales. From the German by M. Wilson, 1 v. The Dead Lake and other Tales. From the German by Mary Wilson, 1 v. Barbarossa and other Tales. From the German by L. C. S., 1 v.

Wilhelmine von Hillern: The Vulture Maiden [die Geier-Wally]. From the German by C. Bell and E. F. Poynter, 1 v. The Hour will come. From the German by Clara Bell, 2 v.

S. Kohn: Gabriel. A Story of the Jews in Prague. From the German by A. Milman, M.A., 1 v.

G. E. Lessing: Nathan the Wise and Emilia Galotti. The former transl. by W. Taylor, the latter by Chas. Lee Lewes, 1 v.

E. Marlitt: The Princess of the Moor [das Haideprinzesschen], 2 v.

Maria Nathusius: Joachim von Kamern and Diary of a poor young Lady. From the German by Miss Thompson, 1 v.

Fritz Reuter: In the Year '13: Transl. from the Platt-Deutsch by Chas. Lee Lewes, 1 v. An old Story of my Farming Days [Ut mine Stromtid]. From the German by M. W. Macdowall, 3 v.

Jean Paul Friedr. Richter: Flower, Fruit and Thorn Pieces: or the Married Life, Death, and Wedding of the Advocate of the Poor, Firmian Stanislaus Siebenkäs. Translated from the German by E. H. Noel, 2 v.

J. V. Scheffel: Ekkehard. A Tale of the tenth Century. Translated from the German by Sofie Delffs, 2 v.

H. Zschokke: The Princess of Brunswick - Wolfenbüttel and other Tales. From the German by M. A. Faber, 1 v.

Series for the Young.—*Each volume 1 Mark 60 Pf.*

Lady Barker: Stories About. With Frontispiece, 1 v.

Louisa Charlesworth: Ministering Children. With Frontispiece, 1 v.

Mrs. Craik (Miss Mulock): Our Year. Illustrated by C. Dobell, 1 v. Three Tales for Boys. With a Frontispiece by B. Plockhorst, 1 v. Three Tales for Girls. With a Frontispiece by B. Plockhorst, 1 v.

Miss G. M. Craik: Cousin Trix. With a Frontispiece by B. Plockhorst, 1 v.

Maria Edgeworth: Moral Tales. With a Frontispiece by B. Plockhorst, 1 v. Popular Tales. With a Frontispiece by B. Plockhorst, 2 v.

Bridget & Julia Kavanagh: The Pearl Fountain. With a Frontispiece by B. Plockhorst, 1 v.

Charles and Mary Lamb: Tales from Shakspeare. With the Portrait of Shakspeare, 1 v.

Captain Marryat: Masterman Ready; or, the Wreck of the Pacific. With Frontispiece, 1 v.

Florence Montgomery: The Town-Crier; to which is added: The Children with the Indian-Rubber Ball, 1 v.

Ruth and her Friends. A Story for Girls. With Frontispiece, 1 v.

Mrs. Henry Wood: William Allair; or, Running away to Sea. Frontispiece from a Drawing by F. Gilbert, 1 v.

Miss Yonge: Kenneth; or, the Rear-Guard of the Grand Army. With Frontispiece, 1 v. The Little Duke. Ben Sylvester's Word. With a Frontispiece by B. Plockhorst, 1 v. The Stokesley Secret. With a Frontispiece by B. Plockhorst, 1 v. Countess Kate. With Frontispiece, 1 v. A Book of Golden Deeds. With a Frontispiece by B. Plockhorst, 2 v. Friarswood Post-Office. With Frontispiece, 1 v. Henrietta's Wish; or, Domineering. A Tale. With a Frontispiece by B. Plockhorst, 1 v. Kings of England: A History for the Young. With Frontispiece, 1 v. The Lances of Lynwood; the Pigeon Pie. With Frontispiece, 1 v. P's and Q's. With Frontispiece, 1 v. Aunt Charlotte's Stories of English History. With Frontispiece, 1 v. Bye-Words. With a Frontispiece by B. Plockhorst, 1 v.

Tauchnitz Manuals of Conversation.
Each bound ℳ 2,25.

Neues Handbuch der *Englischen* Conversationssprache von *A. Schlessing.*

A new Manual of the *German* Language of Conversation by *A. Schlessing.*

Neues Handbuch der *Französischen* Conversationssprache von *L. Rollin.*

Nouveau Manuel de la Conversation *Allemande* par MM. *L. Rollin* et *Wolfgang Weber.*

Tauchnitz Dictionaries.

A complete Dictionary of the English and German languages for general use. By *W. James.* Twenty-eighth Stereotype Edition. crown 8vo sewed Mark 4,50.

A complete Dictionary of the English and French languages for general use. By *W. James* and *A. Molé.* Twelfth Stereotype Edition. crown 8vo sewed Mark 6,00.

A complete Dictionary of the English and Italian languages for general use. By *W. James* and *Gius. Grassi.* Eighth Stereotype Edition. crown 8vo sewed Mark 5,00.

A New Pocket Dictionary of the English and German languages. By *J. E. Wessely.* Tenth Stereotype Edition. 16mo sewed Mark 1,50. bound Mark 2,25.

A New Pocket Dictionary of the English and French languages. By *J. E. Wessely.* Eleventh Stereotype Edition. 16mo sewed Mark 1,50. bound Mark 2,25.

A New Pocket Dictionary of the English and Italian languages. By *J. E. Wessely.* Eighth Stereotype Edition. 16mo sewed Mark 1,50. bound Mark 2,25.

A New Pocket Dictionary of the English and Spanish languages. By *J. E. Wessely* and *A. Gironés.* Seventh Stereotype Edition. 16mo sewed Mark 1,50. bound Mark 2,25.

A New Pocket Dictionary of the French and German languages. By *J. E. Wessely.* Second Stereotype Edition. 16mo sewed Mark 1,50. bound Mark 2,25.

A New Pocket Dictionary of the Italian and German languages. By *G. Locella.* Second Stereotype Edition. 16mo sewed Mark 1,50. bound Mark 2,25.

A New Dictionary of the Latin and English languages. Third Stereot. Ed. 16mo sewed Mark 1,50. bound Mark 2,25.

Technological Dictionary in the French, English and German languages, containing about 90,000 technical terms employed in more than 250 departments of industry, by *A. Tolhausen,* of the Patent Office, London. Revised and augmented by *L. Tolhausen,* French Consul General. Complete in three Parts, crown 8vo sewed Mark 24,00. Each Part (French, German, English [*Second Edition*] — English, German, French [*Second Edition*] — German, English, French [*Second Edition*]) sold separately at the rate of Mark 8,00.

A Hebrew and Chaldee Lexicon to the Old Testament. By Dr. *Julius Fürst.* Fourth Edition. Translated from the German by *Samuel Davidson.* Royal 8vo sewed Mark 19,00.

www.ingramcontent.com/pod-product-compliance
Lightning Source LLC
Chambersburg PA
CBHW031153120726
47905CB00006B/1933